IT NEVER FELT SO GOOD

FOR THE LOVE OF FIBER ~ BOOK 2

KATE BOWMAN

Print ISBN: 978-1-7334674-2-1

ABOUT THE BOOK

Struggling artist Cara Olson is called home to Wisconsin to care for her ailing grandmother who is showing signs of Alzheimer's disease. Leaving behind her mentor//boyfriend, Stefan, she begins to look at her unsuccessful career and relationship in a new light.

Surprised to find her Gram's doctor is her high-school crush, Peter Andreson, she fights her reignited feelings. When Chicago critics dismiss her artwork as a poor imitation of Stefan's, she is devastated and vows to give up art.

While caring for Gram and running her small Scandinavian gift shop, the Wool Gatherers, a local group of fiber artists, help her find new outlets for her creativity, designing works of art with hand-made felt and her re-emerging love of landscape and portrait painting.

Along the way, her feelings for Peter grow, and she realizes she has once again fallen for a man only dedicated to his career. When the opportunity arises for her to return to Chicago with the promise of a new career, she seizes it. But even her success can't fill the void she experiences without Gram, her new friends, and Peter.

Can she return to Shoreview, the place that inspires her art, and be satisfied with a life that doesn't include him?

PRAISE FOR 'IT NEVER FELT SO GOOD'

Failure is a gift...when there are better choices to be made.

Cara Olson has spent her years since graduating from art school honing her painting under her mentor-turned-lover only to realize he's steered her into creating paintings of his ilk, not hers. Now her grandmother, who lives several hours away from the city, needs her help.

Stinging from a disastrous premiere showing of her art, she escapes to Door County, Wisconsin only to be greeted by a mentally slipping Gram. She must help her grandmother, but for how long? She has a career in the city, doesn't she? And then there's her teenage crush, Peter Andresen, now the town doctor. Sparks fly, but she already has a boyfriend back in the city...who's never bothered to meet her family and treats her like a maid. Sounds like an easy choice except Peter believes his career leaves no room for a wife and family.

Choices. Would returning to her roots as an artist be settling? Should she fight for Peter's love? I highly recommend you read Kate Bowman's wonderfully family-centric *It Never Felt so Good* to find out which choices Cara makes.

~Barbara Raffin, Award-Winning author of The St. John Sibling Series

To my sister Lois and niece Patti Lefebvre.
Thank you for your enthusiasm and help in spreading the word of this new author.

ACKNOWLEDGMENTS

Once again, thanks to my daughter Molly Bowman Johnson for her art expertise and for another awesome cover and my son, David Bowman, photographer extraordinaire.

And to Maria Connor who puts it all together.

And of course, a thank you to Zeke, my favorite llama. I still miss you, buddy.

1

"SOMETIMES THE ONE THING YOU WANT IN LIFE IS THE THING YOU *can't have. That doesn't mean you give up. It means you change direction."*

How often had Gram said those words? Often enough that they became my personal mantra, to be repeated nightly before falling into bed. But how many times would I have to change before I lost myself in the process?

I lay under the covers, those words echoing again when my cell phone rang so early on a Monday morning, along with a premonition of bad news. The only person ever to call me this early was Mom.

I let the phone ring three times before doing a log roll off the lumpy futon and turning half-closed eyes toward the bedside clock. Taking a deep breath, I grabbed the phone and sat up.

I wasn't disappointed. It was my mother.

"Hi, Mom."

"Cara, you've got to get up to Shoreview right away to see Lucy. Something's happened to your grandmother."

"*What?* How?" Wide awake now, I transferred the phone to my right ear and took a deep breath. "Did she fall? Is she in the hospital?"

Even though Gram was my mother's mother-in-law, they'd always been close.

A picture of the tall, slender Gram of my youth, always so confident and sure of herself, flashed through my mind, followed by TV commercial images of an elderly lady writhing on the floor in pain, calling for help.

Or was it a car accident? She still drove her Buick like it was 1959, and everyone in town would get out of her way. But things had changed, even in her little corner of the world. Everything but Gram, I suspected.

"No, of course not." Mom clicked her tongue. She'd always accused me of being a drama queen and jumping to conclusions.

"One of her friends called last night," Mom said. "Some new woman I've never met. They found my number in Lucy's address book. They're worried about her. It seems she's been acting strange lately—not like herself at all."

"Strange how?" I got up from the edge of the futon and paced across the narrow room, phone in hand.

"She's getting forgetful, driving erratically—they're afraid she'll hurt herself. She drove that big Buick of hers into the side of her shop. Luckily there was only minor damage, but someone heard the noise and called the police. The O'Brien boy was on duty and gave her a warning—said he'd be watching her driving. She was upset and embarrassed, according to her friend.

"I called Lucy as soon as I hung up with her friend, but she didn't even seem to know who I was." She paused, almost as if to let me know she was thinking things over. Unless she was trying to make me feel guilty for not visiting more often?

"Mom, that really doesn't sound like Gram, does it?" I closed my eyes for a moment, immediately regretting using that sharp tone with her. She was worried about Gram, that's all.

After pulling a double shift at the Daily Grind the previous evening, I'd stayed up for hours working on my latest art piece at the studio of my boyfriend-slash-mentor, Stefan. Too tired to drive back to my own place, I'd crashed here on his lumpy futon, not even bothering to undress. My head throbbed, and my shoulder muscles ached. I'd need a double shot of espresso before my mind could even begin to function.

"Cara Eileen Olson, don't you get snotty with me. You're

beginning to sound like that Steve person you're dating, or whatever you call him these days."

I decided to ignore the jibe about Stefan; we'd been down that road so often it had ruts. I raised my eyes heavenward in a silent plea. I'd be using a walker before Mom stopped talking to me like I was a teenager. I couldn't hold back the sigh.

It wasn't that I didn't worry about Gram...I did, immensely. I couldn't quite put my finger on it, but when I spoke to Gram last month there was something lacking in her voice. The spark was missing. Gram always showed an interest in my artwork. But her voice had sounded flat, uninterested at times, and she kept repeating herself. I'd tried to dismiss it because I couldn't bear to think anything was wrong. Gram had been the one stable person in my childhood. The one who was always there, encouraging my dreams of success in the world of art when no one else cared.

Now I was feeling guilty. I should have called her last week to check in. I'd expected her to always stay the same. For a woman her age, Gram's clear skin wore the wrinkles well. As a child, I'd hoped I'd miraculously turn into the tall, athletic girl I saw in her family pictures. The girl with the straight, shoulder-length silvery blond hair, cool blue eyes, and lanky Scandinavian build. But no, I was a definite throwback to my mother's Irish ancestors—short, a tendency to roundness, with curly black hair. My blue eyes and fair skin were the only things Gram and I shared in looks. But we had our love of art in common.

"You'll have to go up to Shoreview and straighten things out," Mom continued. "Lord only knows what's going on in that shop of hers."

"Isn't it normal to be a little forgetful at her age?" I waited in vain for Mom's reassurance.

"Really, Cara. That's all you have to say? It isn't as if you'd be giving up some great career."

"You're right, Mom. Gram is more important."

"I can't expect Dave to give up his life here in Florida to care for my former mother-in-law. His health isn't all that great."

That was the first I'd heard about any health problems, and my chest muscles immediately tightened. Mom had finally found a new life for herself with Dave, and I didn't want to do anything to jeopardize their happiness.

"What about the boys? Could one of them check things out until I get there?" Caught by surprise, I'd said the first thing that came into my head.

"Don't be silly. Lucy's always adored you, and you know it. You're the only one she'll listen to. Besides, your brothers have wives and children to consider. They can't leave their jobs and families to fly across country to stay with their grandmother. It's only a four-hour drive for you. At least you'll get free room and board there, and Lord knows you probably need it."

Ever practical, my mother. She was right, and I wouldn't trust anyone but me to look after Gram.

All during art school I'd worried about Mom's prediction I wouldn't be able to support myself with my art. Turns out she was right. But it would take slivers under my fingernails before I'd admit I'd made a mistake and give up painting for a more practical career. Art was my life. It had been since the first time Gram put a paintbrush in my four-year-old hand and guided it across the paper. Something came alive in my soul that day, something that has sustained me through all the ups and downs of my so-called career. Giving that up would be like stealing my very breath. I couldn't do it, even if it meant I'd be the oldest barista in Daily Grind history.

Still, her words hurt. Probably because they were so true. Seven years in Chicago and what did I have to show for it? A few showings in a minor gallery, and a relationship going nowhere. If it weren't for the job at the coffee shop, I'd be panhandling.

"I'm sure Gram is just fine."

She had to be. I couldn't bear to think otherwise. I was tied to Chicago for the foreseeable future because my chance for success was here, with Stefan and his expertise. A dark cloud of doubt closed around me when I thought of my work. Something was missing. I felt it. I could almost taste it. Stefan was the only one I knew who could help me find what that was, and he was more than willing.

"Remember how Gram took us in after your dad died?" Mom

asked, stabbing me again with that familiar dagger of guilt. She didn't have to remind me. Gram had been our savior when Dad died.

"I'll go up tomorrow and check things out," I promised.

"Let me know what you find out, kiddo." Relief rang loud and clear in her voice. "I gotta go. It's a beautiful morning here, and we're going for a bike ride."

So much for Dave's poor health. And there it was. As always. Had Mom manipulated me into doing her bidding or were her concerns valid?

I closed my cell phone with a snap and looked out the rain-drenched window at a grey Chicago day. As I watched from the third-floor window, a CTA bus raced by, spewing water in every direction. A smartly dressed woman stood at the crosswalk, shaking her fist in anger before brushing off the water dripping from her tweed suit jacket. I felt her frustration.

I dragged myself into the studio where Stefan was hard at work on his latest project, girding my loins for the upcoming flap. Monday morning and rain. Yup. It had *bad day* written all over it.

The bright white walls and fluorescent lights made my half-opened eyes blink in defense. Stefan worked with his back to the large windows, the grey light slanting through the rain-blurred glass of little help today.

"I have to drive up to Wisconsin to check on my grandmother tomorrow. Want to ride along?"

He stood back, eyes squinting as he stared at the paint-smeared canvas, lost in his usual myopic vision. His distracted, "Hmm?" told me he probably hadn't heard a word I'd said.

"I have to drive up to Wisconsin tomorrow to check on my grandmother," I repeated, emphasizing each word. "One of her neighbors called Mom. They're worried about her."

"Tomorrow? But my friend Frank has his opening at the Fitzgerald gallery in a few days." Stefan turned, paintbrush in hand, an annoyed frown crossing his narrow, esthetic features. "You shouldn't miss that. It's a chance for you to mix with a lot of influential people. And Ted Beaupry will be there. I'll introduce you. It'll give you a chance to meet him on a social level before he judges your entry in the museum art show. You are planning to enter a piece, aren't you? Could give you an extra edge."

"I know, but Mom sounded pretty upset. She thinks Gram's in trouble. I have to see what is going on there. I feel bad enough that it's been months since I've visited Gram. You know how I feel about her. She's always been there for me when I needed her."

"I'm sure she'll be just fine without you. Didn't you say she had lots of friends?"

"We could be back in time for the opening," I said, running a hand through my out-of-control curls, smoothing my hair down. Why I bothered, I don't know. Stefan wouldn't have noticed if I wore a paper bag over my head at this point. "We have a few days."

"For God's sakes, Cara, you can't keep putting your family before your work."

What? Where the hell had Stefan been all these weeks while I'd spent every spare minute in this studio? In la-la land?

"If you want to be a serious artist, you have to act like one," he said, the words followed by a heavy sigh.

"We could be there tomorrow evening, check on Gram, and leave the next day if all is well," I insisted. Only now did I realize how much I'd neglected Gram, always expecting her to stay the same and be there for me when I needed her. How selfish was that?

"But what if she isn't well?" he asked, widening his eyes and raising his eyebrows. "Then how long are we going to be there?"

"What's one lousy opening?" Leave it to Stefan to accentuate the negative. I raised my voice in frustration. "Missing Frank's opening won't damage my career."

"As usual, you just don't get it, do you, Cara? Can't you see how your family manipulates you? You're never going to make it as an artist if you don't change that attitude."

"Oh, I see," I said, my fingers digging into my palms. "I'm supposed to be totally self-centered?" I bit my tongue before *like you* slipped out. Not the best way to treat a mentor, the working part of my brain warned.

"Dedicated to your work is the way I'd put it," Stephan said.

"I put as much time as I can into my art. You know that."

"Sure, when you're not working that dead-end job at The Daily Grind or worrying over your family."

"I've hardly been able to spend any time with my family this past year. We don't all have rich daddies to pay our bills."

"Cara, cut it out. I told you to quit that job and move in with me. I can pay the rent and buy the groceries."

"I know." It was true. He'd been after me for a long time to quit, but I wasn't about to give up my independence, even when things were at their bleakest with my artistic career. I needed to keep my own identity and freedom. And besides, I liked working at the coffee shop. If I didn't, I'd end up doing all his household chores out of guilt, taking over the responsibility for his everyday life, just as I'd done for my brothers. But now my two brothers had wives to change those long-established habits. I'd learned, to my surprise, just how well they got along without me. I guess I'd assumed Gram could, too.

"Let's not argue again. It only upsets me, and there's nothing I can do about it." I was torn between my feelings for the dark-eyed, brooding artist who appealed to the romantic in me and the petty boy he became when thwarted. He was as determined to make me a protégé of his style as I was to prove myself worthy of his time, only it didn't seem to be working.

Frustration over my work and my life built up like a soon-to-erupt volcano. I knew if I didn't get out of here fast, words would come spewing out of my mouth like red hot ashes, burning up my feelings for him forever.

"Maybe time away will be good for me, help me get back on track." Oh, how I wanted to believe it.

"That isn't even logical." He curled his lip and turned back to his canvas. "What you need is more time spent on your art."

"Let's talk about it later. I have to go home and change before work." Grabbing my raincoat off the hook by the studio door, I pushed my arms through the sleeves. Being late for my shift at the coffee shop wouldn't help me get unscheduled time off.

"When will you get that piece for the museum contest finished? You only have a month left," he shouted after me. "This could be your big break. You know Ted Beaupry is one of the judges. If he likes it, you're a shoo-in for national recognition."

I glanced back into the studio, my hand on the open door. My half-finished canvas sat on the easel, waiting.

What if Gram needed me for more than a few days? How would I ever get the piece finished in time? Would it ever really be finished to my satisfaction? I'd worked and reworked it so many times that I was beginning to despise the damn thing. It just wasn't right, no matter what I did. Suddenly sick of it all, I turned my back on the studio.

"Yeah, right," I murmured and shut the door behind me. *Oh, God. What if he was right, and I missed this chance for success? Would I ever get another?* The thought burned a hole in my gut.

THE FAMILIAR JINGLE of the coffee shop door jarred me back to the reality of my life as I entered, almost overpowered by the sweet nirvana of freshly ground beans, brewed coffee, and cinnamon. Was there any other place on earth that smelled as good? Not to the caffeine addict in me. I hurried behind the counter and grabbed a mug, sighing with pleasure as that first jolt of warm caffeine streamed through my blood. It was a relief to get away from the studio and the constant reminders of my failure.

My thoughts were foggy the rest of the day, consumed with fear over Gram and the argument with Stefan. I'd called Gram on my lunch break to tell her I was coming, but she had that same distracted air about her and cut me off after a brief conversation.

The dinging of the cash register, the grinding coffee beans, and the loud chatter of customers seated at the bistro tables didn't afford me quiet brooding time. Probably a good thing because the more I thought about the forthcoming conversation with my manager about time off, the more I dreaded it. Maybe it was the coffee I'd sipped all day, or maybe it was something else.

I finally caught her alone at the end of my shift. Things had been dicey between us lately because I had been offered the manager position —a job I turned down because of the time commitment.

"Could I talk to you for a minute?" I asked.

"What about? It's been a long day, and I want to get home." She pulled the hair net off her dull blond hair and narrowed her pale blue eyes.

"I need to take some time off to visit my grandmother in Wisconsin. She's ill." I took a deep breath and tried to keep my cool.

"How much time are we talking here?" She snapped her gum in my face. "We're pretty shorthanded, and the owners say I can't hire anyone new."

"I'm not sure. Hopefully, only a few days, a week at the most," I mumbled, rubbing my hands together. Was I being realistic? I could only hope so.

"You can take the time off, but I can't guarantee your job, especially if it's more than a week. It isn't fair to your coworkers. There are a lot of people looking for work right now."

"Thanks, I appreciate it."

"Just don't make a habit of asking for favors, Olson." Another snap of her gum, and she turned away.

I swallowed what was left of my pride, promising myself I would someday mimic the words of that old song and tell her to "take this job and shove it."

WHEN I RETURNED to his apartment that evening, Stefan was still at work in the studio. He finally set down his brush and looked my way. Fatigue lines were etched around his deep-set, dark eyes. Running his hand through his too-long black hair, he glanced up at the wall clock. "Is it that late already?" he asked, surprised. "Whew!"

The artist in me couldn't help but admire his dedication. And the romantic in me recognized him as every young girl's fantasy of the struggling artist in need of loving care.

"I hope you brought food. I forgot about dinner again." He flashed his lost boy look.

"No, I didn't. I had to wait to talk to my manager about leaving tomorrow. She was pretty ticked and said she couldn't promise to hold the job for me.'

"So, did you tell her you'd stay?"

Looking at Stefan, the view through the rose-colored glasses I usually wore in his presence faded even further. How many years would it take for this man to know me?

"Of course not. Didn't you hear me this morning? I said I had to check on my grandmother."

"And you're going to go, even if it means losing your job."

"What did you expect?" He was too clueless to understand when it came to relationships. That had always been part of his charm, too involved with his art to be bothered with the mundane problems of the masses. But it wore thin today.

The phone rang, and as usual he let it go to voice mail. "Stefan, please call and let me know your decision about the Fitzgerald opening. I'd like to get my plans confirmed." The throaty feminine voice brought up images of satin, chocolate, and wine, all things sexy in my mind.

"Who was that?" I asked.

"A new graduate who wants mentoring. Not important." He shrugged, suddenly interested in a canvas propped against the wall.

"Why was she asking about the Fitzgerald opening?" It was only this morning I found out I might miss it.

"I guess she heard I might be going alone and wanted me to introduce her around." Color rose up the back of his neck. I'd never seen him blush before. Something was up. If I had the time or energy, I'd try to weasel it out of him. But it would have to wait.

"Stay the night, Cara. We can talk more about your plans after dinner," he cajoled.

"You can't talk me out of going. I have to go home and pack. I came by to see if you'd changed your mind about coming with me. Obviously, you haven't, so I'll just leave."

I slammed the door behind me with a burst of satisfaction and ran down the steps before he could follow. He never opened the door.

. . .

EARLY THIS MORNING, I'd thrown most of my personal belongings into my car, not knowing how long I'd be in Shoreview. Who would've thought they all would fit into the trunk of my ancient Ford Escort? How depressing. But then, the life of a struggling artist and barista didn't call for an extensive wardrobe.

I'd come to Chicago filled with plans for great adventures and artistic success. Those plans shattered, like most of my dreams, with the slamming of the trunk. Wait. Do broken dreams make a sound when they shatter? Or is there just this silent aching deep in your soul?

My life had taken a U-turn, and I could very well end up exactly where I started, back in small-town Wisconsin with a head full of dreams and not much else.

I refused to obsess about it. This was just another bump along the road to success. I'd be back soon. And to prove it, I'd leave all my work and supplies at Stefan's studio.

I drove over there to say goodbye and make one last plea. Maybe I hadn't given him enough credit. Maybe he *did* care.

A part of me still hoped I was wrong about him.

I stood in the doorway and shouted into the studio. "Stefan, I'm leaving for Wisconsin now."

He was painting, of course. Probably had been at it all night, oblivious to the rest of the world. I imagined the argument we'd had hardly ruffled his feathers. I'd always envied that quality of detachment before, but right now it annoyed the hell out of me.

"Okay, babe. Give my regards to your grandmother."

His distracted voice kept me from crying and begging him to come along. Five years together, and he couldn't come to the door to see me off? Most likely he wouldn't miss me until he got hungry and I wasn't there to prepare a meal.

Or maybe it had something to do with that phone call I wasn't supposed to hear. One more thing to add to my list of worries.

"Goodbye, Steve." Now I was imitating my mother's earlier dig. A childish retaliation, but I knew he hated his oh-so-ordinary given name. It felt good.

. . .

I MADE it to the Wisconsin border before the tears started to fall, not even sure why I was crying. I had so many reasons. The stormy weather of yesterday had passed, and varying shades of green could be seen in the frequent fields now visible along the highway. I rolled down the window and sucked in a deep breath of the fresh, clean air. It made me feel better.

Was I really going to miss out on the chance for future success?

It didn't matter at the moment. I knew I had to pull myself together to face my future and Gram's—so I continued the long drive toward my hometown of Shoreview, Wisconsin. Right now, Gram was more of a concern.

Hours later, I slowed the car to a near crawl as I reached the crest of the hill leading into town, and my nerves started jumping. *What would I find?*

The town of Shoreview spread out below me like a picture postcard, like one of those on the racks in every drugstore in tourist country. So perfect it made my teeth hurt. No litter, no panhandlers, and not a Starbucks in sight.

What would Gram say when she saw me? Was she upset that I'd been gone months without a visit?

Would he be there? The one person I'd carefully avoided on my previous visits? I managed to keep him out of my thoughts while busy in Chicago, but whenever I came home, memories of him returned like a newly ripped-off scab.

"You can do this, Cara," I whispered. I took a deep breath and plunged my car down into the deep abyss of small-town living and my never-to-be-forgotten insecurities over a young love lost before it ever had the chance to blossom.

2

THE TOWN HADN'T CHANGED MUCH SINCE MY CHILDHOOD. MY OLD high school looked the same—imposing red brick and a double set of stainless-steel doors, surrounded by student cars parked up and down the narrow streets. The golden spire of St. Anthony's church remained visible above the houses in the distance. The yellow Victorian bed-and-breakfast, with its white gingerbread trim, nestled off on a side street still looked comfortable among the ageless homes surrounding it. And serving as a backdrop to it all was the gleaming harbor in the distance.

Shoreview was located along the shore of Lake Michigan, near the Door County peninsula, that little thumb of land that juts out between the bay of Green Bay and Lake Michigan. It's a beautiful, scenic area of farmland, fishing villages, sandy beaches on the bay side, and rugged shoreline on the lake side. Except in the winter, when the cold wind blows off the lake, churning ice in massive piles along both shores.

The ice had disappeared and trees were turning green again, but Main Street was still quiet. The tourists hadn't yet arrived for the weekend with their overtired children and strollers loaded with purchases.

I drove straight to Gram's shop, talking aloud to myself all the way. *Things couldn't be as bad as the neighbor told Mom. I would've noticed when I was there during the holidays. I took a reassuring breath. People around here always exaggerated, making small town living more exciting. Gram and I will have a nice visit; I'll spend the night and be back in Chicago by tomorrow evening.* That's when I'd worry about my changing relationship with Stefan and whomever this new student was who'd called him.

My grandmother's little Scandinavian gift shop was on a side street, and I pulled into a parking spot along the side of the building next to her vintage Buick, that boat of a car in which my brothers and I had learned to drive. Indestructible, Gram called it. And we'd proven her right on several occasions. I parked and opened my car door to the raucous call of circling gulls. *A forewarning of what lay ahead?*

Uninvited fear lodged in my throat, but I swallowed it down. *Ridiculous.* I looked up from the parking lot into the shop window with its rows of imported glassware displayed on clear shelves and felt better. Nothing had changed.

The Scandinavian chime above the door tinkled merrily as I entered her shop. Gram looked up from the register where a customer stood waiting, and I relaxed. After months, it was good to be home.

I looked forward to the visit now, glad Mom had forced the issue.

"Surprise!" I shouted across the room.

And it clearly was.

The smiling face I'd expected looked at me blankly, as if a mad woman had entered her shop.

A tall, angular woman, Gram had developed a comfortable roundness in her later years, true to her Scandinavian background. She was normally all hugs and warmth, smelling of cinnamon buns and ginger cookies, the direct opposite of what I remembered of her son, my reticent Norwegian father. Her long white hair still had blond at the tips, and she kept it wrapped in a loose bun on the very top of her head. I can't remember her ever having it cut.

"Cara?" Her face lit with recognition after a few moments and creased into a welcoming smile. The middle-aged customer puckered her lips in annoyance.

"My change, please," the woman said. "I'm in a hurry."

"Oh, yes, of course." Gram looked at the price tag on the Norwegian knickknack in her hand and pushed keys on the computer.

"You've already rung it up. I just need my change."

"Sorry, how stupid of me." The look of confused panic on Gram's face was new and caught me by surprise. I crossed the room and stood behind Gram as she struggled to complete the transaction, both of us sighing with relief when she successfully gave the woman her change.

"I hope you're here to help," the woman said crisply. "She needs it."

A crestfallen expression crossed Gram's face as the woman made her way toward the door, looking every inch the dissatisfied customer.

"Come again," Gram called in a weak voice.

And that was when it hit me.

As I looked around the shop, the place where I'd spent so much of my childhood, I could see it was the same, only different, as if the love that had made the shop unique had gone missing. It looked so neglected; this place could have belonged to any stranger. Not to *my* Gram who had filled every nook and cranny with things she loved and cared for like they were her children.

The glass shelves that normally displayed Swedish glassware with artful precision were dusty and the wares haphazardly arranged. Disorganized was too kind a word. Piles of stock sat in boxes on the floor while skeins of gorgeous handspun yarn lay in a confusion of color on shelves and the counter.

What was going on here?

The woman facing me was not my sweet-faced Gram, but a thinner, anxious version of her, nervously pulling on her fingers and wearing an expression that told me she didn't know what was going on either or what to expect next.

After the customer had slammed the door behind her, I put my arm across Gram's shoulders in comfort, surprised at the thinness I found there.

"Not a very happy camper, was she?" I asked.

No response.

"Why don't you close early? You look tired. Let's go in the back and have a cup of tea."

Gram looked doubtful at first. Then abruptly she walked to the door and turned the CLOSED sign outward and locked the door. She turned without a word and walked toward the back of the building.

Gram's shop consisted of three rooms, two filled with items for sale and a small kitchenette/storage room in the rear. I followed her there.

The lines on her face melted away as she got out the teakettle and cups. She prepared the tea with her usual deftness. She was the old Gram I knew and loved—at last.

Could I have caught her at a bad time? Would things be normal again?

"So, how have things been?" I asked as I scanned the small room. It was as jumbled as the shop, and I couldn't stop the frown of concern from flashing across my face. Guilt overwhelmed me.

I shouldn't have stayed away so long. The old Gram never would have tolerated such clutter. There was no way this confused mess had happened overnight. How long had this been going on?

"Why are you here?" she asked, her eyes narrowing, hands planted defiantly on her hips. "Did your mother tell you to come and spy on me?"

She surprised me again. This was not my beloved Gram talking.

"N-n-no." *Oh, dear God. This was bad. Really bad.* I fought for an excuse for being there. "Things were not going well in Chicago. I thought I'd come home for a while. If that's all right with you?"

Her shoulders slumped in relief, but there was still a hint of suspicion in her eyes.

"You're always welcome here. You know that."

I expected her to ask what was going wrong in my life, but she didn't. I guess I should've been grateful.

"You didn't answer my question. How are things with the

business? Did you have many customers during the winter season?" I asked.

She had that vague look again. "I think things have been going well. I seem to have money in the till."

This was not good.

"Well, maybe I can help out while I'm here. It'll be like old times, the two of us together again," I said with what I hoped was a bright smile.

But judging from her skeptical look, she wasn't buying it.

"Humph," was her only comment.

We sat in the back room, drinking our tea and munching on the cheese and crackers she'd found after going through the small refrigerator and cabinets. I continued to ask questions about the shop, but all her answers were guarded.

Enough already. I had to say it.

"Gram, maybe a woman your age should retire and just enjoy life." I could see my mistake the moment the words left my big mouth. "I mean, you've worked hard all your life and it's time to relax."

She bristled with indignation. "You expect me to walk away from my life's work just like that?" She snapped her fingers. "What am I supposed to do then? Sit alone in my house? Not my idea of fun."

"You have your animals and your gardens."

"In case you haven't noticed, they're not big on conversation," she said, crossing her arms over her chest.

"You're right, of course," I soothed, getting up from the small yellow chrome table and dropping the subject. "Let's go home and cook some dinner. I'm still hungry."

FOLLOWING GRAM'S old Buick back to her house was a heart-breaking experience and watching the old tank of a car weave in and out of traffic was downright frightening. Luckily it was a weekday, so traffic was fairly light. *Had she always driven that way?* It was a miracle I hadn't caused a ten-car pileup on the expressway when I first moved to Chicago with her as my driving instructor. I breathed a sigh of relief when she pulled into her driveway.

Gram lived in a white clapboard farmhouse on the edge of town that had been in my grandfather's family for generations. At one time, they'd farmed 120 acres, but most of that had been sold off over the years following my father's death. She'd managed to keep five acres of wooded land and a small field surrounding the house.

The brazen squawk of Florence and Fritz, Gram's pet geese, greeted me when I parked and opened the car door. A short distance away, her llama, Zeke, ears back in confrontation mode, poked his head out of the half-door of Gram's small barn. He fancied himself a guard dog. I grabbed some of my stuff from the trunk and headed toward the house.

Gram was already in the house when I opened the door, bags in hand.

The place looked like the aftermath of a hurricane. "Oh, my God. You've been burglarized," I said. "Don't touch anything until I call the police."

Her usually neat, tidy house was in chaos. Drawers and cupboard doors hung open, couch and chair cushions were turned out onto the floor.

She looked around herself, in shock, and then her face relaxed. "I think I was looking for something this morning when I was running late," she said in that vague voice I hadn't quite gotten used to. "It must've been something important."

"Did you find it?'

"I don't remember." That's when I saw the first sign of panic in her eyes.

"Never mind. I'm sure it'll come back to you. Having a senior moment, were you?" I said lightly as I closed one of the drawers.

"I have a lot of them lately," she whispered.

"Try to remember what it was you lost. Maybe I can help. A fresh set of eyes."

Her face screwed up in thought and then lit with relief. "It was the car keys."

"Obviously, you found them."

"Yes, I'd left them in the car."

Immediately, I showed my worry for her safety. "Gram, you can't do that anymore. It's too dangerous. Things have changed, even around here."

She shrugged my chastising off.

We walked farther into the room. "I'll start cleaning up." I picked up a couch cushion and put it in place. What could I possibly say to make her feel better? I was in over my head.

While reaching for another cushion, I asked, "What were you planning for dinner?"

That same distressed look spread across her face. Looking at her now, I realized exactly how much weight she'd lost these past months since I'd seen her last. Her clothes hung on her once-rounded body. I had to admit the neighbors were right to be concerned.

"I don't remember."

My stomach had been complaining for hours. The cheese and crackers I'd had in Gram's kitchenette hadn't done much for me.

"I guess I forgot to take something out of the freezer," she mumbled.

"We'll find something, I'm sure." I went to the kitchen and searched the open cupboards. "Do you have a can of baked beans? That's always good with toast." It'd become a staple of my diet since my student days.

She snickered. "That was a favorite of my father's since the depression. I vowed as a child I would never serve beans as a main course to my family." She opened the refrigerator door and removed a carton of large brown eggs, her mood visibly lightening. "Just got these yesterday from the neighbor. You're in farm country now, girl. Scrambled eggs and buttered toast always make for a healthy meal."

"Some would argue with that, Gram."

Dinner was light but filling. After Gram went to bed, I cleaned up the house as much as I could before sinking into bed, praying tomorrow would be a better day.

. . .

THE NEXT MORNING, I awoke to a Gram who seemed more like herself—feisty and ready to go to work, the anxiety and confusion of yesterday forgotten.

"Time to get up," she'd called through my closed bedroom door. "If you're coming with me, you can't be late."

Yes, this was a good thing. Could yesterday have been just a bad day, a lapse in her normal behavior? Having me arrive so unexpectedly and dealing with that nasty customer may have thrown her off stride. That was my theory and I was sticking to it. The state of her shop and home would have their own explanation. I so wanted to believe that.

After dressing in my one new pair of jeans, I threw on a sweater, pulled my hair back into a ponytail, and went down to the kitchen. I'd have to wait until a later time to unpack and check out my room more thoroughly. It looked the same as I'd left it, not at all like the confused mess downstairs.

"This coffee is awfully strong." Gram slammed her mug on the table.

That was putting it mildly. My hair curled in ways I'd never seen before after just one cup. Even caffeine addicts like me would have trouble drinking two cups.

"I think you put too much coffee in the pot, girl." She'd made the coffee, but I didn't bother to correct her. Why stress her out again? She looked her usual neat and trim self today, bun in place, a handknit cardigan covering her dress pants and blouse. I wasn't about to start trouble.

We had breakfast, finished straightening up, and prepared to leave for the shop. I'd decided while lying in bed the night before that I couldn't leave Shoreview until things were back to normal with Gram. I had to make sure that what I'd witnessed yesterday was just an aberration on her part. And it looked today that could be the case.

"I'll drive," I said.

She looked relieved, but I sensed that suspicion again when she said, "I could do it, you know."

"Of course, you can."

We got to the shop and immediately started straightening up the stock.

"Honestly, this place gets into such a mess some days. I don't know why people can't leave things where I put them," Gram said.

"Maybe you need to hire someone to keep an eye on things while you're handling the cash register."

"I've always run the shop on my own, since you left anyway. Never had a problem." She straightened her back and gave me the "look" I remembered from childhood. But she wasn't going to subdue me so easily today.

"But what happens if you get sick?" I raised my eyebrows, keeping my tone soft.

"What do you mean by that?"

"Well, you're not indestructible, you know. You can get the flu or a bad cold, whatever. What do you do when that happens?" I frowned. Surely, she had a backup plan for the shop.

"I call Nancy. She helps me out if she's not working at the restaurant."

"Who's Nancy?"

The chimes above the front door tinkled, and our conversation was interrupted by the entrance of a few customers. Gram dropped the skein of yarn she was holding to greet them with a smile.

From then on, customers came in at a regular pace. Gram handled them while I continued to bring order to the shop, always with one ear cocked. She was relaxed and "with it" mentally in the morning. But as the day wore on, I could see her getting more agitated. Her sentences grew shorter, her answers to customers' questions more abrupt.

It was late afternoon when the door chimes tinkled again, and a smartly dressed middle-aged woman entered the shop. Her hair was the color of nutmeg and pulled back into a tortoise-shell clasp, a perfect complement to her hazel eyes. She wore a beautiful handknit sweater in an Aran cable pattern over freshly pressed knit slacks. I immediately pegged her as suburban Chicago, one of the hordes of Chicago tourists who regularly visited Shoreview during the summer months. I'd heard it was a year-around thing now and a boon to the local economy.

"Hi, Lucy," the woman said. "I brought in more of my handspun."

Indecision flickered across Gram's face, but she quickly covered.

"Give it to my granddaughter—she'll put it out somewhere," she said and waved a hand breezily toward me.

"Is it labeled?" I asked.

"You must be Cara. I've heard so much about you." The woman motioned with her head for me to follow her to the other room. "I'm Martha O'Connor. We've never met. I only moved here from Chicago a few years ago. So, I'm not one of the locals you grew up around. I guess we never crossed paths during your visits home."

When we were out of Gram's hearing, she said softly, "I'm the one who called your mother. One of the ladies in our spinning group, Joan Berglanc, found her number. She's a long-time friend of Lucy's, I believe."

"Yes, I know Mrs. Bergland. Thank you for calling and thank you for caring."

"We're all worried about your grandmother. She doesn't seem like herself. I thought her family should know. I hope I didn't overstep the boundaries of our friendship." She looked toward the other room. "As I said, I'm new here, but even I noticed a change in Lucy lately. Can you see it?"

Oh, I'd seen it all right and it was frightening. At least to me. Still, I was reluctant to discuss Gram with this stranger. How much was concern and how much idle curiosity? Sometimes I forgot I hadn't lived in Shoreview for nine years. "She does seem a little...different."

The woman looked back at me with a determined expression. "I would never forgive myself if something happened to her and I hadn't warned her family."

"You're right. I'll see that things are taken care of before I leave."

"What are you two whispering about back there?" Gram

called out.

"We're not whispering—you need a hearing aide," I yelled back, "which I've told you for the past ten years."

"I was just telling your granddaughter about the Wool Gatherers. You should bring her to the next meeting." She gave me a conspiratorial wink.

Gram walked closer and looked at me speculatively. "I don't know—she's an artist, not a crafts person. Graduated from a fancy art school in Chicago, you know." My heart swelled at the obvious pride in her voice.

"Why can't she be both? You haven't come to a meeting yourself for quite some time. Are you still doing that Rosemaling style embroidery?"

"No. I haven't had time." I knew Gram well enough to recognize the flicker of interest in her eyes while she talked about it though.

"Well, bring Cara to a meeting. You know we always have a fun time, no matter what's going on in our personal lives." She turned back to me. "How long are you staying?"

"I haven't decided yet."

"Please come to the meeting and bring Lucy. We miss her."

"I'll see what I can do." I wondered at Gram's feelings about her friend as the woman walked toward the front of the shop.

"She seems very nice," I said, looking to Gram for confirmation.

"She's married to the local sheep shearer, Riley O'Connor. Best thing that ever happened to him and his boy was when she moved here from Chicago."

"I don't recall hearing their names."

"Of course not. You've been gone a long time." Was that a rebuke or sadness in her voice?

"You never told me you were doing embroidery," I said when Martha closed the door behind her. "I only remember you painting."

"You never asked."

That stung. Had I been that neglectful? Had our telephone

conversations been all about me and what I was doing? I knew the answer immediately. Guilty as charged.

Well, that was about to change. I was learning there was more to my grandmother than I remembered. She wasn't a little old lady who stayed home and baked cookies and waited for grandchildren to visit.

What else was I about to learn?

"Tell me about the Wool Gatherers."

"Oh, they're a group of women who get together occasionally on Friday nights. They're all interested in the fiber arts—spinning, weaving, knitting—that sort of thing. We work on crafts, talk, laugh, and have a potluck supper."

"That sounds right up your alley, Gram. How long has this been going on?"

"For several years, now that I think about it."

"How come I never heard about it?"

"Didn't think you'd be interested." She shrugged her narrow shoulders. "You weren't here long enough at a time anyway."

Oh, boy. Phone calls and short visits hadn't been enough to keep our relationship as close as I'd thought.

3

"I've decided to stay home today," Gram said the next morning.

"Why? Aren't you feeling well?" I turned from the stove and the bacon I'd found in the freezer, now sizzling. She'd just come into the house from feeding her animals, her cheeks flushed with a healthy glow. Clear-eyed and with a bounce to her step that was missing yesterday, she made me want to believe things were back to normal.

"I feel better than I have in months. Knowing you'll be here to run the shop if anything happens to me is the lift I needed. There isn't anyone I'd trust more to take over."

Did she think I was here to stay? With tongs in hand, holding aloft a slice of half-cooked bacon, I stared in disbelief. I had planned on being here for only a few days. But how to tell her that? I didn't want her to fall back into the fragile mood of yesterday. I closed my eyes for a second while I tried to find the right words, knowing I couldn't really leave if she needed me and it seemed pretty obvious that she did.

"You have to think about selling sooner or later," was the only thing I could come up with.

"Now, why would I do that when you're here?" She looked down at the floor. "Be careful, you're dripping grease all over. Slippery floors are dangerous for old people, you know."

I looked down and made a mental note to wipe the floor. "Gram. I'm not sure how long I'll be staying. Things are unsettled right now."

"You have all your things with you, don't you?"

"Not everything. Anyway, that's only because I'm in transition. I told you, things haven't been going so well in Chicago." I turned back to the stove, avoiding her scrutiny. This new person in Gram's body could very well pitch me out on the porch, luggage and all, if she learned the truth.

"I think there's more on your mind than you're admitting. You're searching for something, girl, and came home to find it."

If only it were that simple. The answer to my problem didn't lie in Shoreview but in my work. Five years working alongside Stefan hadn't produced any great results. When I got back to Chicago, I had to find out exactly what was wrong. I was wasting my time and Stefan's until I did.

"What's the name of that boyfriend you're always yammering about, René or Jacques?"

"His name is Stefan. Why?"

"I notice you haven't mentioned him since you got here. Something you want to talk about?" She widened her eyes with the question.

I swear, the woman could see into my soul. Was my Gram finally back from whatever place she'd been hiding?

"There's nothing to talk about. A minor disagreement, that's all."

"Ahh, I thought it was something like that." She nodded, a pleased smile twitching at her lips. "It took you long enough to face facts. I was beginning to give up hope."

"What are you talking about?"

"Do I have to spell it out?"

I always hated it when she said things like that, as if she knew without my saying exactly what was bothering me. I ignored her comment. "I fixed breakfast. Eat before it gets cold."

We ate.

.   .   .

LATER, when it was time to leave for the shop, I asked, "Are you sure you'll be all right here alone all day?"

Her crossed arms and narrowed eyes gave me her answer, and I left in spite of my misgivings.

But Gram's words upset me all morning as I tended customers —like a canker sore under the tongue. Was she referring to Stefan? How could my working with him be anything but helpful —someone on his way to being recognized as a top Abstract Expressionist? To have one of the instructors at the Art Academy my senior year offer to mentor me in his new studio after graduation was a thrill and validation of my talent. It was my good fortune that Stefan took me under his wing, patiently explaining that the work I'd been doing was more like illustration than *real* art.

Of course, the fact that he was devastatingly handsome and totally devoted to his art only added to his allure. I was the envy of my contemporaries for the first time in my life. Stefan turned me from landscapes and portraiture to a more passionate use of color and form, always willing to critique my work and make suggestions for improvement. I'd never find a better mentor. I needed him if I was going to succeed, and once again I reminded myself that the little things he asked in return were minor annoyances.

I huffed out a breath and slammed a cabinet drawer after arranging the colorful threads inside during a lull in customers.

Gram might well be slipping. This place was a good example. Nothing was displayed to advantage. It was obvious now that she needed help here. Had I been so concerned with my art that I neglected the one person who believed in me?

By late afternoon, I'd rearranged all the yarn bins, sorting the gorgeous handspun by weight and color. There were skeins in the bright primary colors of red, yellow, and blue, and a multitude of blends, resulting in just about every color of the rainbow. Just handling them gave me a sense of peaceful energy and a yearning to create.

Next, I tackled the Swedish glassware and figurines. They were in need of a good dusting, maybe even washing. I picked up a red wine glass and marveled at its distinct and classic design. It was a gorgeous example of the thousands of hours spent in perfecting the glassblowing technique. I should rearrange every piece to show off its uniqueness. Then again, maybe I'd better not touch anything else until I saw Gram's reaction to what I'd already done.

I called her again.

"Gram, where do you purchase your office supplies?" It was my third call of the day, and I was running out of excuses in order to check on her.

"At Manny's Office Supply, as always," she said irritably. A long pause followed. "What's going on, Cara? I'm trying to get organized here, and you keep interrupting me."

Busted. "I thought maybe you'd changed things since I've been gone. That's all."

"You're sure that's all?"

"Yup." The door opened just then, and three young women sauntered in. "Gotta go, Gram. Customers."

I put down the phone and smiled at them in greeting. They only stayed long enough to give the inventory a cursory glance and were gone. Not too surprising. The inventory was geared more toward the older generation.

A few minutes later, as I bent over a shelf in the back room of the shop, I heard the door chime signaling someone new had entered the shop. Setting the Christmas ornaments gently back in their packing box, I went into the front to greet the customer.

I recognized him immediately. Thank goodness I wasn't holding one of the Christmas ornaments. It was Peter Andresen, my brother Jack's boyhood friend and my long-ago but not forgotten school crush. The one person I'd been avoiding in Shoreview like the flu since his return to town as a new doctor. And wouldn't you know, dressed in jeans and a t-shirt, I didn't look much different from the adoring teenager he'd remember. I felt my smile go stiff in an effort not to lose it.

He wore his sandy blond hair shorter now. That was the only change at first glance. I swallowed the thought after a closer look. His face had lost the youthful roundness that made every woman want to mother him, but when he flashed that familiar boyish grin, I could see he still possessed the seductive quality of a snake charmer. Thank goodness, I was beyond the temptation now. Or was I?

"Hi, Peter," I managed to chirp, my pulse picking up an irregular beat. His lean frame towered over me, making me feel like the "little sister" again.

"Hey, Squirt. When did you get home?" he asked. "It's been a long time." His look softened and he came up closer. "How long are you staying? A little longer this time?"

I decided to cut him some slack for using that hated childhood nickname, seeing as how we hadn't seen each other since he left for college after my sophomore prom. I took a calming breath. He wasn't to know I still harbored hurt feelings after that night. It had taken me a long time to regain any self-confidence

"I got here a few days ago. I'm here to visit Gram."

"How's she doing? I haven't seen her for a while. She's not sick, is she?"

"Well, not exactly." Kicking myself mentally, I pressed my lips together, sorry I'd let even that much escape. Gram would have a fit if she heard me.

"What does that mean? Is something wrong?" His brow furrowed.

Was he as concerned as he appeared? Wait a minute. Hadn't that been his M.O. as long as I'd known him? I once believed he thought I was someone special, blissfully ignoring all the older girls who'd clung to him like Saran Wrap. Those childish feelings of betrayal rose up like acid reflux in the back of my throat, reminding me.

Grow up, Cara, about time to leave those childish feelings behind.

"Don't worry about it. She has plenty of people watching out for her." Oh, crap. Now I sounded like a shrew. If I wasn't careful, he'd guess I still carried bad feelings and wonder why.

"Are you here to shop?" My voice squeaked. Groaning inwardly, I continued, "I mean, can I help you with anything?"

The tips of his ears had turned red, and I remembered my mother's long-ago teasing. *I can't believe with those leprechaun ears there isn't some Irish in you, Peter.* Oh, God, how he must've hated that. But it was better than being compared to a Norwegian troll, wasn't it?

"I came in to buy a gift," he said.

"What did you have in mind?"

"Something a woman would like. I haven't a clue. That's why I hoped Lucy would be here."

"In case you haven't noticed, I'm a woman now." I smiled to soften my words.

"Oh, I noticed, Squirt." His heated look confirmed it.

"Give me a hint," I said in my most business-like voice. I refused to slide into the old trap of hero-worshiping. It would be beyond embarrassing if he knew how long I'd harbored feelings for him.

"Well, I want something she'll think is pretty. Something that isn't useful." He looked around the room helplessly. "Something she wouldn't buy for herself."

"Hmm. Let me see." I walked toward the glass shelving in the window. Gram had a lot of Norwegian glass pieces there, where they'd catch the light and sparkle. At least they would when they weren't covered in dust. I picked up a vase. "This is lovely."

He hesitated. "Something a little more colorful, I think."

I spotted a beautifully carved wooden box covered in rosemaling, that Norwegian art form that Gram specialized in. "How about this? It's rather unique, unless she's Norwegian, of course."

"Yes, that's more like it." His fingers brushed mine as he picked up the box, sending a rush of unwelcome warmth up my arms. I pulled my hand back so quickly I almost hit the shelf behind me. He inspected the box carefully after giving me a side-long glance that told me he'd noticed. "Would you like it?"

"Of course, I'd like it. Otherwise I wouldn't have suggested it," I quipped. I'd treat him like a brother if that's what he expected.

"Whoa. As snippy as ever, I see." He raised one of those exquisitely shaped eyebrows, and I could see the laughter dancing in his navy-blue eyes. Memories of how he'd loved to join my brothers in teasing me surfaced. He'd been like a third brother until teen hormones got in the mix.

"Sorry. That came out before I remembered you were a paying customer." Gram would kill me if she'd heard that exchange. She'd always had a soft spot for Peter, never mind he was also a customer in this case. He'd spent a lot of time at our place as a kid, hiding out from the unhappiness of his own home, from what I'd heard.

I wondered whom the gift was for. A little imp of jealousy raised its head. His girlfriend? Or maybe a wife? I tried to see his ring finger, but it was hidden. Out of habit maybe?

Jeez, what was the matter with me? I'd been too long in the city, mingling with a crowd that didn't have the same morals I'd learned in my childhood. I'd ask Gram tonight. This was Shoreview. She'd know whether or not he was married and any other pertinent personal information. That's supposing she remembered, of course. I sure wasn't about to ask him.

The door chimes pealed again, and I excused myself. Another customer.

"Look around some more. Maybe something else will catch your eye," I said to him before walking away in the direction of the new customer.

"Oh, something already has." He winked and moved into the other room, hopefully before he saw my blush.

The customer was a younger woman, and her interested glance in Peter's direction was pretty obvious.

"Can I help you?" I asked politely.

"I'm just browsing," she said with a flick of long blond hair.

I watched as she wandered through the aisles, picking up knickknacks and setting them back on the shelves again, working her way closer to Peter, where he examined a blue vase. Finally, she stopped right next to him and smiled.

"Hello," she said.

The blatant invitation in her voice was obvious even from where I stood. Peter looked up from the other piece he'd been examining and gave her the wide smile I remembered so well from the past.

"Hi," he said and edged toward the counter with the carved box in his hands.

"I'll bet you don't remember me," she said, her cherry-red lips in a pout.

He gave her a slow, appraising glance. "Oh, I'm sure I'd remember if we'd met."

"I was with my mother, Mrs. Saari?"

A shuttered look replaced his open expression. "Oh, yes. Now I remember. How is she?"

"She's fine, thanks to you."

"Well, give her my regards." He set the box on the counter. "I'll take this, after all."

I hid the smile. So, things hadn't changed much. He was still a babe magnet. I wondered how his wife or girlfriend felt about that? I said a quick prayer of thanks that at least he wasn't my problem. I could only imagine how well his medical practice thrived.

"Tell Lucy to call me. I'm concerned," Peter said.

"Sure, and thanks for stopping." My eyes followed his departing figure thoughtfully.

4

I LOCKED UP GRAM'S SHOP EARLY THAT EVENING, DROPPED THE KEY in my oversize bag, and straightened my shoulders. I'd done something to help Gram, even if she wasn't aware of it. Every little bit would help.

The episode with Peter was another matter. I cringed at the memory of my reaction at seeing him after all these years. Thank God, no one else was there to witness it.

When I got home, I found Gram standing out in the pasture with her animals—petting Zeke and talking softly to the geese. Her voice carried softly across the evening breeze, and her relaxed stance was like the Gram I remembered. I closed my eyes, and some of the tension in my shoulders eased.

Zeke's ears went back close to his head when he noticed me, and the geese honked softly in irritation as I drew near the fence.

"Shush, you silly animals," Gram said in that same soothing voice. "It's only Cara." She kept a hold on the llama's halter.

I threw a leg over the fence and called out, "Hi, Gram."

Suddenly, loud and raucous honking shattered the tranquility. My feet had barely touched the ground when a flash of white feathers caught my eye, racing in my direction. I leaped back over the fence. The pair flapped their wings, still honking loudly.

Damn, but those birds were annoying.

"Don't let them intimidate you; that's what they want," Gram called as she walked over to the fence, still holding the llama's halter.

"Those two are meaner than a Chicago junkyard dog," I shouted above the noise.

"Just stand your ground and shake a finger at them. They'll back down," Gram said. "They're more bark than bite."

"If you say so." I gingerly climbed back over the fence, pretending to be brave, and shook my finger at the white creatures. "Don't even think about it," I snarled.

Surprisingly, Gram was right. They waddled away, honking softly to each other in disapproving tones.

"Get over yourselves," I yelled to their retreating backs.

"You got a phone call," Gram said. "That young man in Chicago wanted to know when you were coming home." She snorted indelicately. "I said you already *were* home. He didn't like it."

Rats. How could I have left my cell phone behind this morning? Further proof of my state of mind. The device had become a lifeline these past few years, connecting me to family, work, and Stefan.

Had Stefan stepped out of his self-indulgent world long enough to realize I might not return for Frank's opening and decided to reopen our argument? Gram didn't look upset, and I sighed in relief. He'd kept quiet about why I left Chicago.

"Did he leave a message?"

"He went on and on about some art gallery and how you were supposed to be there with him. Something about important people he wanted you to meet." She gave me a sidelong glance. "Does that mean you're leaving?"

The opening was tomorrow. Dare I leave Gram alone for a few days? She went back to brushing the llama while whispering something in his ear. If only all that dithering at the register and confusion about the car keys was only a temporary memory lapse. How could I know for sure?

I wanted—no, I *needed*—her to be normal again, back to the old Gram who took care of me, not this person who slipped in and out of her mind and needed my help. I also knew I deserved to be shot at sunrise for such a selfish thought. But it wasn't about my leaving, was it? It was about my loving Gram being herself again.

"I won't be leaving, Gram."

"He wants you to call him back—seemed put out when I told him you were working at the shop."

"I'll call him." I went into the house and grabbed my cell phone off the table where I'd left it that morning.

A picture of Stefan flashed in my head, standing in front of his easel, paintbrush in hand, squinting in the north light at the canvas. He wouldn't answer the rings; he never did. He waited for the machine to pick up to see if it was worth his time. After the fourth ring, I hung up. A perverse part of me made me do it. I didn't know what I wanted to say anyway. Maybe subconsciously, I'd left the phone behind on purpose. Let him call me back. He had caller ID. I knew I couldn't leave Gram in her condition—I didn't want to.

Gram had made soup for dinner, and the smell of savory chicken, onions, and parsley brought not only hunger to my stomach, but a sense of homecoming. At last, I felt like my world had righted. This was the warm, neat kitchen I remembered— light-years away from the chaotic mess I'd found on my arrival. I took a deep breath as we sat down at the table. I'd talk to her about leaving after dinner. It was still early.

The soup tasted as good as it smelled. After a few spoonsful, I took a crusty hard roll from the breadbasket and broke off a piece, spreading it with the creamy Wisconsin butter I'd grown up on.

"Peter Andresen came into the shop today," I said.

Gram's head snapped up, and she smiled brightly. "Oh, I'm sorry I missed him. I haven't seen him for ages. He's a pretty busy guy these days—with a new practice and all."

"Why is that, Gram? Does he have a family?" I asked casually, taking a bite of the roll. It still didn't seem real that Peter was a doctor. I'd pushed it out of my mind as soon as Jack told me.

"Heavens, no. I don't think the man takes time away from his work long enough to get close to a woman."

"Really?" That sure didn't sound like the Peter I remembered. She made him sound like another Stefan. I gave a snort, and Gram threw me a disapproving look. "How long has he been back in Shoreview?"

"Long enough to build up a thriving practice. What is your problem, girl? You've always had a bad attitude toward Peter. I don't understand it." With a sly look crossing her expressive face, she said, "Unless you're covering up something?"

I felt myself flushing. "Please, let's not go there. You know I have a boyfriend—you talked to him yourself today." No way was I giving her any ammunition for that line of thought.

She didn't reply, just bent her head over her bowl of soup and continued eating.

Peter stayed in my mind while I ate, and I remembered all the meals he'd shared with us, almost like one of the family. Everyone knew his father as an upstanding, wealthy, and extremely involved businessman, while his mother pretty much kept to herself and her lovely home, never attending school or sporting events or mixing with the locals. And as for his sister, Nancy, I didn't even want to go there. She'd had a grudge against me since our teen years for some unfathomable reason. I couldn't seem to get up the nerve to find out why. Was it their family dynamics that had driven Peter to spend so much time at our home during his growing-up years? Had she resented that?

My brothers and I had lost our father at a young age, but we'd had each other and Mom and Gram, always there to take an interest in their activities. And even though Mom worked long hours, she'd managed to keep a tight rein on her boys. And I had had Gram. We were pretty content.

It was in the later years that my social life took a turn for the worse. My brothers decided they had to take the place of my father and came to the conclusion there wasn't a boy in the county good enough for their little sister. It didn't take the local boys long to figure that out. Everyone knew Cara Olson was *hands off*. As a result, I ended up going to prom my sophomore year with the only boy they considered safe. That was Peter Andresen, two years older and looking bored out of his mind. He spent most of the evening ogling the senior girls. Even with the passing of time, the memory still cut.

We finished eating, and I started stacking the dishes on the counter.

"Don't bother with that, girl. I can do it. You'd best get upstairs and do your homework. Your mother will be home from work soon, and you know how upset she gets if you haven't finished by nine."

I prayed it was an odd joke. But judging from her expression, she was dead serious. My poor Gram. What was happening to her?

Gram couldn't be left alone. That was now obvious. Would she want me to give up this opportunity if she was in her right mind?

But that was the problem, wasn't it? She wasn't in her right mind. I knew that now. Somehow, I had to find an answer to this predicament.

There'd be no trip back to Chicago until then.

As I left the room and walked up the stairs, leaving Gram in her delusion, I thought about the things I would have to do for a longer stay.

"No, I won't be coming back anytime soon," I said, walking out onto the porch as I talked to Stefan later that evening. "Things aren't going as well as I hoped here."

"*What?*" Stefan's frustration vibrated in my ear all the way from Chicago. "You can't just throw away your career to take care of an old lady."

"She's not any old lady. She's my Gram."

"Well, put her in a nursing home if she needs someone with her all the time."

I gulped huge breaths of air. He didn't mean what he just said. He couldn't. Not in the way it sounded anyway. I could never love someone that callous.

"I have to go. I'll call you in a few days—when I know exactly what's going on."

"You're doing it again, aren't you?"

I felt my spine snap straight at his self-righteous tone. "What are you talking about?"

"You're letting your family take precedence over your career."

"I really don't have a choice here, Stefan." How could he be so clueless? The pain in my heart made my voice thick. "But you wouldn't understand that, would you?"

I'd been spending all my available time in his studio, with him. I was just now realizing how I'd replaced my family's dependence on me with Stefan's. How could I have been so blind?

After disconnecting, I hurried back into the house, desperate for help. I had to call my mother. I needed advice.

Mother, of course, was *Not available at this time. Please leave a message.* That just about summed up our relationship these days.

The one person who'd always been available was incognito, hiding somewhere in the recesses of her mind. Panic clawed up my throat. Who could I call? Who around here cared enough about Gram to be bothered? It'd been so long since I'd seen her friends, I didn't know how many were still in the area.

Then I remembered the woman who'd come into the shop that first day. The one who called Mom and started this mess. Martha O'Connor. She seemed like a sensible, caring woman. At least, that was my first impression, and first impressions usually turned out to be my best. I'd call her.

I ran up to my room and searched for the number she'd written on a scrap of paper for me that day in the shop.

"I'll feed the animals tonight, Gram," I yelled through the open door on my way outside. I pulled my cell phone out of my jean pocket and walked toward the barn where I'd have privacy. Taking the crumpled paper out of my pocket, I stopped just inside the door where Gram wouldn't see me. The sun was low in the west, shining through the weathered slats of the old building, and the dust from straw, hay, and grain floated endlessly through the still air as I walked farther into the structure.

"O'Connors'." The voice sounded friendly. I'd take the chance she'd be as helpful as she'd appeared.

"Martha? It's Cara Olson. I wonder if I could ask your opinion concerning Gram." The geese honked in the distance as soon as I spoke. Luckily, they toned down their squawking to a low grousing as they rounded the corner of the barn, and I shook my finger at them, just to be safe.

"Of course. Ask away. I'll be happy to help any way I can."

I'd felt a connection to the woman as soon as I met her—was it because we'd both spent years in Chicago? I didn't know, and did it matter? Maybe she could give me advice that Gram's long-time friends couldn't. They'd be like me, letting our hopes for the best cloud reality.

"Could we meet for coffee sometime soon?"

"Sure, it happens I'm not working tomorrow. How about in the morning? I have a ten-year-old stepson who's in school then. It would be a disaster if I wasn't home in the afternoon to meet the bus."

"That would be great. Before I open the shop if possible. Please keep this in your confidence. Gram would be very upset to hear I was talking about her to her friends."

"I understand completely."

Now I was left to feed Gram's critters. I threw some corn to the geese, and that stopped their complaining. Zeke watched with a baleful eye as I got his grain out of the locked bin but crowded against me as I threw it in his high feeder, out of the reach of the geese. Gram spoiled them terribly. They should've been out foraging in the pasture. But Gram said it was too early and too green and they had to adjust slowly, so I gave them a bit of hay, too, all the while obsessing if I was doing the right thing by discussing her condition with Martha.

WE MET EARLY that Friday morning at the Cuppa Joe café, the place where all the locals hung out, away from the trendy tourist spots. The familiar smell of fresh coffee assailed my senses and made me long a bit for the life I'd left in Chicago. I'd had no idea how uncomplicated it would seem after dealing with Gram. After looking around to make sure none of Gram's friends were there to see me, I took a seat in the worn booth where Martha waited, feeling like a covert operator in a thriller novel. I'd told Gram I was leaving for work extra early so I could get some cleaning done in the shop before any customers arrived.

I skipped the conversational niceties and jumped right in with my concerns. "I'm having a hard time figuring out exactly what is going on with Gram. She seems to go in and out of reality. When did you first notice a change in her behavior?"

"Looking back on it now, I can see there were gradual changes for months, but none of us put it together—because they were so random. Joan stopped at the house one Monday because that's the day the shop isn't open for business. Lucy made instant coffee because she'd been searching for her electric coffeepot all morning and couldn't imagine where she'd put it. When she opened the fridge for cream, she found it on the top shelf. She'd evidently put it there the night before. Joan said she seemed perfectly rational and just embarrassed. We all laughed about it when Joan told us the story—teased her about having a 'senior' moment.

"Another time, she put a mug of water in the shop microwave late one afternoon and hit the button for ten minutes instead of one and it shattered That's when we decided something had to be done before she hurt herself." She looked sympathetic. "I won't even go into the driving thing. I'm sure you've seen that for yourself."

"Oh, God. What is happening to her?" Fear hung like an oppressive weight over my shoulders. I couldn't rationalize away these behaviors.

"If you can forgive my butting in," she continued, "I suggest you take her to see her doctor. There are so many things that could cause her symptoms. We suggested it, of course, but didn't get anywhere. She seems determined to prove that nothing is wrong. I'd say she was in strong denial. She's pretty much shut herself off from her friends. I'll call her today and invite both of you to the Wool Gatherers meeting at my place tonight. It'll be good for her to be with friends."

"Okay, thanks, Martha. I appreciate it."

"Let me know if there's anything I can do. I know this can't be easy for you."

I left the coffee shop with a hollow feeling in my chest. How would I get this new Gram to the doctor's office, much less take away her car keys if it came to that? It would take an order from the Pope himself. But then, she might not listen to him either. Not this new Gram, anyway. Somehow, I would have to talk her into it.

5

GOING TO THE WOOL GATHERERS WITH GRAM THAT FRIDAY NIGHT would be as much fun as a bikini wax, but what choice did I have? Imagining what could happen to Gram driving alone on those dark country roads in her mental state was enough for me to grab my jacket.

Socializing with her friends would be a good thing for her. Martha was right. We piled into the vintage Buick and took off into the blue shadows of a cool spring evening. We'd already had the familiar argument over who would drive and ended up in the navy-blue boat with me at the wheel. Gram sat beside me, perfectly calm and balancing the cake on her lap she'd baked after much reading and rereading of an old family recipe.

"I don't bake anymore. What's the use when there's no one around to eat it but me," was her explanation for her memory lapse.

She had a point. Shoot, I could hardly remember how to make Stefan's favorite chocolate mousse without the recipe in front of me. And how many times had I done it?

I started to make a left-hand turn at the highway, only to find the automatic turn signal didn't work.

"Use your arm to signal like you do with a bike," was her reply to my shriek as I looked into the rearview mirror. Luckily, no one was close behind us.

"What if someone decided to pass me right now?" I snapped. "I could lose an arm."

"They're not supposed to pass near an intersection," she said smugly.

"Oh, and isn't knowing that going to give me a lot of satisfaction when I'm wearing a prosthesis, Gram?" I gave a gentle swat to her arm, so she'd know I was joking.

After much winding up and down and around country roads and several dead ends, we finally arrived at Martha's. I wanted to turn back several times, but Gram insisted we keep looking. The log house was new, and the country setting picture-perfect. A lowering sun gave the logs a warm, polished look, and the weathered porch swing with its bright pillows was very inviting, a combination of old and new. As I carried the cake in for Gram, I took a deep breath. *Maybe this night wouldn't be so bad.*

Martha opened the door at Gram's knock, and her face lit with a smile. "Oh, I'm so glad you made it. Did you have any trouble finding us? I was beginning to worry."

You aren't the only one, was on the tip of my tongue, but before I could answer, Gram said, "Oh, no. We had a lovely drive here."

Martha took the cake from my outstretched hands and set it on the kitchen counter before giving Gram a welcoming hug. The tight lines around Gram's mouth visibly relaxed. She'd told me on the drive over that Martha was a part-time teacher. It was easy to see why kids would love her. I repeated a silent prayer Gram would never learn it was Martha who had called Mom and also that Gram would be able to keep her wits about her this evening. I seemed to be doing a lot of that lately. Asking for divine intervention, that was. Hopefully, God still remembered me from the days when prayer had been more of a habit.

Voices echoed from the great room as I stepped farther into the home. I was pleasantly surprised to see a few of the women looked close to my age. When one of them turned around, I recognized Sue Ellen Johnson from my high school years. I hadn't seen her since but remembered her as having a great sense of humor and an easygoing manner. Could be a fun evening after all. I started to relax.

"Cara Olson, it's so great to see you," she said, walking over and grabbing my hands in hers.

Sue Ellen still wore her hair in a ponytail, and there was no makeup glamorizing her face that I could see. I was right in my first estimation. Things hadn't changed much around here. I felt even more at home.

"When did you get into town?" she asked.

"A few days ago."

Tapping the shoulder of the woman standing next to her, she said, "Nancy, look who's here," before turning away to answer someone else's question.

Oh no, not Nancy Andresen. If only I'd recognized her sooner, I could've been forewarned. The woman had the cool blue eyes and blond hair of her Scandinavian ancestry but the temperament of a stereotypical green-eyed redhead. She could've fallen out of my mother's family tree. I'd planned to avoid her like I did her brother.

"Peter said you were back in town. Are you here to honor us locals with your presence?"

Whoa, my nose almost had frostbite. Her attitude hadn't changed a bit.

"I'm visiting my grandmother, and in case you've forgotten, I'm a local, too." I said it with a smile, hoping to lessen the tension that had always been between us.

"Really? Is that why you've spent so much time here these past years?" She managed to turn her nose up even further. "Lucy tells me you're all wrapped up in your artist boyfriend and his art. I'm surprised you even found the time to have a conversation with my brother."

"Peter and I were friends when we were kids." I narrowed my eyes. What was her problem?

"Were you? I wouldn't have guessed."

Okay, now I *was* confused. "Well, anyway, I'm here to visit my grandmother."

She looked over at Gram, and her features softened. "That's good for Lucy," Nancy said before she abruptly walked away.

I looked from Gram to her. What was that all about? The

name Nancy and the half-forgotten conversation about Gram needing help in the shop came back to me. Was this the Nancy she'd referred to? Nah, that was too much of a stretch, even for someone with my imagination.

I followed behind Gram as she wandered across the room. She finally sat down next to Joan Bergland. They'd been friends for years. Joan had waved a greeting to me earlier. The cane next to Joan's spinning wheel reminded me that Gram had told me she'd had a stroke a while back. Joan was an expert hand spinner and often gave lessons to beginning spinners. As they talked, Gram pulled an embroidery hoop out of the gigantic purse she carried, along with multicolored swatches of embroidery thread, and began to thread a needle. I stood closer.

"When did you start embroidering?" I asked. "I don't remember you doing needlework."

"I probably did a lot of things you never noticed," she said in a dry tone.

What else would I learn about this woman I thought I knew so well? That familiar guilt settled in. She was right. I had become so desperate to succeed in art that I'd devoted myself entirely to Stefan and work, same as I'd devoted my younger self to family until they no longer needed me on a daily basis.

Before I could get too deeply engrossed in my thoughts, I was interrupted. "C'mon." Sue Ellen had returned with Martha and began pulling me around the room. "I want you to meet everyone."

The women were involved in a variety of crafts—spinning, knitting—one even had a portable loom set up on a small table. As much as I admired their handiwork, what really caught my eye was the glorious mixture of colors and fibers they worked with. I stopped to run my hand over a few balls of the wool, amazed at the softness and clarity of color.

"Hi, Cara. I'll bet you don't remember me." It took a moment for me to place the friendly face of a girl in the class behind me in high school.

"Of course, I do, Lila." I offered my hand. "Nice to see you again."

"We're so glad you're here," she said in a whisper. "Lucy looks better already."

I gazed across the room at Gram again. She did look more like herself, engaged in conversation with her friends. "I sure hope so."

Glancing back at Lila, I asked, "What are you working on?"

"I'm spinning this wool for a sweater I plan to knit for my husband." She picked up the ball of wool sitting at her feet and handed it to me. "Did Lucy mention that I raise sheep? This wool is homegrown merino. I'm the one who got Martha involved in raising her own wool." She smiled devilishly. "Which, of course, led her to meeting the local sheep shearer, who is now her husband."

"I'd like to take *some* credit, if you don't mind." A woman who'd been introduced as Carol chimed in. She was the one with the small loom. "I'm the one who got her the job at Jake's school, after all."

"Okay, you all had a hand in it, and I'm really grateful. Most days anyway," Martha said with a grin.

"Where is Riley, by the way?" Carol asked.

"He's hiding out upstairs with Jake and Maeve," Martha answered. "Maeve is our border collie," she explained. "A real sweetheart now that she's out of the puppy stage. I have Sue Ellen and her husband to thank for her. That puppy was a godsend when I first moved here alone. They were right when they said I needed her company."

The woman next to Lila had been watching us with interest as we talked. I murmured a soft greeting when we reached her.

"Cheryl, show Cara the vest you're working on," Martha said. She turned back to me. "I think you'll like it since you're an artist. It's becoming a real work of art."

Cheryl lifted up the garment. It was made of multicolored wool—shades of blue, pink, and green—somehow blended in layers to make the most interesting fabric I'd ever seen. She'd embroidered a pattern over the wool with different colored threads. "This is a vest I made out of hand felted wool. I'm just embellishing it with some old jewelry. Trying to 'fancy it up', as my youngest daughter would say."

"Hand felted? I never heard the term before."

"It's when you make felt out of carded wool—using soap, warm water, and friction. It's actually a lot of fun, and you can come up with some amazing designs."

"Have you been doing this for a long time?" It looked pretty complicated to me. In fact, all the projects I'd seen that evening looked like the women had put a lot of thought and effort into them. Even Nancy, busily knitting on what looked like an intricate Nordic ski pattern.

"Actually, I just started felting a few months ago. I don't have a lot of time for long, involved projects. I took a class in Green Bay, and Carol was in it. She told me about this group and invited me to a meeting. I love it."

My excitement level shot up at the sight of all those brilliant colors and textures. I suddenly missed my paints more than ever. I picked up a corner of the vest, noticing the dyed curls felted into the wool. "What a beautiful color. And so soft."

"Those are curls from the fleece of a mohair goat." Cheryl looked up from her handwork. "We usually set aside a day in early summer for dying the fleece and spun yarn. It's a lot of fun. You should join us. I can teach you to felt that day if you'd like," she said shyly.

"I don't think I'll be here long enough for that," I said. My throat started to close at the thought. "I have my work waiting for me in Chicago."

"Of course, you won't," Nancy said with a smirk. "Things will be much too boring around here for you."

"I'll have to get back to my part-time work at the coffee shop before then," I explained uncomfortably.

"I understand," Cheryl said with a sympathetic nod.

As we were eating the potluck dinner later that evening, I watched Gram and Nancy, heads together, talking and smiling like two old friends. I pulled Gram aside when she returned to the kitchen for a piece of cake. "I didn't know you were such good friends with Nancy Andresen."

"Such a sweet girl. She helps me in the shop sometimes. Remember, I told you that the other day?" Gram said with a gentle look in Nancy's direction.

I don't know which shocked me the most. The use of the word sweet and Nancy in the same sentence, or that she really was the "Nancy" who helped Gram in the shop. I barely kept my plate from slipping out of my hands.

I had to confirm this with Nancy. Maybe Gram's mind was wandering again. But dare I risk another slash from that barbed tongue? The decision was made for me later when I caught Nancy alone in the kitchen and had the perfect opportunity to question her.

"Sure, I help her,' she said. "She's a wonderful, caring woman. Practically abandoned by her family."

I should've anticipated her answer, but the last part was over the top, even for Nancy.

"What? No one *abandoned* her."

"Really? Then why did it take her friends to notice she has a problem? Where were you? Oh, that's right." She rolled her eyes in an annoying way. "You were off in the big city. Pursuing your 'art' career. How's that working out for you, by the way? I haven't heard about any great awards, unless I somehow missed the news?"

The rising cloud of hurt and anger almost cut off my vision. Who was she to judge me so harshly?

"I was doing it for Gram. It was what she wanted—for me to succeed at something when she never had the chance." I clamped my lips shut. Where had that come from? I didn't need to justify myself to this woman.

"You keep telling yourself that if it makes you feel better. Just do me one favor, will you? Stay away from my brother. He's had enough heartache."

What was that all about? Her tirade played over and over in my mind the rest of the evening, and I was barely able to carry on an intelligent conversation with anyone. When Gram said she was ready to leave, I bolted for the door. Now, if only I could avoid any left-hand turns in the blue demon on the way home.

.   .   .

I "BIT THE BULLET"—AS Gram was fond of saying—the next morning when I was pretty sure she would have her wits about her. She'd slipped into the past again on the ride home last night. "I'd like to make an appointment to see your doctor."

She gave me a sharp look. Oh, yeah, her wits were in order now. I'd begun to notice a pattern here. She was my old Gram in the morning, pleasant and easygoing and placid. At least, most of the time. But as the day wore on, she became more distracted and agitated. By evening, she passed in and out of reality.

If I wanted to get her in to see the doctor, I had to make a morning appointment. Or maybe the late afternoon, when her symptoms were at their worse, would be better?

"Why? What's the matter with you that you have to see a doctor?"

"Not for me. I think it would be a good idea for you to get a physical and an opinion."

"Opinion on what? You're talking in riddles, girl."

Once again, I'd let my mouth move faster than my brain. If I didn't step carefully here, I'd end up in deep llama dung. But there was no turning back; it had to be done. I took a deep breath and plunged in.

"Gram, I've noticed a change in you since my last visit."

Her head shot up. Was that a sudden flash of fear I saw in her eyes?

"Explain yourself," she snapped in a tone she'd never used with me.

"Well, I couldn't help but notice you've been having trouble with your memory." How far dare I go? I didn't want to scare her unnecessarily. "Maybe you need a thorough checkup. When was the last time you had one?"

"There's nothing wrong with me," Gram insisted, but I could see the worry in her eyes. "I might be slowing down some, but that doesn't mean I'm ready to be put out to pasture."

"That's not what I'm suggesting." I walked on eggshells. One slip-up could bring disaster. "I'm merely saying that a thorough checkup might find a problem that could be easily fixed."

"Hmm, it might not be a bad idea at that." There was that sly look again. "I'll call and make the appointment first thing Monday morning if it'll make you feel better," she said.

What? No big argument? This was going a lot easier than I'd hoped. Maybe Gram had just needed an extra push. I breathed a sigh of relief. Dr. Martin had been her physician for as long as I could remember. He'd notice any changes in her.

When my brother called later that evening, I didn't have much to report except that Gram was open to a doctor's visit. I promised to call as soon as I had anything definite to report.

FATE or maybe the alignment of the stars or possibly the angels had a hand in getting Gram an appointment because the clinic just happened to have a cancellation that Wednesday. We closed the shop early and drove over in the late afternoon. Gram insisted we take her Buick.

"I'm not riding in that tin can you drive." She crossed her arms over her chest, and I knew arguing would be useless. I'd had to agree anyway since she'd had the turn signals repaired after much complaining she didn't drive enough to warrant the expense.

"Well, at least let me drive."

She mumbled something about me needing "time behind the wheel", and I realized she'd slipped into the past again. Would her doctor be able to bring my Gram back to stay?

6

GRAM AND I DROVE UP TO THE SAME CLINIC I'D VISITED throughout my childhood—a one-story, red-brick building located at the bottom of the hill near the harbor. We got out of the parked car and walked from the newly paved parking lot to the double white doors. The ever-present gulls swooped overhead, searching the nearby restaurant parking lot for leftover crumbs. They had a few weeks to wait before the outdoor tables were set out and dining alfresco began.

I walked up to the desk with Gram and waited in the queue to register. My palms sweated as much as they had when the two of us stood in line for my school immunizations. After some fumbling, we found her Medicare card and other pertinent information in the zipper pocket of her oversized knit purse.

"I'm coming in with you."

"So, now you think I can't even remember what's wrong with me?" The old Gram was back, at least temporarily.

"I thought you wanted me to talk to the doctor?"

Her expression brightened. "That's right, I forgot."

The nurse came in and took her blood pressure. Luckily, they didn't have to check mine. My nerves jumped around like bare feet on hot pavement. I was so scared for Gram.

"Dr. Andresen will see you in a few minutes," the nurse said with a friendly smile. My head snapped up, and I looked at Gram. She looked away, fidgeting in the contoured plastic chair.

"I thought you made the appointment with Dr. Martin."

"Didn't you know? Dr. Martin retired and moved to Florida. Peter is the new doctor on the clinic staff." Gram stopped moving long enough to laugh at my surprised gasp. "That shocks you, hey? I don't know why. Dr. Martin was getting old."

"You're kidding me, right?" Her smirk would've been comical if I wasn't on the receiving end. Why hadn't I looked closer into the matter of Gram's doctor? "How come no one told me Peter was your doctor?"

"Well, why would we? You were never interested in him. Or were you?"

"I'm just surprised, that's all. I would've thought someone would tell me."

"He's a wonderful doctor. Everyone loves him," she said, still wearing the smirk.

I sat up straighter. Could I trust him to diagnose Gram when her condition could be so serious? "He's awfully new at this, isn't he? Isn't there another doctor on staff we could see?"

"Peter is the doctor I want to see," she insisted. "I always liked him when he came over with the boys. Did I mention he's single?"

I wasn't about to argue. If he was the doctor she wanted, I'd go with it. At least it was a start.

"I can just imagine all the women lining up to see him," I said, doing my own eye roll.

Gram's eyes lit up at that remark, and I could've bitten my tongue. "Yes, and he's still single."

"I heard you the first three times, Gram."

I wasn't prepared for that same rush of adrenaline I'd felt in the shop when Peter walked into the exam room. *Get over it,* I chided myself, grateful nonetheless that I'd worn my favorite blue cotton jacket over my t-shirt. Stefan had even complimented me on the color choice, and that was pretty unusual.

"Good morning, Mrs. Olson," Peter said. He wore the requisite white jacket over a blue shirt, the stethoscope around his neck and the chart he carried making him a far cry from the playboy I remembered. But the penetrating depth of his glance hadn't changed.

"Call me Lucy, Peter. No need to get all professional." Her look was almost playful.

"Of course." He took Gram's hand gently and gave her the full force of his intent scrutiny. "Are you having a problem? You haven't been in for a check-up for quite some time."

Wow. He was a regular Dr. Phil. It didn't take a psychologist to see why he was so popular with his patients. I was impressed.

"Someone seems to think so," Gram answered with a tip of her head in my direction.

"She gets a bit confused at times," I chimed in.

"Hi, Squirt. Nice to see you again." Thankfully, the look he gave me wasn't nearly as intense.

With that nickname, I was back to the little pest that followed my brothers around all summer, enamored with their handsome friend. Was this payback for my behavior in the shop?

I could feel the heat in my face as the memories of the crush I'd had on him, the boy who'd always encouraged my brothers to let me tag along when they went fishing or to the beach. He'd been my knight in shining armor then. I wondered if his annoying sister had ever divulged my dark secret or if she even knew? Most of my friends had guessed I was madly in love with him. That's why his behavior at the prom was so devastating. I had hoped that evening would prove to him how I'd grown up. Instead, I'd been forced to watch him flit from girl to girl, barely blinking an eye in my direction. It had taken me years to get my self-esteem back. Until Stefan had asked me to join him, in fact.

"Put on the gown, and I'll be right back to examine you."

I snapped back to reality and looked at Gram. She seemed more relaxed now. Wish the same could've been said for me.

After doing a thorough physical exam, Peter asked Gram a lot of questions, which she answered quite coherently, even though I could see she was becoming a little agitated. I quietly thanked God. If only he could tell me that my worries were exaggerated.

"Can you count from one to ten for me?" he asked.

"Well, of course, I can." The question annoyed her, and her face flushed. She started counting.

"One, two, three, four, five," and then she hesitated, looking at me with a flash of panic on her face before continuing. "Six, seven, eight, nine ten, Jack, Queen, King." She smiled triumphantly.

He and I both laughed, and I was sure he also remembered the many hours we'd spent playing cards on Gram's porch on those long-ago summer evenings. Card games were like one of life's lessons to Gram. She'd never cut us a break, expecting us to do our best and take our losses like a grownup.

After a short memory test which gave Gram problems, Peter left the room, saying he'd return after Gram dressed, his expression once again professional. She didn't speak as I helped her on with her clothing. Finally, in a voice just above a whisper, she asked, "It's pretty bad, isn't it?" Her hands shook as she buttoned up the high collar of her cotton blouse.

I didn't know what to say. I was frightened myself at his seriousness when he left the room. "Peter will know what to do."

And in my heart, I prayed it was true. After watching Peter with Gram and her reaction to him, I was reminded that it wasn't his looks or bad boy attitude that had attracted me to him all those years ago. It was the innate caring for others I'd sensed in him, even then. He'd made a good career choice. I had to admit it.

Our hands clung to each other as we waited in the office chairs. After what seemed like ages, he returned, a sheaf of papers in hand.

"Well. This is where we stand." He put Gram's chart on the desk and looked directly at us. I knew by his somber expression there'd be no sugarcoating the diagnosis.

"Physically, you're just fine. In fact, for a woman your age, you're in excellent health. I do, however, find signs of the early stages of dementia."

Gram's face lost all color at those words.

"Is it Alzheimer's?" she asked in a barely audible tone.

"It's too soon to tell. First, I'll study your lab work, and we'll get a CT scan of your brain to check for any tumors or minor strokes you may have had and not noticed. There could be various other reasons for the problem—maybe a lack of vitamins or low thyroid function to name a few causes. So, let's not think the worse until we have to.

"The good news is that if it is Alzheimer's, there are medications now that work quite well to lessen the symptoms—for years in some patients. And you're in the earliest stages if it is dementia, so you have an excellent chance of the medications working. I won't say that it's a cure because that would be lying. But medication will lessen the symptoms so that hopefully you can continue to live your normal, productive life for a long time."

Peter rose from his chair and put a comforting hand on Gram's shoulder. "The nurse will schedule all the tests with the lab. We'll talk again after I have your results." Turning to me, he said, "I want you to call me right away if she has any problems."

As Gram gathered her purse and sweater from the chair, he pulled me into the hall. I tried desperately to think of him merely as Gram's doctor, but the way my pulse shot up at his nearness told me that wasn't going to happen anytime soon.

"I'm glad you're here to take care of her. She'll need you," he said. "As I said, I'll call when I have the test results, and you can make another appointment then."

"I'll watch her carefully," I muttered, thankful he couldn't read my wayward thoughts.

"Thank you, Peter," Gram murmured when she reached us.

"I'll do my best for you, Lucy. You know that, right?"

"There's no one I'd trust more than you, Peter. By the way, you can come over and spend some time with Cara and me, you know. She's kind of lonely, I suspect, with just a confused old woman for company."

Give me a break. She wasn't fooling anyone with that self-deprecating attitude. My face heated again with her blatant proposal and I held my purse in a death grip.

"I imagine you'll be hearing from the boys," I said, desperate to change the subject. We both knew Jack would be calling him as soon as he heard the news, badgering him endlessly about Gram's condition.

"I look forward to it—haven't talked to Jack in ages." He gave me that engaging smile that probably melted hearts all over Door County. I sighed inwardly. Whatever gave Gram the idea he'd be interested in me? I still smarted from the last time the family had arranged for us to spend an evening together.

"What would you think if I took Lucy's suggestion and came out to the farm one night?" he asked softly for my ears alone.

Danger, danger, danger, flashed through my brain. How was I supposed to answer that without looking like another desperate female? I quickly conjured up a picture of Stefan hard at work in his studio.

"That's fine, but just so you know, I do have a boyfriend." The blurted line sounded embarrassed, even to me. Laughter glinted in his eyes, proof he still thought of me as a little sister. My resolve strengthened. I could and would remain immune to his magnetism. He was merely an old addiction left over from adolescence.

"Don't worry. I don't bite."

"You won't get the chance." Good grief, you'd swear I was back in junior high. I marched out behind Gram, toward the lab and her tests, my head held high, even though I heard his chuckle behind me.

"IT'S HIM AGAIN," Gram said the following Monday as she handed me my cell phone. "That Steve person, or whatever his name is these days."

I had to remember to keep my eye on the thing while I worked. I'd set it on top of the glass case in the main part of Gram's shop because my pockets were so shallow. I could never be quite sure what Gram would say to any caller. Even though I didn't miss Stefan as much as I'd expected to, I owed him big time for the help he'd given me these past five years and didn't want Gram to unknowingly insult him.

"Hi," I breathed into the phone, trying to sound more enthused than I felt. Being Monday, the shop was closed, so we'd decided to do a bit of spring cleaning. I was dressed in an old pair of cut-offs and a sleeveless shirt I'd found in the back of my former closet. Gram had worked with me, washing glassware and shelves. She'd laughed, just like old times, while I told her about my adventures in the art world.

"I've got good news," Stefan said, more excitement in his voice than I'd heard in a long time. "I had a meeting with the owner of the Lincoln gallery. They've accepted me as a client."

"Wow." I'd never been in that gallery but heard it was quite prestigious. I was impressed. "That's wonderful."

"But that's not all. He's willing to add your best piece to my opening and showcase it as the work of an up-and-coming artist."

"Oh my God. I can't believe it." I jumped up and down in my excitement. "Are you sure?"

"Have you been working on anything new?"

"I've been so busy here the past two weeks that I haven't had a chance." Already, my mind was racing through possibilities.

"Babysitting?" The disdain in his voice immediately raised my hackles.

"I've been helping Gram with the shop, getting things back in order."

"In other words, you haven't been working at all."

"I've been working all right, just not on my paintings."

"Well, you'd better get going on a new piece because you've only got about two and a half weeks. Do you think you can do it?"

"Of course, I can."

"I hope so because I've put my reputation on the line here. It's imperative that you show up. You've already missed the deadline to enter the museum contest."

I knew I'd missed the deadline. It'd been preying on my mind for days.

"When will you be back?" he continued.

Oh, damn. I didn't have an answer for that question. "I don't know...things are still unsettled." I'd walked to the back of the shop by this time, worried Gram would overhear our conversation. "The doctor hasn't given Gram a diagnosis yet. He's waiting for test results," I said softly. "It sounds like things are really happening for you, though."

"I've been extremely busy, as you can imagine. I have all these paintings to get framed and boxed. I sure could use your help. But I guess you've got more important things on your mind."

Had he always had that pronounced whine in his voice or had it just developed since I left? "I'm afraid Gram has to be my number one priority at the moment. All I can do right now is hope for a good diagnosis." I looked up at the ceiling for patience.

Maybe I didn't actually owe Stefan all that much. But still, there was that guilt. And I really didn't want to lose out on this opportunity. It would be a major loss. I'd probably never get a chance like it again. And now that Stefan was talking to a new student....

"I'll try my hardest to get there as soon as I can, but things are looking doubtful for a quick return," I said. "Maybe in a week. We should hear the results of Gram's tests any day. That will give me a clue as to what's going on with her." I tried for an upbeat tone, but truthfully, I didn't see how things could turn around that fast. But I could start painting again. Gram had some supplies in her shop, and I could scrounge around the house for more. "In the meantime, I'll start to work right away on a new piece. I have something in mind. If nothing else, I can always ship it."

"Remember what we discussed...how the color conveys the emotion. Don't fall back on your old, easy way of seeing things."

"Yes, of course. I remember all you taught me. Did you think I'd forget it in a few weeks?" He'd been pounding that abstract style in my head for so long that some days I felt like throwing an open jar of paint on the canvas and calling it quits.

"Okay, call me when you're ready to come back. It's really important that you're here in person, Cara."

"Of course, Stefan. I'll see what I can do." I rolled my eyes and closed the phone as I walked back to the front of the shop.

"What did he want?" Gram asked.

"He's all excited. He was offered representation by a prestigious art gallery." I wanted to tell her about his offer to show one of my works at his opening. We'd never kept secrets from each other. But if I told her, she'd insist I leave right away. I couldn't. Not if I wanted to be able to face myself in the mirror each morning. My heart and mind would be on Gram...painting wouldn't even be a close second.

BY EVENING, I'd devised a plan. I called my mom and told her about the offer.

"For heaven's sakes, Cara. When are you going to give up that ridiculous pipedream and get a career that will sustain you in your old age?"

"I have a career, Mom. Success isn't all about money, you know. I'm an artist." Why did I even feel the need to justify my life?

"Oh, right. That and fifty cents will get you a cup of coffee, or whatever it is they charge for coffee in that fancy coffee shop," she sniffed.

"It's not fifty cents, Mom. I can guarantee that."

"Who's going to stay with Lucy if you go?"

"I don't know, Mom. That's why I'm calling you."

"Well, isn't it just like that Steve person to muck things up like this." Mom had this habit of getting angry with anyone who messed with her life plans. Kind of like Stefan, actually. "Well, I can't leave. Dave hasn't been feeling well enough to travel." She gave a great sigh. "I'll call your brothers. They're very concerned about Lucy and you. Have they called?"

I'd talked to Jack last week. They seemed pretty busy. "Not yet."

"Well, expect a call any day. I think they're making plans to visit soon."

Oh, wait. Hope sprang up unbidden. Maybe one of them could stay with Gram while I went to Chicago. It could happen. It was obvious Mom wasn't going to help me out.

"By the way, did you know that Peter is still single?" Mom said.

"Goodbye, Mom. I'll call if there's any news."

My brothers were my last hope. Otherwise, I'd have to ship my painting and miss all the fun and excitement of the opening.

.   .   .

WEDNESDAY MORNING GRAM and I arrived at the shop early, loaded with art supplies I'd dug out of my closet and filled in with a stop at the local art supplier. We went straight to the back room and unloaded our supplies. I could work on my new project between customers. It would be a small piece because of time and space limitations. Stefan and I had discussed my ideas for hours in the weeks before I'd left Chicago, and I was confident this new one would please him and the critics. Now, I only had to get myself motivated to begin. *What was I afraid of?*

It would have to be something different—unique—if it was to catch the eye of a dealer. Stefan leaned toward bright, almost garish colors and loose design. I could never quite get a handle on that style, even after all this time.

But I pushed my doubts aside. *You can do it*, I repeated over and over until it became my new mantra.

Gram sold unfinished paper-máche boxes and other objects ready for decoration in the shop, along with a small supply of paints and brushes. It was still early so I set her up in the back room with a small box to decorate like she'd done for me years earlier. Meanwhile, I began the study, hoping to get the colors and shapes I wanted on the small canvas that day. It would be abstract in design, of course, and as I layered on the vivid blue, I planned to intersperse it with soft yellows and flame-like flashes of vibrant red. I could envision it coming together as the day went on. This time, I would get it right. Stefan would be pleased. I finally had a vision of my success.

Being in the small kitchenette with Gram brought back a lot of childhood memories. I'd spent much of my summers in this very spot. Mom had often dropped me off on her way to work the noon shift at the local Swedish restaurant, and Gram provided me with brush and paints to keep me busy. The late summer afternoons had flown by as we painted, side by side, between customers. This was the place where I first discovered my love of art, totally immersed in the blending of colors and the manipulation of my brushstrokes.

Gram was into rosemaling, that beautiful three-hundred-year-old Norwegian art form. She practiced the Telemark style, named after the region in Norway where it had been initiated. I remembered Gram explaining to me one day as we painted together that in Norwegian, "rose" meant decoration and "maler" meant painter. She showed me how the decoration was based mostly on scrolls and imagined flowers—no roses involved.

I could still hear her soothing voice in my head, explaining when I wanted to use bright reds and yellows, that the palette used was very limited, usually only three or four colors in earth tones and subdued shades. We had looked at pictures in her cherished books that described how it began as a way for early Norwegians to decorate their churches and log homes and then spread to the beautifully carved furniture and other objects in their households.

It wasn't until years later that I realized Gram was an absolute master of the brush, due to the rhythm of Telemark outlining that set it apart from other types of rosemaling. She taught me many things in the back room of that little shop. The most important being my love of color and design.

Mom had never wanted me to go to art school, scared to death I'd end up working as a waitress like she did, barely making ends meet while trying to raise a family. Mom wanted me to have what she considered a real career—like nursing or teaching—and job security. We'd argued long and hard about it, but it was the one thing I was determined to do with my life.

Gram always kept out of our arguments, but I'd felt her support. She believed in my art and was full of encouragement. She and Mom were at opposite ends of the spectrum on this, and I felt the pull—practicality on one side or following my dream on the other. The dream won out. I was doing it as much for Gram as for myself. Yet, I understood why Mom was so upset with my working at The Daily Grind; it wasn't the life she'd planned for her only daughter. *But what could I do?* I couldn't give up on my dream. I wasn't starving, and I got to paint almost every day. I was actually quite satisfied and probably would've gone on forever if fate hadn't made the change for me. Now I'd been given several chances for success. I couldn't let myself screw up.

Before I knew it, it was late afternoon, and I was far from

where I'd planned to be. Customers had been in and out most of the day...usually a good thing. Today, not so much. I still had hopes of finishing the small study tomorrow so I could begin the actual painting soon after, depending on how busy we were in the shop.

"What do you say we close up and go out for dinner?" I asked Gram. Life was looking good. Gram had kept busy painting most of the day, although I could see her focus and attention waning as the afternoon wore on.

Surprisingly, she didn't give me any argument, so we closed up and went to Ina's Swedish Restaurant, the same one my mom had worked at years earlier. I hadn't visited the place in several years, so I felt like a tourist seeing the waitresses dressed in Scandinavian costume and looking in the gift shop with its many Scandinavian imports with new eyes. Gram, of course, would always love the décor, as it was lush with rosemaling.

The waitress had just brought our meal—Swedish pancakes, light and fluffy and covered in syrup—when Peter and his sister walked in. I turned my head quickly, pretending I hadn't seen them.

"Oh, look. There's Peter and Nancy," Gram said in that voice of the hard-of-hearing. They turned around, and she waved madly. Naturally, they came over.

"Join us," Gram said.

I wanted to kick her under the table, but heaven only knew what kind of a reaction that would get. Instead, I gave a generic smile, using a mouthful of food as an excuse for not seconding the invitation.

"Thank you, Lucy, but I can see you already have your meal. Some other time perhaps," Peter said.

Nancy looked as relieved as I felt at his answer.

"You haven't been over to see us, Peter," Gram scolded.

"It's been a busy week at the clinic. What can I say?" he said with a slight grimace.

"How about we set a date for dinner—say, next Monday— since that's the day the shop is closed?"

Alarm bells went off in my head. Monday was close to the

time I should be leaving for Chicago with a completed project. Gram didn't know anything about my trip, and I couldn't tell her. Not until I had a working plan for her care.

"You're welcome, too, Nancy." Gram was being her old, gracious self, and while that made me happy, I dreaded the thought of spending an evening with the two of them at any time, much less that day.

"That's nice of you to include me, Lucy, but I'm busy that evening." Our eyes met, and we gave a collective sigh of relief.

I glanced down at my watch. Six o'clock, and Gram still had her wits about her. Maybe the painting today had been good for her.

"I'll check my schedule, but it should be fine," Peter said. "We'll let you get on with your dinner. Nice to see you again, ladies." Peter left us with his usual engaging grin and walked toward an empty table. Nancy followed close behind.

"Now don't forget about dinner, Peter," Gram called out to their retreating backs.

I watched them with mixed emotions, longing for the easy camaraderie of those long-ago summer evenings spent playing cards with Gram, my brothers, and Peter. The evenings had usually ended with lots of shouting and laughter.

Funny, how I'd never thought about Nancy and what she was doing during those evenings. Was she left alone with her reclusive mother? Why hadn't Peter brought her along? For that matter, I could've invited her. Could that be part of her animosity toward me? I wondered how she felt about Gram's dinner invitation. Would I be in trouble now for not staying away from her brother?

7

GRAM AND I ARRIVED AT THE SHOP AN HOUR EARLY AGAIN THE NEXT morning. I set up my paints and equipment in the back room on the small table I'd found in Gram's garage last evening. I planned to finish my study painting that morning and begin on the actual work by afternoon. Depending on the number of interruptions, of course.

Luckily, the shop's back room had the perfect window open to the north light. It was small but helpful.

We set up Gram's work next to mine, and we both began painting, our hands and minds working in harmony. Looking at Gram, I could see the small worry lines between her brows had all but dissolved. I hadn't seen her that content since I'd arrived in Shoreview. I was really tempted to ignore the time and keep painting when the ticking clock said ten a.m.—opening time for the shop. I set down my brush with a sigh and covered my paints, knowing I had to get my mind in another place for a while.

We took turns helping customers that morning, although I took care of any actual sales and Gram was happy to let me do it. Most of the customers were tourists, more interested in looking than buying. That was fine with me today, but not with Gram.

"At this rate, I'd better start painting for money," she groused. I nodded in sympathy.

By late afternoon, I could see Gram spent more time looking

at her work than actually making intricate brushstrokes. It was time for her to quit for the day.

But not for me. I'd finished my study by early afternoon and now worked on the actual painting. I didn't want to quit. I was having my best painting day in a long time. If I could just finish this one section before we left, I would feel so much better.

"Gram, why don't you make us a cup of tea? I think we need a break."

She looked up then, that confused expression in her eyes momentarily. "Yes, that does sound good."

The bell chimed just as she started filling the kettle, and I groaned, setting down my brush again. This back and forth painting was totally frustrating.

The woman who'd entered dawdled through the aisles, picking up item after item and then setting them back down. She was a customer, doing what customers were supposed to do but frustration seeped through my pores. In the meantime, the teakettle whistled, and I knew Gram would soon have the brew ready. We were supposed to close in fifteen minutes, and I didn't know if I could get Gram to stay any longer. She looked exhausted. Finally, the woman came up to the register carrying a glass vase.

"I'll take this," she said.

"It has a beautiful flowing shape, doesn't it?" I said as I scanned the bar code. "That'll be $39.99 plus tax."

"But that's not the price. It says $14.99."

I turned the vase over and read the sticker on the bottom. Sure enough, the original price was covered by black marker, and it was now marked $14.99. "I'm afraid there's been a mistake. Someone marked it wrong."

"Well, that's your mistake, isn't it? It says $14.99, and that's what I should pay for it," the woman said, a tightness to her expression now.

I stared at her in confusion, my mouth opening and closing while I searched for a solution. How many other items had Gram lowered in price? Once again, disaster loomed on the shop's horizon.

"I'm very sorry," I said softly, "but my grandmother hasn't been well, and it seems she made a mistake and put the wrong price on the vase."

"Like I said, that's your problem, not mine."

She was right, of course, but that didn't make it any easier. Would this nightmare ever end? What would happen to Gram and her shop if this continued? My cell phone rang as she left. It was my landlord. His raspy voice conjured up smoke-filled rooms and tobacco-stained fingers.

"When will you be back?" he asked. "You said you'd only be gone for a few weeks. I have someone else interested in renting the place, and I'm giving you notice."

"You can't do that. I still have two weeks left on my paid rent." I didn't want to make this decision until I was forced to. The place was perfect for me—completely furnished, reasonable rent, and no lease. The landlord lived downstairs, and we'd never had any problems, except when his cigarette smoke managed to seep through the vents. Where would I ever find another place like it in the city?

"Yes, I can," he said. "In two weeks, I go into your deposit. We didn't have to sign any city rental agreement, remember?"

The truth was, I didn't have the money for the next month's rent and no way of getting it now that I'd taken an unpaid leave from my job at the coffee shop. My head pounded as I searched for a way to put him off. I had to get back to Chicago as soon as possible. We'd always gotten along. I was positive I could convince him to allow me to stay in the apartment if only I could talk to him in person.

"Please, I'll be there as soon as I can. Don't do anything until I get there."

After disconnecting, I went back into the kitchen area. I was in desperate need of the tea by this time. What I wouldn't give for a little Jameson Irish whiskey to throw in, like Mom had done occasionally after a long day at the restaurant.

"I guess we'd better call it a day, Gram." I walked over and picked up the mug of tea sitting on the counter. "I'm too upset to do any more painting."

"If you say so, dear. But I'm just getting a good start on fixing this."

I looked over to where she stood in front of my easel, paintbrush in hand. Dread rose up from my toes and wafted its way slowly up my body. I didn't want to look but knew I had to. I walked across the room with zombie steps, coming to a stop behind her. Yup. It was the worst-case scenario. She'd painted all over my canvas.

I put my clenched fist up to my mouth, choking back a sob. I'd finally connected with a painting and been inspired for the first time in a long while...and now this. The canvas was totally ruined. She'd painted over all my vibrant colors with swirls of a muted brown.

"I don't know why I would've done such a painting in the first place. All those gaudy colors and straight lines—it's enough to give me a headache," she said.

I couldn't speak for a moment. Disappointment and frustration waged a battle with my compassion. Finally, I found my voice. "Let's get out of here. It's time to close."

I didn't bother cleaning up. What was the use? My life as an artist was over, at least for the foreseeable future. Depression covered me like a shroud.

"Will your mother be home? I hope she's started dinner. I'm hungry."

"It's just us tonight, Gram," I muttered, putting my arm around her shoulders as we walked out to the car.

I'd been kidding myself, hoping against all logic that Gram's illness would disappear as mysteriously as it had appeared. It no longer mattered if I couldn't leave her in a week to go to Chicago; I would never have a painting finished in time. At least, not one that would portray my best work.

WHEN WE GOT HOME, the answering machine flashed. I hesitated to play back the message. Could this day get any worse? *Well, yeah, that's why I didn't want to answer the damn machine.*

Finally, I got up the nerve and pushed the flashing button,

expecting the worse. Peter's voice filled the room, warm and laced with excitement.

"Hello, Lucy. I've got your test results, and I'd like you to make an appointment to come in and discuss how to proceed with your treatment."

"Who's that, and what's he talking about?"

"It's Peter, your doctor. Remember? You had a physical the other day, and they did some lab work and a scan. We have to go back and see if they found any problems. I'll call the clinic in the morning."

"Oh, yes, now I remember." She didn't look very happy about it. "I'm going to bed."

"Not yet, Gram. We haven't had supper."

I found some leftover soup in the refrigerator and warmed it up. We were mostly silent while we ate as Gram only answered my attempts at conversation in monosyllables. As soon as she finished, she headed upstairs to bed, leaving me to clean up and feed her animals.

"Good night, Gram," I said in a flat voice and watched her leave, my heart weighing heavy in my chest. My life was changing and there wasn't a thing I could do about it. There'd be no sleep for me tonight.

EARLY THE NEXT MORNING, I called Peter's office and was told to bring Gram in later that day. Still reeling from the loss of my painting, I plodded through the day in a fog of depression. Only the optimism I'd heard in Peter's voice gave me a bit of hope. We closed the shop and went in late that afternoon.

We sat in the waiting room, both pretending absorption in the months-old magazines when Carol, one of the women I'd met at Gram's fiber group, walked in, carrying a bright red, oversized leather bag. I guessed weaving wasn't her only hobby.

"Well, hello." She sat down next to Gram and pulled out a partially knit sweater and knitting needles. "Are you waiting to see Dr. Andresen?"

We nodded in unison, Gram's face as expressive as a bobble-head on a dashboard. I knew mine must be the same.

"Me, too." Grinning our way, she said, "You both look as nervous as I feel. You'd think I'd get over it by now, but these regular check-ups still make my heart go into high fibrillation."

"There hasn't been a change, has there?" Gram asked with a concerned frown.

"No, my last scans were clear. I should explain," Carol said as she turned to me. "I'm a breast cancer survivor. Most of the time, I can just put it out of my mind and get on with life, but when it's time for a check-up, those old fears come raging back."

"I can't even imagine," I whispered.

"I don't know what I would've done without Peter. He's become as much of a friend as doctor. He's the very best. We're so lucky to have him here."

"That's good to hear." A growing fear that Gram and I would soon need any and all support loomed like a dark cloud overhead.

"Well, dear, you had an awful lot on your plate then," Gram said, patting Carol's hand.

"You're right, Lucy. I was such an emotional wreck at that time in my life, even before the cancer," Carol said, fixing her gaze on me. "You might as well hear it from me. There are no secrets in this small town. My husband had just left me for a younger woman, and they were expecting a baby. My three sons and I felt abandoned as it was, and then this diagnosis threw us off into the outer space of despair. I didn't know what to say to them or how to explain what was happening to me during my treatment. I was so scared myself. They were afraid they were about to lose both their parents.

"Peter was amazing. He had the oncologist talk to them and explain as much as he could. It was a definite turning point in our lives—actually brought us closer. Well, as close as you can get emotionally to teenage boys," she grimaced. "I'll be eternally grateful to Peter for that."

"But everything's all right now?" I asked, hoping for a positive response. I needed to hear good news.

"Oh, yeah. I just have to have these follow-up exams every six months for several years. So far, everything is clear, and I haven't any reason to think it won't stay that way."

"Lucy?" The nurse had stepped into the room, a chart in hand. Gram and I rose up in unison, like sheep to the slaughter, and followed her into the exam room.

"Good luck." Carol's words rang out behind us.

"I'm sure Peter will have good news," I said as we took seats. "Couldn't you hear it in his voice last night?" Inside, my heart ached for Gram. She looked so grim. My petty problems didn't amount to much in comparison to hers and Carol's. I could do another painting anytime.

I'd been doing research on the internet on Alzheimer's disease for these past two weeks after Gram had gone to bed, and it was difficult to put any kind of hopeful spin on it. If that was the diagnosis, watching her deteriorate would be hell. Peter had been honest about the medications. They could be helpful in delaying the worst symptoms, but there was no cure. I found myself pulling on my fingers, unable to come up with any light conversation while we waited. Gram was in the same agitated state, her lips moving silently while she waited in the chair. I knew she was praying for a miracle herself.

When Peter entered the room, he flashed that golden smile, and even under these circumstances, my heart did that funny leap.

"I have good news," he said.

I wanted to jump up from my chair and grab him by the shirt collar and scream, *Tell us already, for God's sake.*

"You have a condition called hypothyroidism, which we can treat with replacement therapy. That could be the cause of many of your symptoms." Peter put his hand on Gram's shoulder in a comforting gesture. "I know how frightening this has been for you—for both of you." His sympathetic glance included me. "I'll start you on medication, but it will take some time to know how many of your symptoms will be alleviated. I also need you to take extra vitamins and a brisk thirty-minute walk at least three times a week."

Now Gram and I were smiling. I felt almost giddy with relief and could barely keep myself from planting a big kiss on his tempting lips. But I did manage to restrain myself.

"Does this mean I don't have Alzheimer's?" Gram asked.

"I think we can safely rule that out for now. However, you could still have memory problems associated with MCI." At our blank stare, he continued. "Sorry. Sometimes I forget and fall into medical jargon.

"MCI is short for Mild Cognitive Impairment. It's an intermediate stage between the usual cognitive decline of normal aging and the more pronounced decline of dementia. Usually, these changes aren't severe enough to interfere with your day-to-day life and activities. It can lead to Alzheimer's down the road, however, but some people with MCI never get any worse and a few eventually get better. Only time will tell, and everyone is different."

I grabbed Gram and gave her a big hug. She was laughing through her tears. I could see Peter was having difficulty maintaining his professional persona—the huge grin on his face gave it away.

"Thanks, Peter," I murmured, giving his hand a tight squeeze. The feel of his hand in mine was so much more than I'd anticipated—a warmth, a connection—on so many levels. I looked up at him in surprise.

"Don't thank me. It's my pleasure to give you some good news." He tightened his own grip. Was it my imagination or had he felt the connection, too? "I know how worried you've been—both of you."

Gram and I left his office feeling like we'd just won the lottery. It was difficult not to think of Peter as a hero.

The entire two weeks I'd been in Shoreview had been like a roller coaster ride—the ups and downs leaving me breathless and confused.

I called my brothers and Mom with the good news as promised as soon as we got home. I even felt good enough to broach the subject of their staying with Gram while I returned to Chicago. No takers though—all tied up with work and family.

.   .   .

"How are things?" Martha pulled me aside that Friday at the Wool Gatherers' meeting. "She's looking better," she said, nodding in Gram's direction.

"It's hard to say; she's so up and down. Peter says it'll take some time, but if his first effort at diagnosis is correct, the next few weeks should show a slow improvement."

"Does that mean you'll be leaving for Chicago soon?"

"That depends on Gram," I said. "She is getting up in years. Someone in the family should be close in case she needs them, and right now, I'm the only one available." That truth had been hammered home to me these past weeks. "But I'm still working on a solution. Who knows?"

"But what about your boyfriend and your career?"

"They're kind of up in the air."

"She's going back in a few days." Gram had come up behind me without my realizing it. "Jacques or Henri—whatever his name is—wants Cara to be in some kind of a show."

I swear the woman's hearing was getting more selective every day.

"It's Stefan, Gram. And I haven't said I was going."

"You're going, no question about it." She'd been paying more attention than I'd realized. Now what was I going to do? She'd never accept some lame excuse for my refusing.

"If it's me you're worried about, forget it. I've taken care of myself all my life, and I still can." Gram crossed her arms over her chest in that now familiar stubborn stance.

"I can help out at the shop," Nancy offered, her green eyes uncharacteristically soft when she looked at Gram.

"We'll all make it our business to see that Lucy is well looked after," Martha assured me.

"Quit talking about me like I'm some kind of an invalid. I don't need people hovering over me like I'm completely senile. I can take care of myself, I tell you." Gram was getting angry; little spots of red appeared on her apple cheeks and her eyes narrowed.

God, how I wished that medication could take immediate effect.

"You listen to me, Lucinda Olson, and stop being so stubborn," Joan called from the back of the room. "We're both getting older, and sometimes we're going to need help. Nothing wrong with that. You just behave yourself now, and let your granddaughter do her thing. Your family is worried about you, and the brunt of it has fallen on her shoulders. Cara needs to go without worrying about you every minute."

"She's right, Lucy, and you know it." A murmured agreement went up. Gram looked around the room, then threw her hands up in defeat.

"Okay, I give up," Gram said. "Someone else will be taking care of the old lady."

"We'll see how things go, Gram." I turned to the group. "I really appreciate the offer, everyone."

Was there still a possibility of my going to the art show? A glimmer of hope raised its seductive head. Only, I didn't have a new piece to hang. I'd left several canvases with Stefan, however. I reviewed them mentally. My only option was to go through them and choose the best.

Knowing Stefan, he'd have an opinion about my choice. That should've made me happy. Only, the times I'd had to squash my own feelings about my work and defer to his opinion had rankled. Usually, the problem was I thought the piece lacked something—but I couldn't figure out how to fix it. After five years as his protégé, I had to admit he was the expert. I also knew I should be grateful for all he'd taught me. Defer to his expertise.

I spent the rest of the evening wandering around the room, watching the others do their thing, especially Cheryl, who was now working on a felt purse. It was made of a mix of bright cherry-red and natural colored wool, and she was adorning it with small beads in an intricate pattern. I couldn't take my eyes off it.

"What a beautiful color. Did you dye the wool yourself?" I asked.

"Yes. I used an acid dye instead of a natural one," Cheryl said. "It gives a clearer, brighter color."

"You use acid? Doesn't that ruin the fibers?"

"Oh, no," she laughed. "The acid is vinegar—it's the mordant used to set the color."

There was a lot more to this dyeing stuff than I'd realized. I asked many more questions before the evening ended, and Gram and I piled once again into the Buick.

WE DIDN'T GET HOME until late that night. I'd had a million questions for Cheryl about felting and dyeing. It was something new and different, and I now wanted to give it a try. Crafts sold well among the tourists in this area. It could be the way for me to make a little money while minding Gram's shop. I needed to raise rent money before I could return to Chicago to stay. Finding an apartment loomed in the future.

Gram had just gone up to bed when the phone rang. It was my brother Jack. "Hey, Squirt, how's it going?" He was as bad as Peter.

"Isn't it about time you gave up that childish nickname? It's really annoying." Jack laughed. He still loved to tease. He was the brother nearest to me in age, and we'd been quite close as youngsters. "Things are okay, I guess."

"Thanks for keeping us posted on Gram—glad you're there, kid." He drew a deep breath. "Listen, after talking to Mom and Peter, Elizabeth and I have decided to bring the kids up for a weekend, and Joe hopes to do the same as soon as he can. Unless you think it would be too much for Gram."

"Are you kidding? She would be ecstatic. You know how she loves the kids." This could be the answer to my prayers. Gram hated feeling obligated to her friends. It was a matter of pride, and something I could understand. "How soon can you come?"

"Why? Has something happened that you need us right away?"

"Stefan has this opening at a gallery coming up in a couple of weeks, and I want to be there. He's offered to hang a piece of my work. It would be a great opportunity for me."

"Oh, yeah. I heard you were still hanging out with that guy.

How many years has it been? And why haven't we met him? Makes one wonder what you're hiding."

I couldn't answer that because I didn't know or want to face the answer myself. "Jack, this is really important. Stefan has arranged this great opportunity for me."

"Okay, if you say so. Did you know that Peter is still single? You couldn't do better than that, kid," Jack suggested.

"If one more person in this family says that to me, I'll..." I could hear him chuckling, and it set my teeth on edge. "Just tell me you can come this weekend, please."

"I'm sorry kid, no can do. Work is still really hectic now, and the kids have all these end-of-schoolyear projects. We'll be there as soon as we can, I promise."

"Thanks, Jack. I'm sure Gram will be happy to see you."

Back to square one for me and the Wool Gatherers. It wasn't as if I didn't appreciate their offer. I just hated leaving Gram now that I knew she was still having problems.

Much to my surprise, Nancy came into the shop the following afternoon. Her blond hair was tied back in a loose ponytail, and she looked unusually cool-headed as she carried in a bakery box.

"I want to talk to you about your trip to Chicago. Where's Lucy?" she asked softly.

"She's in the back room."

"Listen, I meant what I said about helping out while you're in Chicago. I've worked here with Lucy on several occasions so I know the routine. And I could even spend the nights at her place if that would work for her."

"Really?" I felt my eyes widen in surprise. "We'll need to make a financial agreement."

"Lucy and I already have an agreement from when I worked here before. We talked things over after you and Lucy left last night, and we all agreed it was the best for both of you. Everyone offered to help so you don't have to worry about it."

Could this really be happening? It took a moment for me to

find my voice. "Are you sure?" That giddy feeling pulsed through my veins.

"Yes, we worked it out. I'll be at Lucy's on Tuesday morning so you can leave then."

"I've put the kettle on for tea." Gram came in from the back, noticed Nancy and the bakery box, and clapped her hands. "Is that what I think it is?"

"If you're thinking chocolate-raspberry cheesecake, it is."

"Perfect timing," Gram crowed.

"Would you like me to watch the register while you take a break?" Nancy asked and lifted the box for inspection. "I've brought Lucy's favorite dessert."

"Are you serious? I would like to pick up a few office supplies," the pragmatic side of me said. "We've had people in and out of here all day, and I never did get the chance to have lunch."

"No problem. That's why I'm here—and to bring Lucy dessert, of course."

I picked up my purse and put my hand on Nancy's arm before leaving. "This is very nice of you. I won't be gone long."

"Take your time." She brushed aside my thanks with an uncomfortable grin. "Lucy and I can visit."

I thought about their relationship all the way to the store. Why was it she could be so affable and friendly with Gram and so uncomfortable around me? Was it something I'd done in the past? Whatever it was, I had to get to the bottom of it.

RETURNING to the shop later with my packages, I could hear Gram and Nancy talking and laughing. I felt a stab of envy at their relationship. I walked into the room to tell them I'd returned, but they already knew it was me who'd come in.

"Sit down. We've saved you a piece of cheesecake," Gram said, pulling out a chair.

"Maybe Nancy wants to take it home?" I asked.

"Nonsense. She said it was for you. Isn't that right?" Gram directed the question to Nancy.

"Yes, of course." Nancy nodded. "We saved it for you, and you'd better eat it before the two of us decide not to be so nice after all."

"Thank you." I picked up the fork Gram had set out for me and took a bite. "Mmm, this is delicious."

"I'll get you a cup of tea, Cara." Gram got up and turned to the kettle.

"What's going on here—why have you changed?" I whispered.

Nancy shrugged. "It makes Lucy happy."

Gram set the cup of tea in front of me, smiling genially. "Isn't this nice? My two favorite girls enjoying tea with me."

Nancy and I exchanged looks. Poor Gram. If she only knew the undercurrents raging between us.

Nancy didn't stay long after that, promising to be there on Tuesday morning.

8

BETWEEN WORRYING ABOUT GRAM AND RUNNING THE SHOP, I'D given up on doing a new painting while in Shoreview. I could do it in Chicago now that I was free to leave tomorrow. I couldn't come up with a good excuse for canceling Gram's dinner invitation to Peter for Monday evening though. Something else to stress over.

Gram had been on her medication for a week, and I noticed a little improvement. She didn't seem to get as restless and confused as the day wore on. Hopefully, that meant she'd carry on most of the conversation with Peter during his visit. I knew he didn't want to spend the evening discussing Gram's condition with me. The problem was, I hadn't been living in the area since high school and I couldn't imagine what else we'd talk about.

I spent way too much time in my room late that afternoon, trying on slacks and jeans with abandon and throwing them around the room, all the while berating myself for my lack of wardrobe, which basically consisted of jeans in several colors, t-shirts, and sweaters. By the time I finished pulling clothes on and off over my head, my hair was standing up straight with static electricity. Finally, I came to my senses and pulled on a pair of black jeans and threw a blue sweater over my head. I wasn't in the city anymore. People here didn't dress formally for dinner at a friend's house.

Since when had my wardrobe become so important anyway? I gave myself a mental slap against the side of the head. What was I doing? Joining the queue for Peter's attention?

Peter's car pulled into the driveway at five, right on the mark. I'd guessed he'd be punctual, and I wasn't wrong. Gram was nowhere in sight, so I went out to greet him. He'd just stepped out of his car when I saw Zeke careening out from behind the house, Gram chasing after him.

"Come back here, you beast." The more she yelled, the faster the animal ran. I swear, I saw Zeke smiling.

Peter stepped in his path and grabbed his halter with one arm as I made my way down the front steps. The llama had something flopping around his long neck as he ran, and Peter lifted it off easily.

"What have we here?" he asked, and I saw my red lacy bra fluttering in his hand. I had hung it on the clothesline behind the house earlier that afternoon and forgotten about it. It was a Victoria's Secret number that Stefan, in a totally uncharacteristic move, had given me for my birthday.

"Is this what a well-dressed llama wears these days?" Peter asked with raised eyebrows.

Oh, how I wanted to wipe that smirk off his face. "It's Gram's," I said, daring him to contradict me. I grabbed it out of his hands and folded it tight between my hands. By this time, Gram had reached us.

"It certainly is not," she said in a horrified tone. "Even *I'm* not that crazy." She reached for Zeke's halter. "Thanks for catching him," she said, her breath coming in short spurts.

"Are you okay, Gram?"

"I'm fine. I'll just put this bad boy back in the barn where he belongs. You two go on inside."

I heard the angry honking of the geese coming along the side of the house and had half a notion to slow my steps just so I could watch Peter's reaction to their attack. But I took pity on him in the end and led him into the house. It wouldn't do for Gram's doctor to be laid low by her guard birds.

Peter had brought a bottle of local Chardonnay and a box of

dark chocolates from my favorite sweet shop. Did he remember me standing open-mouthed with longing at the candy display in the window all those years ago?

"Isn't it nice to see some men still have good manners?" Gram asked when she came in, giving me that knowing look before setting the gifts on the kitchen counter. I knew she was referring back to her phone conversations with Stefan. She just didn't understand Stefan like I did. Or maybe she was right. But I wasn't about to admit it.

Peter looked from me to Gram. "Am I missing something?"

"Nothing important," I muttered.

We opened the wine with dinner. Gram didn't drink any. "My mind's muddled enough," she said, refusing a glass when I poured for Peter and myself.

Peter finished off a piece of Gram's apple pie in record time after dinner and set his fork on the now empty plate.

"Nancy tells me you're off to Chicago tomorrow," Peter said.

"Yes, I have things to take care of there." I chugged the last of my wine. Could I get this meal over with and Peter out the door before anything disastrous happened—such as me making a fool of myself.

"Something pretty important, according to Nancy."

Gram stayed my arm as I reached for her plate. "Just leave the dishes, dear. I'll take care of them in the morning. I'm feeling quite tired."

"Oh, no, you made dinner. I'll clear up. Why don't you visit with Peter?"

"I'll help her, Lucy," Peter said. "You rest." He got up from the table and began carrying plates to the counter. "Playing cards wasn't the only thing I learned from you."

"Well, if you're sure..." She hesitated, looking at me for assurance. "I might just go up to bed."

"You go ahead, Gram. It's been a long day, I know." *Oh my God, now what? How could I get rid of Peter without being rude?*

"You don't have to stay," I said to him in a low voice. "I can have these few dishes washed before your car even gets to the highway."

"Oh, no. You're not going to get rid of me that easily. I told Lucy I'd help, and I'm staying. I don't need her angry at me."

"Stay then." I shrugged.

The first time our fingers brushed as we passed dishes back and forth, I almost dropped one of Gram's fine china plates.

"Oops, sorry."

"No, I'm sorry," he said with a grin.

I began to wonder if he was doing it on purpose the next time it happened.

What was the matter with me? It was only Peter; he was like another brother, for crying out loud. I knew that was how he thought of me; hadn't he proved it many times over?

We certainly weren't looking to develop any kind of romantic relationship. Our past actions had proven that. I'd just begun to face the flaws in my relationship with Stefan. Why would I want to step into another disaster? We'd finish up these dishes, and he would head home. End of story.

There was still light in the sky as I put the last dish in the cupboard. Peter picked up the wine bottle and two glasses.

"Why don't we sit on the swing and kill this bottle. I hate to go home so early on a beautiful spring evening."

"Sure, why not." Did I actually say that? As I was the only other person in the room, it would seem so. I followed him out the door and settled next to him on the old wooden swing, as close to my side as I could get without falling over the edge. He poured a little wine into my glass.

I'd loved spending evenings here as a child, watching the few cars that passed down the county road, always hoping someone exciting would pull into our drive. "Traffic seems to have picked up," I said, watching the fourth car whiz past.

"Not quite like Chicago, though, is it?" His arm rested on the back of the swing, and I picked up the scent of his spicy after-shave. I could swear it was the same one he'd used in high school, only subtler. "Are you anxious to get back?" he asked.

"I am missing out on some great opportunities," I confessed, trying to ignore the warning beads of sweat popping out along my hairline. "And of course, I need to straighten things out with my landlord and my supervisor at work."

"And there's the boyfriend to consider." His hand played softly with a tendril of hair that lay on my shoulder. Not very brother-like behavior. All my senses went on high alert, and my body stiffened in reaction to his touch. I shook my head lightly in an attempt to dislodge his fingers, but he didn't take the hint.

"How come you've never brought him home to meet Lucy and the family?"

"I don't know. The time was never right." I was growing uncomfortable.

"Your brothers think you're afraid to introduce him to the family." He looked off into the distance while he talked and just kept playing with that strand of hair as if it was an afterthought, which was all right with me. I didn't want to look at him either, afraid of what I might see in his eyes.

This time, I jerked my hair out of his reach. I wasn't about to try to explain that Stefan's sometimes pretentious behavior was due to his artistic sensibilities that my family wouldn't understand.

"Is there some other reason then?" he asked, keeping his tone light.

"Stefan was always busy with some project when I came up here. I told you, it just never worked out. Can we please talk about something else?" His hand snaked across my shoulder now, and I knew it was no accident. Common sense told me to pull away, but for once, common sense and I didn't seem to be on the same page.

"Okay. So what are you going to do about your apartment and job? Will they both wait?" he asked.

"I plan to smooth things out while I'm there, once I explain the circumstances of Gram's condition. Hopefully, they'll keep the status quo until I find out if I can get back for good. I can always stay with Stefan if I lose the apartment; that's no big deal. But the job is another matter. If I lose my place there, it'll mean searching for another job. That could mean commuting anywhere in the city or surrounding area."

Of course, my real worry was all the opportunities I'd have to give up to stay in Shoreview. But I wasn't about to go into that with Peter. His hand tightened on my shoulder for a moment and then moved to the back of my neck, gently massaging away the tightness that I'd carried for days. I hadn't been this relaxed for a long time.

"What'll you do if Lucy continues to need help? Will your boyfriend leave Chicago and move up here?"

"Heck, no," I said without thinking. What a ludicrous idea. I had a vision of Stefan being chased by the geese and giggled. Maybe I'd had too much wine. I was feeling way too at ease with Peter.

"What's so funny?" Peter asked, smiling himself. Before I knew exactly how it happened, his arm had lowered, and I was cuddling up to him, both of us laughing like the kids we used to be. Suddenly, we were kissing, and it was definitely not like siblings.

Our eyes met in shock, but instead of running for the hills like a sensible woman, I grabbed Peter by the shirt collar and placed my lips to his again, as if to prove nothing could possibly feel that good. *Wrong.* Oh, so wrong, and I closed my eyes in ecstasy.

This was the kiss I'd longed for all those years ago when, in the throes of teen-aged lust, I'd dreamed of Peter. I felt his kiss all the way down to my toes and back up again. His arms were wrapped around me now in such a close embrace that I could feel the rapid beat of his heart against my chest. Or was it my heart beating against his? We were so close it was hard to tell. I opened my eyes and stared back into the navy-blue depths of his eyes.

Maybe it was a good thing we hadn't connected in our teen years. I couldn't have handled these feelings at that age. I didn't know if I could handle them now.

Something in Peter's eyes scared me. Was it passion or disgust? Whatever it was, his eyes suddenly shuttered, and he looked away.

But that kiss awakened me to what I'd been missing. He

wasn't the man for me, but there must be someone out there with whom I could share this newly found passion of mine.

I pulled back and turned my head away, embarrassed, only to see Gram peering out between the curtains inside the house, wearing a wide smile of white teeth. Oh, boy, I was in big trouble now.

9

"You're sure you'll be all right? I don't have to go, you know. There'll be other openings." I'd rolled down the window to give Gram one last searching look. She and Nancy stood next to the Escort, waiting for me to pull away. What were Gram's true feelings? She'd never mentioned last night's kiss. Did she even remember?

"Go on now, girl. You know better than that," Gram said.

"We'll get along fine, don't worry. I'll keep a very close eye on her." Nancy put her hand on Gram's forearm, resting now on the open window, and winked at me.

"All right, that's enough, you two. Don't make me feel even older than I am." Gram withdrew her arm. "Off with you now. And try to have some fun while you're there."

Pulling out of the drive, I glanced back at them in the rearview mirror. I was so torn. A part of me wanted to stay here with Gram, not only because I worried about her, but also because I knew these people really cared about both of us. I wasn't just some wannabe artist to them. I'd been sucked back into that small-town atmosphere of family without my realizing it. Even Nancy had mellowed toward me these past few weeks. I knew she cared deeply for Gram, and maybe that was the reason.

My hands tightened on the wheel. *No.* I couldn't go back to my old life here. It was too late. This was my big chance. I had

over a week to finish one of the paintings I'd left behind in
Stefan's studio. I simply had to concentrate on choosing the best
one for the show. He'd help me.

The painting was only one of the problems facing me now. I
had to meet with my landlord and my boss, and I still didn't have
the answers they wanted. I could easily lose my apartment and
my job. And the time away had given me a chance to think long
and hard about my relationship.

Sure, it'd been easy to tell Peter that I could move in with
Stefan, but it wasn't something I looked forward to doing—in
fact, I dreaded the thought. It would mean giving up my independence.

I could give many reasons why I'd stayed so long with Stefan,
including my appreciation for all he'd done for me and my admiration of his work. Was that enough to sustain a long-term relationship? When had I given up my search for intimacy and
settled for complacency? What kind of a boyfriend in this era of
cell phones didn't call every day? And why wasn't I beside myself
with longing to be back with him? Hard questions with no
answers.

To add insult to injury, I nursed a slight hangover and guilt
about the kisses I'd shared with Peter. Had I been added to the
list of women chasing after the young, single doctor? *Argh!* If I
weren't driving, I'd beat my head against the steering wheel.

After years of trying to get everyone to forget that long-ago
crush, I'd managed to reignite all the speculation with that one
wayward kiss. That was assuming Gram would remember and
tell, of course. Who was I kidding? You could bet the rest of my
family already had smug smiles of satisfaction plastered across
their matchmaking faces.

I ARRIVED in Chicago later that afternoon at the peak of rush hour
traffic, tired and frazzled. It sure hadn't taken me long to get used
to long country roads and minimal traffic again. I parked behind
Stefan's building and walked up the familiar stairs. But now,
everything seemed different, unwelcoming. It could've been years

instead of weeks since I'd been here. My life had changed in ways I wasn't even aware of until this very moment.

I knocked on the door instead of just walking in, though I wasn't sure why. Okay, maybe it was guilt from that kiss.

Stefan had that usual little furrow between his brows when he opened the door. "Since when do you knock? I almost didn't answer."

He held a paintbrush in his hand, and I knew I'd committed the mortal sin of making him leave his work to answer the door.

"Sorry, Cara." Stefan sighed at my look of disappointment and set the paintbrush down before putting his arms around me in a fierce embrace. "I missed you," he whispered. "Things just aren't the same when you're not here." He draped his arm around my shoulder as we walked into his studio.

I saw what he meant an instant later. The place was a disaster. Pizza boxes, Chinese take-out cartons, and empty pop cans vied for space on the countertops and floor. I could only imagine what his bedroom looked like. On second thought, I didn't want to imagine it. If this room was any indication, it wouldn't be a pretty sight.

Stefan looked behind me. "Where's your painting?"

"I didn't have time to do a new one. I started, but things happened."

"Oh?" He raised an eyebrow in that familiar way—which now struck me as quite pretentious. Why hadn't I noticed that before?

Telling myself I didn't owe him an explanation, I continued as if he hadn't spoken. "Anyway, I decided on my way here that I'd submit the last piece I'd been working on before I left. I should be able to finish it in time."

"I doubt the paint will even be dry," he said, twisting his mouth in an ugly expression.

"Stop being so negative. You said you liked it." I walked to the back of the studio where it was still propped against the wall. Looking at it critically, I suddenly wasn't so sure. Gram's words— *all gaudy colors and straight lines*—came back to haunt me. She couldn't have meant it. It was her illness talking.

Stefan had been my mentor for years, and he'd taught me so

much about Abstract Expressionism. He liked to explore with different mediums, often going for a three-dimensional surface. His work was really getting noticed now, and consequently, the critics adored him. He'd made several big sales in the last few months. He expected me to ride the waves of his success and style. I picked up the canvas and propped it on an empty easel.

"What do you think?"

"It has potential but needs tweaking. You can do it." When he put his hand on my shoulder, I felt more confident. He wouldn't give his approval to something he didn't believe in; it wasn't a facet of his personality.

"I'm going over to my apartment," I said. "I have to meet with the landlord. He called last week to say he has someone else interested in the place and doesn't want to hold it for me."

"After all this time, he owes you. Tell him that."

"I'll tell him I'll pay him any back rent when I come back to stay. It isn't as if I'm asking for charity—just an extension on my rent." I wasn't sure if I was trying to convince the landlord or myself.

"How many times have you been through this?" Stefan said with a feigned look of ignorance. He knew darn well how often I'd had to hide out at his place while waiting for my paycheck. Granted, it happened more than I liked but not often enough to cause problems with the landlord.

I shrugged in reply. "Wish me luck." I had to get out of there before he started on that same old diatribe about my moving in with him. Looking around the place, I could see why he found the idea so appealing. Thank God, I'd resisted. No way was that going to happen.

"Pick up some dinner on your way back, will you?" he asked.

"I'm going to stay at my apartment if I can," I said. "Maybe squatter's rights will win out."

"Your first night back, and you're not staying here with me?" The look of surprise on his face was classic.

"I don't think there's room for me." I gestured to the mess.

"Oh, c'mon. We can clean up the place in ten minutes." He bent down and picked up an empty pizza box.

"If it's so easy, why didn't you do it before I got here?" I asked, widening my eyes innocently.

"What's the matter with you?" His face creased in confusion. "Are you angry about something?"

"Sorry, it's been a long drive, and I'm not looking forward to meeting with the landlord or my boss. I'll be back tomorrow morning. I still have my key in case you're sleeping."

"You could always join me there," he said with an uncustomary leer. I almost choked on a wave of revulsion. *Oh, my God. What had happened to me these past weeks?*

THE LANDLORD WAS WAITING when I got out of my car and not looking too happy. Was he hoping I wouldn't show up?

"Listen, I'm sorry, but as I said, I can't rent the apartment to you any longer." He threw the opening salvo, his eyes not quite meeting mine. "You have only one week of paid rent left."

"Couldn't you just hold it a little longer? I've explained about my grandmother. She's getting better every day. It shouldn't be long before I can come back to stay." It wasn't easy to plead, not when I knew I was in the right. But what choice did I have?

"There's one week left before I go into your deposit so, as I said, that gives you the two weeks of that. I gave you thirty days' notice, the letter's in your box. You didn't leave a forwarding address. Besides, like I told you, I have someone else who needs the place." He still wouldn't meet my eyes, and that gave me some hope.

"So you said. Does that mean you've been advertising the place while I'm still renting? That doesn't seem fair after all the years I've been here."

"Fair doesn't have anything to do with it." He darted a look at me. "It's my niece. She's having problems living at home, and my sister wants her to move in here, where I can keep an eye on her." His lips tightened in a stubborn line. "I don't have a choice. Blood is thicker than water. You'll get what's left of your deposit back if you leave soon," he said in a conciliatory voice before walking away. As if that would make it all better.

At least I had the place while I prepared for the opening. Who knew what could happen after that? Maybe the critics would fall all over my piece and make me famous. Or maybe one of the gallery's rich clients would buy it for an exorbitant price, and I wouldn't even want to come back to this dump. Oh, yeah, I was good at weaving pipe dreams. Spending the night here was a necessity.

I'd brought bedding and toiletries with me so I could move right back in to my old apartment. Being around Stefan during several of his gallery openings had prepared me for his mood swings from euphoria to high anxiety, and I knew I'd need a place to escape to reality. I'd had mixed emotions about staying with him anyway. Something had definitely changed in our relationship while I was gone, and I needed to get things straight in my head.

Stefan and I met at Art School. He was just Steve then, a teaching assistant who totally impressed me with his dramatic style and work ethic. I was thrilled beyond belief that he could be interested in mentoring a newbie like me. From there, our relationship grew until I spent all my free time with him, painting and studying. All my passion for my art somehow got mixed up with my feelings for him. It was hard to explain now, even to myself.

But after seeing him today, I finally realized whatever sexual excitement had been in our relationship had long since left…if it had ever been there. It was more a case of hero worship. We were like an old married couple on the brink of divorce. More acquaintances than lovers, each engrossed in our own lives. The only thing holding us together now was our passion for art and maybe his need for an adoring groupie.

I looked around the apartment I'd called home for five years. The walls were bare of decoration, the furniture dark and utilitarian. It looked soulless and empty with most of my personal belongings already in Shoreview. I guess it had never really been home, more like a place to keep my clothes. I recognized my subconscious had an inkling I wouldn't be returning. Why else had I so callously thrown every memento into the Ford that day three weeks ago when I left for Wisconsin? My body sagged on the edge of the unmade bed. Now what? What recourse did I have? The landlord was right. I remembered now. There hadn't been a Chicago Rental Agreement to sign because I was the only tenant in an owner-occupied building, and it didn't apply. The cold, hard truth was it wasn't worth fighting over, and I probably wouldn't win anyway. Moving into Stefan's studio was easy to say, but not easy to do. Having my nights alone made it bearable. I had to find another solution. But first things first. I had a painting to do, and it had to be my best.

THE NEXT WEEK FLEW BY. I spent every day and most of the evenings working on my painting. I was at Stefan's early one morning, my fingers itching to get started. I'd used some iridescent acrylic paints, trying to achieve that amazing color and light I saw in my head—a mixture of bright to soft reds, deep blues, and yellows. It was a painting meant to bring joy. It took several days and tons of anguish before I'd called it finished, but even then, I didn't feel satisfied. Four years of art school and five more as Stefan's protégé and I still wasn't proud of what I'd done.

Stefan had put aside his own work periodically to critique. He suggested lengthening a shadow here, intensifying the color there, adding a little more dimension, and so forth.

"I just don't know. Something's missing." I hesitated, loath to send anything but my very best. As much as I loved all the colors, it just didn't seem to belong to me.

"It looks great. Come on, we have to get it framed and crated. Luckily, it doesn't need much drying time." Stefan crossed the room with impatient strides. "I only have a few more pieces to get over to the gallery. I'm spending the day tomorrow supervising the hanging of the works. You're welcome to come along."

His words didn't encourage me this time. My instinct told me the painting could be better. Was it the work or my state of mind? I couldn't decide. It didn't help that Peter's face popped into my head whenever I looked at Stefan. It was ruining my concentration. Yes, that was it. *Of course*—it was all Peter's fault.

.   .   .

THE NEXT DAY, I left Stefan at the gallery, hanging pictures with a promise to return as soon as I could. I had one more thing on my agenda for this week, and that was a visit to my supervisor at the coffee shop. The thought of begging her to hold my position indefinitely had festered long enough. I couldn't put it off any longer.

The familiar scent of fresh brewed coffee and fresh baked scones greeted me as I opened the door. I took a deep breath. Believe it or not, I had missed this place and the people I'd worked alongside for the past few years. The shop teemed with customers, and I could tell by the frantic wave of the staff as they hurried about that they were short of help. *Oh, crap.* Not a good time for me to be requesting more time off.

As I expected, my request wasn't well received. The supervisor barely had a minute to spare for me.

"Do you know how many people in this city are looking for work?" she vented. "I have applications sitting on my desk that have been there for months." She snapped the always-present wad of gum in her mouth. "You've already been gone four weeks. Sorry, but no can do. I need help, and I need it now. You have to make a choice here. Either come back now or don't come back at all."

Well, that wasn't going to happen, was it? Two strikes down, one to go. That only left the painting hanging in the gallery. What would the critics have to say? Would anyone even give it a second look? A part of me hoped they'd totally ignore it. Especially since I knew in my heart it wasn't my best work. No review was better than a bad review, right?

The phone call to Gram didn't help.

"Things are going along just fine here, don't you worry. The shop's been quiet this week, and we've had a lot of time to spend painting. It's been fun."

I envisioned Gram and Nancy, laughing and telling stories in that cozy kitchenette as they painted, and I felt a twinge of envy. Would I ever be able to express that joy in my work again?

. . .

THE NIGHT OF THE OPENING, I stood before the mirror, dressed in my usual black jeans and high-heeled boots, wishing I'd bought a new outfit, for good luck if nothing else. After pulling on the sequined t-shirt, I had even more misgivings. I looked shop-worn. Stefan had assured me the black leather jacket was totally appropriate, but he was so wrapped up in his art he was totally clueless. I pirouetted in front of the mirror. Hey, I was an artist. *This is the way I'm supposed to dress, not like a society matron.*

As soon as I stepped into the gallery, I could see it was way upscale from those Stefan had worked with previously. I felt myself shrinking into my skin in an effort to become invisible.

I recognized the *Tribune* art critic as he walked around the room, notepad and pencil in hand. A fellow critic joined him. I followed as inconspicuously as possible as they made their way toward the wall where my painting hung. Stefan had left me long ago, surrounded by the rich art patrons who'd come to view his work. No one else in the room had a clue as to who I was, and I suspected they could've cared less.

Just as the critics reached my painting, the gallery owner approached. "What do you think?" I heard him ask.

"Very impressive. I think you've discovered a new protégé."

My heart began to beat loudly. Was he talking about my work?

"Except for this piece." The second critic gestured toward my piece. "It doesn't match up to the rest of the work. It's a poor imitation without the artistic soul." To my utter shame, the *Trib* critic nodded in agreement.

"Yes, well, it's his girlfriend's. He wanted it hung—what could I say?"

I couldn't move; my limbs were locked in place. A horrified gasp escaped my lips. They heard the sound and turned my way. I felt naked...all my insecurities proven right and flaunted in public for all to see. The force of the humiliation spread like wildfire through my body. When I heard the owner's muttered *Uh-oh*, I finally came to life. I had to get out of there. I turned and pushed my way through the crowd and out the door. Nothing and no one would ever induce me to enter the place again. Let the owner explain to Stefan what had happened. I had to get away.

THE NEXT MORNING, I awoke to my ringing cell phone. I'd just fallen asleep after hours of pacing, overwrought with anxiety about my future. I'd lost my job, lost my apartment, and the critics hated my work. Strike three. I was out. A twenty-seven-year-old loser. Now I had to face Gram and tell her that I'd failed her. My mother was right.

"Where the hell did you go last night?" Stefan's voice carried more anger than concern.

"Didn't the gallery owner tell you what happened?"

"No, he just said you left in a hurry."

It was too painful. I couldn't repeat it. "Please, do me a favor. Go over and get my painting, and you can ask him about it."

"Why can't you tell me? And why do you want the painting taken down? This is your chance for recognition."

"Oh, I've been recognized all right. Just do it, please." I disconnected the call before he could ask any more questions.

I got up, dressed, and packed up the few things I'd brought to my apartment. After delivering the key to the landlord, I climbed into the Ford and drove over to Stefan's, knowing it would be a long time before I came back, if ever.

Stefan was waiting at the door for once. He put his arms around me and patted my back soothingly. "They don't know anything. I think it's a great painting. You have to develop a tougher skin."

"Let's face it. You're biased." I tried to smile at his feeble attempt to comfort me.

I'd done a lot of thinking while pacing my miniscule apartment, and I walked over to where he'd leaned the painting against the studio wall. I took another long, hard look at my work. It didn't take a genius to see that the critic was right. I'd done a poor imitation of Stefan's work.

"Stay here, and you can start something new. I'll help you.

You're close, babe. All that's missing is that edge for success. If you didn't spend so much time worrying about your family, you could do it."

"No, he's right. I've tried to copy your style, and it isn't working." It was painful to admit I'd been so caught up in my admiration of the artist Stefan that I'd lost my own style and passion. "I have to get back. Gram needs me."

"Why can't she come here? We could find her a nice place to stay. Why do we have to be the ones to change our lifestyle? What about your brothers? Aren't they responsible for her, too?"

"We've gone through this before. I'm the only one available now."

"What about me? I need you, too. This place is a mess since you left, and I don't know when I've last had a decent meal."

Had he always whined that way?

I turned to look at him and read in his self-indulgent expression what my future would be like if I stayed. It wasn't a pretty sight. Gone was the glamour of Stefan the artist. He was back to plain old Steve.

I realized then he'd never understand me or my relationship with my family. *Did he understand anyone?* He was so wrapped up in his work that nothing or no one else mattered. Exactly how long would he miss me—a week, a day? Or only until he found another eager student to take my place, someone so enamored with the artist that she'd do all the mundane things in life for him. Maybe he'd already found her. I felt sick inside.

What a fool I'd been. Oh, God. I'd spent the past years chasing *his* dream, not mine. All these paintings I'd been doing weren't my creations, just an extension of his. He'd criticized my earlier work so much that I'd lost my own style. I didn't even know what that was anymore.

I was going back to Shoreview. That's where my love of art began. Maybe I'd find something there to keep me happy. I needed time to think about my future, quite sure now I'd never come back.

"Believe it or not, this time it isn't about you. It's about me and my future," I said.

"What future is that? A life in some backwater town taking care of an old woman? You deserve more than that, Cara. We deserve better than that."

"*An old woman?* That's how you describe my Gram?" I started to shake with pent-up anger. Anger at Steve for being who he was, and anger with myself for all the years I'd wasted with him.

"There no longer is a *we* as far as I'm concerned, Steve. Goodbye."

"That's just hurt pride talking. Like I told you, you've got to develop a tougher skin."

I didn't bother answering but walked out the door.

"You'll be back when you come to your senses," he called down the stairs. "I'll be waiting."

I got back in my car and headed north, a mere shell of the woman I'd been when I left there just weeks ago. *What lay ahead for me now?* I felt adrift and rudderless. Painting no longer appealed to me. I'd lost whatever drive I'd had. I felt like Gram—confused, disorientated—afraid of what the future held and unable to go back to the past. Suddenly, I missed her terribly and could hardly wait to be back in that old farmhouse, drinking strong coffee and eating her ginger cookies at the kitchen table, the one place where I'd always felt secure.

10

NANCY AND GRAM HAD ALREADY CLOSED THE SHOP FOR THE DAY and were sitting in the kitchenette when I arrived, doing exactly what I'd been dreaming about—drinking coffee and eating cookies. Nancy looked more relaxed and happier than I'd ever seen her.

How I envied them.

Gram hurried over to give me a hug as soon as she noticed me in the doorway. "You're back," she said, relief heavy in her voice. I felt a flash of guilt for giving her more worry. She put her hands on my shoulders and held me at a distance as she gave me a penetrating stare. "You don't look very happy. What happened, Cara?"

As happy as I was to see my old Gram, I didn't want to spill my guts in front of Nancy. I still had memories of the girl from high school with a chip on her shoulder the size of Cleveland, the one who'd like nothing better than to throw my recent failures in my face. And of course, there was her brother to consider. I couldn't bear for him to know what a loser I'd become.

"I'll tell you all about it later," I said, breaking out of Gram's grasp. "So, how did things go at the shop while I was gone? Any problems?"

"Oh, no, we got along just fine, dear. Nancy took care of the customers while I mostly painted in the back room. You know, like you did when you lived here."

"Thank you, Nancy, for all your help. I really appreciate it." As grateful as I was, a touch of jealousy colored my feelings.

"No problem. It was a fair exchange," Nancy said.

I gave Gram a quizzical look. What had been exchanged?

"I've been teaching her rosemaling. I didn't find out until a year ago how interested she was in learning," Gram said, directing a fond look at Nancy. "All those wasted years that we could've been working together." She shook her head, her lips pressed together. "She was just too shy to ask."

"How did you two ever connect, anyway?" I'd been wondering about that for weeks.

"Lucy finally admitted last fall that she was feeling a bit over-whelmed, what with all the tourists coming through, and needed help," Nancy said with a gentle smile directed at Gram. "I finally got up my nerve and volunteered my services part-time in exchange for lessons."

"It's been good for both of us," Gram said. "She's been doing really well. I think she should go to school and become a master of the art."

"Well, who better to learn from—a woman who was so very close to the title herself," Nancy said, giving Gram a smile of gratitude.

I couldn't seem to move and stood staring at the two of them with my mouth hanging open in surprise.

"Oh, sit down, dear. I'll get you a cup of coffee, and you can tell us all about your trip." Gram bustled over to the stove.

"What do you mean—saying Gram was so close to the title of master?" I asked Nancy while Gram poured the coffee.

"Didn't you know about that either?" She gave me a look that asked where I'd been all my life. "Lucy was working and studying to become a master of rosemaling before she got married and your grandfather needed her on the farm. She said she'd planned to start again later in life, but when your father died, she opened the shop to help you all out." She flashed a sympathetic look in

Gram's direction. "I think when you all left, she felt it was too late."

I didn't know what to feel at the moment. Anger at Gram for sharing a part of herself with Nancy that I never knew, or anger at myself for not caring enough to find out? Did Gram love us so much that she didn't want us to know of her sacrifice or think so little of us she thought we wouldn't help her achieve her dream in any way we could? I'd go with the former because that was the woman I knew, but my heart ached with the pain of not knowing for sure.

On one of Gram's good days, I'd catch her alone and find out more about this dream she'd put aside for us. That must never happen again.

WE WERE PREPARING dinner that night when Gram broached the subject. I knew she wouldn't be able to wait too long.

"Spill it," she said. "You've been moping about like a dog who's lost his favorite bone ever since you got back." She put her hand on my shoulder. "Sharing trouble can cut the weight in half, you know."

"Oh, Gram." I tried unsuccessfully to fight the sob in my voice. "The critics hated my painting, said it was a bad copy of Stefan's work. They and the gallery owner thought it was awful. I think they actually felt sorry for me." It was one of the hardest things I'd ever had to do, share this failure with the one person who'd always believed in me. I related the entire sordid episode of the opening, and she clucked her tongue sympathetically.

"Well, now is the time to take a good look at your work and judge it for yourself. Don't pay attention to what they say; it's what you believe that really matters. You can't plan your future based on what a few critics say."

"That's the thing. They're right. I don't know why I couldn't see it myself. I was copying Stefan's work and didn't even realize it."

"You're a wonderful artist, my girl, and you're at a turning point. Open your eyes and see what's out there. We have a wonderful art colony in this area, you know. Maybe that wasn't meant to be your *real* work?" Her words only added to my pain.

"I don't think I'll ever paint again, Gram. I've lost the desire."

"Nonsense. You're strong; you'll recover."

"I'd like to believe that, Gram, but right now, it doesn't seem possible." Inside of me, there was a hole where my enthusiasm had resided. It had flown away with the words of the art critics.

"Anything is possible, Cara, if you want it bad enough."

Oh, I wanted it bad enough, that wasn't the problem. The problem was knowing I couldn't trust my own judgment. I'd known in my heart the artwork I was doing wasn't my own, yet I kept following Stefan's advice because I'd lost confidence in myself.

"Maybe after some time, Gram. For now, I just want to stay here and work with you." I put on a bright face. "You want me to stay, don't you?"

"Of course, I do, but that doesn't mean I want you to give up your art." She frowned and put her hands on her hips. "Like I said, this is a turning point. You'll find your own way to paint now."

"We'll see, Gram we'll see." I put my arm around her shoulders and gave them a squeeze. "You could be right," I said, but the tightness in my chest wouldn't leave.

JACK and his family arrived the following weekend. It was Saturday evening, and we all sat around Gram's kitchen table, deep in the mellow after-dinner glow that came from eating the family's favorite Scandinavian meal—Swedish meatballs, mashed potatoes, limpa bread, and lingon berries, all topped off with Gram's fresh apple pie. Or maybe we were just too full of carbs to move. Except for the kids. They were getting restless.

Peter had been invited to join us since he and Jack had been best friends forever. I tried my best to avoid eye contact all during the meal, but just the sound of Peter's voice wrapped around me like a warm blanket and I eventually gave up in defeat. The memory of that kiss still burned in my brain like a hot poker, and every time our eyes met, my heart turned over. *How had I let it happen?* And what must *he* be thinking?

I couldn't deny that my dark side was happy to see him, but my more sensible side wished he'd disappear from the planet. Or at least from Shoreview. Since that wasn't going to happen, I'd have to find a way to keep my emotional distance or die trying.

"So, Peter, what's it like to be the most eligible bachelor in town?" Jack's wife Elizabeth gave a sly smile, somehow managing to direct it at both of us. I looked furtively at Gram. Had she told them about the kiss she'd witnessed? Hoping her memory loss would work in my favor tonight, I held my breath.

"Yes," Gram said. "I imagine you're ready to settle down with the right woman by now." She looked guilelessly at Peter, waiting for his answer. *Saved.*

"Do you want the truth?" Peter asked.

"Of course. It's got to be more exciting than the life of an old married couple," Elizabeth said.

"Really?" He grimaced. "How would you like to be constantly bombarded with photographs and phone numbers from every patient or acquaintance with an unmarried female relative over the age of twenty-one?"

Oh, great. And I'd just joined the queue.

"I dunno, it sounds like fun to me," Jack said, studiously avoiding his wife's glare.

"If I remember correctly, I practically had to drag you out of that man cave you shared in college," Elizabeth said. "You were always working on some project or other with your nerdy engineering roommates, Jack."

"Exactly." Peter leaned back in his chair, tilting on the rear legs. "I have plenty to occupy my time just trying to keep my head above water at the clinic. I don't need a woman complicating my life."

"Not even Auntie Cara?" My six-year-old niece, Carolyn, who'd been suspiciously quiet during most of the meal, looked up innocently at Peter as she continued. "Dad says you always had the hots for her."

I choked on my freshly poured coffee. Jack got up and made a big show of patting me on the back. Actually, it was more like a pounding. But not before I saw the wink he directed at his daughter. Maybe Carolyn wasn't so innocent after all.

"Stop already, Jack," I managed to squeak through scalded lips. "I'm going to have bruises."

"Oh, really," Jack whispered for my ears alone. "Too bad it wasn't your head. Maybe I could pound some sense into that empty space you've developed."

I managed to turn and give him a look that should have felled a horse.

"Carolyn, you have to stop listening to grown-up conversations." Gram's face was flushed, and she looked down at the table. Or was that laughter she trying to hide with her downcast look?

"Your Aunt Cara already has a boyfriend in Chicago," Peter said, doing a great sad-clown imitation.

Give me a break. He wanted commitment like a dog wants fleas. Falling for him would be a repetition of my wasted years with Steve. Just like Steve, he was too busy for a wife or family. But then, so was I. Or at least I had been.

"Yeah, but nobody thinks they'll like him," Jack's son added. "Not even Aunt Cara anymore."

"Really?" Peter straightened in his chair, and I swear those leprechaun ears stood at attention.

"Dad says that's why she never brought him around for him and Uncle Joe to meet."

"Your father has had some interesting conversations about my life with you all, hasn't he?" I said, repeating that quelling look. But it was as if Jack was Teflon-coated. Every look and remark just rolled off. "He seems to forget that I have a life in Chicago that I'm going to return to at some point."

I slammed my coffee cup down on the table, preparing to flounce out of the room with as much dignity as I could muster. I hadn't told anyone about my break-up with Steve. Had Gram guessed?

Of course, Peter's cell phone rang at that moment, and he excused himself, spoiling my exit. We were all silent while he took his call. But I managed to send black looks to Jack and his wife, a silent promise that we'd be discussing this later when the children were in bed.

"Sorry, but there's an emergency, and I have to leave. Thanks for another wonderful dinner, Lucy. It was great seeing you all again."

"Our pleasure, Peter. Cara will see you out." The look Gram sent me was a reminder he was a guest in our home.

"Keep in touch." Jack raised his hand in a goodbye salute. "Hopefully, we'll be seeing a lot more of you now."

What did that mean? Extra visits to Gram, or a reference to my eligibility? I could kill Jack.

I got up and charged ahead of Peter to the foyer. As I reached into the guest closet and handed him the lightweight jacket he'd worn, our fingers touched briefly. The jolt of awareness sent little alarm bells off in my head, and I pulled my hand back, almost dropping his jacket. But he was even quicker and whipped the jacket on before I could catch my breath.

While opening the door to leave, he quipped, "Now you know why I shouldn't marry. What woman would want to put up with this? Can't remember the last time I've had an uninterrupted evening out."

"Yeah, well, we all have our problems." Right now, the loss of my art career seemed more important than him missing an evening with friends, and I would've loved to tell him about it. But I wasn't about to whine, not when he had an emergency to get to.

"I'll see you around," he said and left.

Later, after we'd cleared the kitchen and Jack and Elizabeth were getting the children off to bed, churning thoughts of my empty life swirled around in my head. Had the past five years been a complete waste of time? Was Jack right? Could the reason I never insisted Steve come home with me be that I knew, as Gram would say, he'd stand out like the proverbial petunia in an onion patch? I tried to picture him at the dinner table with the family, but it was impossible. I couldn't think of one thing he had in common with any of them, other than knowing me. Who knew what rude remark would inadvertently cross his lips? Remarks about the narrowness of small-town living and the lack of modern art in the area, just to name a few.

Steve wasn't any Peter and never would be.

11

JACK AND ELIZABETH WERE GONE JUST AS QUICKLY AS THEY'D arrived. And now, a few days later, I was dreading the next Wool Gatherers' meeting, where I knew there'd be questions about my quick trip back from Chicago. How would I explain my failure?

Telling Gram how it went was bad enough, but at least I knew she would always believe in me and in my work. Or at least I'd thought so until that remark she'd made about my painting being garish.

It took a few days, but after a lot of thought and soul searching, I had finally made a life-altering decision. I'd give up my art, at least for now. Instead, I would spend my time taking care of Gram and the shop for as long as she needed me. I would let go of that long-held dream of an art career in Chicago. What further proof did I need of my lack of talent than that debacle at Steve's opening?

After making that decision, my soul felt lighter and freer than it had in a long time. Now, I just had to figure out a way to explain it.

"TELL US ALL ABOUT YOUR TRIP." Lila was the first to bring up the dreaded subject as the group sat around, working on their projects.

Gram and I exchanged looks. Thankfully, she kept silent.

"The trip was great. I got everything squared away there, so now I'm free to stay with Gram as long as she'll have me."

A guarded look passed between the women, one that said they suspected why I was giving up my Chicago career to stay with Gram. But, like the true friends they were, they didn't ask. My body sagged in relief.

"Have you thought any more about learning to felt?" Martha broke the silence.

"Not really," I said.

"Well, you're in luck because our dyeing and felting day is coming up soon and you're invited."

Oh, yeah, isn't that just what I needed, another way to be reminded of my artistic failings.

"I can't. I have to be in the shop." Why couldn't they just leave me alone to lick my wounds in private?

Okay, so maybe I *was* a whiny loser. But I didn't want their sympathy. I'd only come to the gathering for Gram's sake and because I owed these women the courtesy after their kindness to us.

"I'd be happy to help out at the shop that day. Lucy and I are in the middle of a project anyway," Nancy said.

I shot her a keep-your-mouth-shut look.

Was that a glimmer of sympathy I saw in her eyes? How different from the Nancy I remembered.

"Okay, it's settled then," Martha declared in her no-nonsense voice. "I'll pick you up early on that Saturday morning. We're meeting at Lila's farm. Be sure to wear old clothes. It gets pretty messy."

So much for my protests. The subject changed before I could come up with another excuse to get out of it. I didn't have the energy to argue anyway. I suspected they'd made it their mission to get me involved, and out of respect for Gram, I acquiesced. It wasn't as though my social calendar was filled.

"Nancy, what's the latest on your brother? I hear he's been seen with a different woman every weekend," Lila asked with a grin.

My ears perked up, and I moved closer. As much as I tried to deny it, I was interested in anything about Peter.

"Please." Nancy grimaced. "I only wish! All he does is work and study his dry medical magazines. Sometimes I'd just like to shake him. He's so afraid of commitment; scared to death he'll choose the wrong woman to fit his demanding career. He made that mistake while in medical school and now he's gun-shy."

I'd never heard anything about a girlfriend. Why hadn't anyone ever let that little detail slip out? What was her name? Where was she from? Did they break up because of his career? I wanted answers, but I didn't dare ask the questions. I chewed my lips in frustration.

"That doesn't sound like the Peter I know," Gram said. "He's longed for a family of his own as long as I've known him."

"Well, that's the thing," Nancy said. "I keep telling him if he's already aware of the type of woman he needs, it'll work out. He's got it in his head that he can't be both a good doctor and a good family man. He's afraid he'll take after our father."

Well, that explained a lot. What was wrong with him? He needed a good clip to the side of the head. He should realize there were a lot of successful career men who also led full family lives. I was beginning to get a better picture of the man he'd become and why.

"I say we should leave the poor man alone. He'll find the right woman in his own time," Joan said. Raising her eyebrows with a sly smile, she continued, "For all we know, he may have already found her."

I looked over at her out of the corner of my eye, only to see that smile directed at me. I ducked my head for a moment, pretending great interest in the spinning. Were my feelings so obvious? But looking around the room, no one else seemed to have noticed.

"At the risk of sounding terribly selfish, I'd say we're pretty darn lucky he devotes so much time to his practice," Carol said. "I know I sure appreciated it when he was there for me and the boys."

There was a general nod of agreement.

"I suppose," Nancy said, her mouth twisting. "But I just want him to be happy."

"I say it's time to eat," I said. "I'll help set things up." I walked into the kitchen, followed by Carol and Nancy. They didn't hear my sigh of relief.

"I'M GOING FOR A WALK, GRAM," I yelled upstairs the next evening. I was sick to death of thinking about my future—or lack thereof. My feet carried me unthinkingly down the path through the woods behind Gram's field, still brooding over what could fill the empty spaces of a life without art.

The air around me pulsed with the scent of verdant life. Tree frogs croaked their evening sounds. Everything teemed with the chartreuse green of new growth.

Tiny violets had appeared almost overnight among the dead leaves on the forest ground, poking their heads up in defiance of the long winter that had buried them deep in the cold and snow. Where did *they* get their strength? Even though all around me the earth had come alive, I felt a part of me had died along with my desire to paint, and I was at a loss on how to resurrect it.

I squatted to the level of the violets. Rebirth after death. So delicate looking, yet so strong. Why couldn't I be like them? Something inside of me wanted desperately to believe I could mimic the strength of the forest wildflowers. The thought carried on the whisper of the evening breeze, and I breathed the scent in deeply, needing to believe it.

The desire to paint clawed at my insides. I could feel it gasping for life. Was it seeing the violets, so determined to thrive in that barren sea of decayed leaves? My fingers itched with the familiar longing to hold a paintbrush and bring that very vision to canvas.

Don't even consider it, a part of me begged. *You don't do land-scapes. You're setting yourself up for failure again.* I could visualize Steve's sneer. But a stronger voice answered, *What's the harm? It could be fun.*

I ran back to the house to get my digital camera. I'd take a few photographs. That way, if I decided to paint the scene someday, I'd have captured it on film.

More excited than I'd been since coming back to Shoreview, I couldn't begin to describe the feeling of satisfaction filming those flowers gave me. I was finally on a new path. Where it would lead, I didn't know, but it felt damn good.

THE PICTURES I took that night were only the beginning. I found myself carrying my camera with me everywhere I went now, capturing scenes and faces so familiar to me that I had no longer noticed them. Now, I saw them through different eyes. Dare I say it? The eyes of an artist.

I downloaded the pictures onto my computer and spent a lot of time studying each and every one when I was alone. The crinkle of an eye, an upturned nose, the special coloring of the sky after an evening rain. I catalogued them all in my brain. But right now, the thought of actually painting remained too painful.

TWO WEEKS LATER, I found myself waiting at the door for Martha, dressed in my rattiest jeans and t-shirt, a navy hoodie slung over my arm and a Chicago Cubs cap on my head, just in case. Even in June, the weather could turn on a dime in Wisconsin, especially so close to the lake. All it took was a shift in the wind. I'd be prepared.

Nancy had already stopped by for Gram, and they were off to the shop. I noticed Gram didn't give her any argument about taking the Buick, unlike every time we left home.

When I saw Martha pull in, I dragged my feet to her car. How did I let myself get pulled into this? I owed it to Gram to be nice to her friends, but wasn't this going a bit too far?

"Are you sure I'm not supposed to bring anything?" I asked Martha as I buckled my seatbelt.

"No, everything was organized before we talked you into coming," Martha assured me.

Geeze, what was this? Another attempt to take over my life and

decide what's best for me? Been there, done that—with Steve—
and look how that turned out.

Guilt over my rotten attitude shut me up. I would find a way
to get through this day *and* keep a smile plastered on my face.

We drove for a few minutes, listening to the local radio station
playing a jazz tune. Finally, Martha broke the silence.

"I know it's none of my business and I don't mean to pry, Cara,
but what the *hell* happened in Chicago to make you decide to give
everything up and stay here indefinitely? That sure wasn't your
plan when you first arrived."

"Well, Gram really seems to need me, and—"

"Give me a break. Whatever you're doing is working.
Everyone can see how much better she is. You might not realize
it, but you're talking to the queen of denial, or at least I used to
be. Sharing your problems with friends can really help, ya
know?"

"Okay," I said after a deep sigh. I liked Martha, and she didn't
seem to be one for the gossip mills. "Here it is in a nutshell. The
critics totally panned my painting, calling it a poor imitation of
Steve's work and completely lacking in soul."

"Were they right?" she asked.

So much for the platitudes and sympathy I'd expected.

"Yeah," I admitted, my face flaming. "They were. I think deep
down I always knew it, but then again, there's that part of me that
made me keep trying."

"What about the boyfriend? What did he have to say
about it?"

"He tried to convince me that the critics were wrong, and I
should stay with him."

"Why didn't you?" She shot me a questioning look before
snapping her glance back on the road.

"Because I finally admitted to myself I've been working in
his shadow for too long, years actually, trying to imitate him and
doing a freakin' poor job of it. I had to get away to try and find
myself before I can even think of returning, if ever. My relationship was over long ago. I was just too stupid to realize it."
Verbalizing my feelings gave them legs, and I realized the pitiful

truth of my life. "God, I sound like I should be a guest on Dr. Phil."

"No, you sound like a woman who's on the verge of self-discovery. Believe me, I know how scary it can be—been there, done that."

"Thanks, Martha, I appreciate it." The smile I gave her was weak, but it was the best I could do at the moment.

When we arrived at Lila's, I followed Martha over to the area where Cheryl waited.

Cheryl had a small table covered with a plastic tablecloth, a rush placemat, a piece of old net curtain slightly bigger than the mat, a larger piece of old cotton sheeting, and a pan of very hot, soapy water. She dove right in with an explanation of felting.

"You can do felting by hand or by machine," Cheryl began in the patient voice of a teacher who knows her subject well. "I'll start out by making a small piece, using a natural colored wool batt. It'll be easier to see the design that way. When I finish, you can try your own hand at it."

Guilt swept over me in hot waves. I wanted to stop her, tell her she was wasting her time, I wasn't interested in anything connected to art. But instead, I watched with the evasive smile of an indifferent student.

"I like to make three layers of the wool to make sure my felt is dense enough, but you can go thinner or thicker, depending on your project." After cutting twelve inches off the fleece batt, Cheryl proceeded to pull it apart, separating it into three layers, which she laid atop one another in opposite directions.

"Now comes the fun part," she said as she pulled out a bag of wool swatches dyed in bright colors. I watched with interest as she began laying them on top of the third layer to form a design. "Let's go a little wild here." She smiled. "It's like painting, you know. I can put any color I want on the white wool—it's kind of like a canvas, a collage with textiles." She laid out wisps of red, purple, and green wool across the batt, alternating thickness and direction. "I like to add a few dyed mohair curls when I have them. They have a special sheen and clarity of color that's different from the sheep's wool. But today I only have the natural curls, so I'll pull them apart and place them in a fine layer across the fabric. That'll give it a nice sheen."

My interest peaked as I watched her lay out the pattern, my fingers itching to grab some colors and take a stab at my own design.

Next, she covered the wool with a piece of old net curtain and sprinkled a little hot soapy water across it, patting the water through to the fibers.

"There are two distinct stages in making felt by hand. This is the felting stage, where you add soap and water and hand pressure to make the fibers start to interlock." Cheryl kept sprinkling and gently patting until all the fibers were saturated. "You have to be quite gentle at the beginning so your design stays in place."

She began working the flat of her hands more vigorously, using a polishing action with her palms. I was intrigued in spite of myself.

"Did you know felt is man's oldest textile?" Before I could answer, she hurried on. "It predates Christianity, at least as far back as 700 BC. I like to picture all those nomadic tents, strong enough to resist rain and snowy conditions, besides being waterproof and warm." Her voice took on a dreamy quality, and I knew she was lost in the beauty of her craft. "And of course, you know it was also an old Scandinavian home craft. We're really into those things in this area," she continued.

She didn't have to tell me that. I'd been inundated with all things Scandinavian my entire life.

After about ten minutes, Cheryl gently peeled the net off the surface. The colored fibers had all been worked into the wool, as if they'd always been a part of the batt, and a fine sheen of mohair covered the entire piece. A square of fabric was taking shape.

"Now we go into the shrinking process. This is where we need friction, so to do that we'll roll the piece in the rush placemat." After wrapping the felt inside like a jellyroll, she rolled the mat back and forth for several minutes. "You want to gradually increase the pressure, because that and the rolling create the friction that shrinks the felt."

Unrolling her piece, she rinsed the wool, laying it out to dry. It had gone from a thickness of several inches to a much flatter piece of fabric in minutes.

"What are you going to do with it?" I ran my hand over her creation, surprised at the softness. The colors had blended into a soft mosaic against the natural wool background, and she was right about the mohair lending a glossy sheen.

"I think I'll make a bonnet for my newest grandchild. I'll line it with a soft batiste and blanket stitch around the edges with a matching yarn. It'll keep her nice and warm this winter without being too heavy."

"It'll be lovely," I said, smiling.

"Now it's your turn."

My hands shook a bit as I tore off the section of fleece. Something had happened to me while I watched her. It was the same feeling I got when beginning a new painting—a mixture of excitement and anxiety. Would I be able to create the vision in my brain or would I mess this up, too?

As I repeated the steps Cheryl had shown me, the design formed in my head. I felt the anxiety drifting away.

An hour later, I was hooked.

IN THE WEEKS THAT FOLLOWED, I became a woman possessed. Using the small wage Gram insisted on paying me, I bought books. I ordered dyes. I experimented with color. I couldn't get enough of felt making and dying. I began with small samples, then progressed to a multicolored layered piece of fabric. I sewed that into a child-size purse and embellished it with old costume jewelry and ribbon. I knew it looked amateurish compared to Cheryl's work, but I was proud, nonetheless. I decided to give it to my niece for her birthday.

A month passed, unnoticed. Gram and I were happy in our little world. Her daytime memory had improved, and she seemed much calmer and more like her old self. We'd followed Peter's instructions to the letter. I made sure she remembered her meds and got physical exercise. She seemed so much better I often forgot all about her memory problems. Except for her anxiety about running the cash register. She didn't want any part of it, and I couldn't blame her. She definitely needed help in that area.

Gram was spending a lot less time in the shop these days, enjoying the time spent with her animals, the house, and cooking. She more or less left the running of the shop to me, encouraging me to make all the business decisions. I wasn't sure if it was because she didn't trust her judgment or if she wanted to make me feel useful.

Steve called a few times, but I didn't have much to say to him. All he wanted to talk about was his work and his growing fame. While I was happy for him, I felt removed, like it no longer concerned me. I had moved on to another life, and Stefan was again just the Steve I'd first met in art school.

I made a few more purses and a hat and took a chance when I decided to place them in the shop. What did I have to lose, after all? Any profit would go directly to Gram. And as my mother had so aptly stated when this all began, I definitely had benefited from the free room and board and small salary.

Surprisingly, the felt items sold. The customers found them unique and practical. It made me feel good to be able to bring money in. I no longer felt totally unproductive.

"You should go online and see some of the beautiful wall hangings by other artists," Cheryl said at a Wool Gatherers meeting.

I was working on embellishing a vest of my own to wear in the shop on cold mornings. The design and texture just seemed to fit into the Scandinavian theme of the shop.

"Really?" I asked intrigued at the possibilities.

I ran to my laptop as soon as I got home. My mouth dropped open in surprise.

A few pieces especially caught my imagination—one that looked like a Monet painting with wisps of vibrant flowers against a green multitextured background and another that depicted a winter evening—stark black wool tree trunks and wisps of grey foggy background set against the white wool canvas.

Something stirred deep within, a calling to create a beautiful palette again. I felt that familiar itch.

"Gram, look at this." I carried the laptop over to where she sat at the kitchen table. "Can you believe it? And the art is all fiber."

"Why haven't you toured the art galleries in Door County? You'd be surprised at the diversity. There are a lot more interesting subject matter and professional artists around here than you realize."

I shook my head. "Thanks, but I'm not interested." I couldn't look at paintings, if that was what she was suggesting. It was still too painful.

"Cara, it's not like you to close your mind like this." Gram shook her head slowly, wearing a frown.

"But I'm not. I'm actually opening my mind to other ways of expressing myself. It's kind of exciting, actually." The possibilities were endless now. Why hadn't I realized sooner how fiber could be used as paint on canvas?

FELT MAKING and dyeing became my new obsession. I gloried in the various color combinations I could create with the vibrant acid dyes and the subtlety of the naturally dyed fibers. Combining them was like painting on my own created canvas, just as Cheryl had said. I especially liked the combination of magenta and violet—resulting in a gorgeous, vibrant purple. Using the natural wool as a background for the dyed mohair curls, I spread a thin layer of their silky sheen to completely change the look of the wool.

"I have to learn to spin," I told Gram a few weeks later. "It's the only way I'll get the yarn exactly the color and thickness I want." One of the designs I had in mind called for a rope-like background. "Maybe even weaving."

She smiled that knowing smile of hers but said nothing.

Bursting with energy now, I was having a difficult time finding enough hours in the day for all I wanted to create. Fiber was my new love.

The gorgeous works of art I'd perused online inspired me to

begin working on a wall hanging of my own. I tried to capture the movement of a tree caught in an early fall windstorm. I used dark wool for the trunk and branches and fine layers of green and yellow dyed merino wool to suggest leaves moving in the wind. A warm glow peeped through a partly cloudy blue sky with just a hint of setting sun behind the clouds.

It took several evenings to dye the wool to the exact shade I wanted and to get it felted. But when I finished, I felt a satisfaction reminiscent of my earlier days of painting. It had been a long time.

When I hung it in the shop with a FOR SALE sign on it, my hands suddenly started to shake. What if no one liked it? Was it too amateurish? *Stop it. It doesn't matter what others think.* I liked it, and that was what counted. I took into account the hours spent producing the piece and priced it accordingly. It would probably never sell at that price, but I loved it so much I didn't care.

Shortly after hanging it up and starting on tidying up the store, Peter came into the shop. I hadn't seen him since that fateful dinner with Jack and his family. My pulse picked up, and I caught my breath for a moment. I realized I'd missed seeing him far more than I should have, and it annoyed the hell out of me.

"I'm looking for another gift," he said. "That box you suggested for my friend's wedding was a big hit with the bride, so I've decided to trust your taste." He favored me with his trademark smile. "You are the artist, after all."

"Well, gee whiz, thanks for the vote of confidence." It was annoying to discover a part of me was gloriously happy to know the first gift hadn't been for a love interest as I'd originally thought. "Is this another wedding gift?"

"No, this is more personal."

A flood of disappointment washed over me at those words.

"Why don't you look around for a while and tell me what catches your eye."

"I like this blue vase." He'd wandered through most of the shop by the time he picked it up and still seemed at a loss.

"It's beautiful. I'm sure any woman would love it."

Then he stopped in front of my wall hanging. "Wow. This is nice." He ran his finger over the fiber. "It's very soft."

"It should be framed, but I didn't want to add on to the price."

"Who did it?"

"I made it." I felt a little thrill at the obvious admiration in his voice.

"I thought you only did paintings—and very modern ones at that," Peter said, looking at me.

"I've learned something new since I've been here. Do you really like it, or are you being polite?" I sounded as eager as a kindergartner showing Mom their school project and gave myself a mental reminder it was only Peter.

"Cara, this is beautiful. I like it so much I'm going to buy it."

"Have you looked at the price tag?" I wasn't sure I was really ready or wanted to part with it. Who was he going to give it to? It felt like I was selling a part of me, and I wanted to grab it back.

"Yes, and it's worth every penny."

"Well, I don't know..."

"What do you mean, you don't know. What kind of a salesperson are you, anyway? You'll be out of business in a month if you keep this up."

I stomped off to the cash register and started to ring up the sale.

"I'll take the vase, too," Peter said.

"Swell. Would you like them gift wrapped?"

"Just the vase, please." He watched me, a grin lifting the corners of his mouth as I wrapped the items with jerky movements. "This is the first time someone's been mad at me for purchasing sale items in their store."

I stopped and took a deep breath, realizing how ridiculous I was acting. It wasn't only the sale of the hanging that bothered me. It was the fact that Peter was probably purchasing it for someone else—a stranger. No wonder he thought I was crazy.

"I'm sorry. I don't know what got into me." There was no way I could explain my reaction. I had to just let it go at that. I should have realized what would happen when I put the wall hanging in the store.

"Hey, would you like to take in a movie some night? Since you already have a boyfriend and I can't date anyone around here without the wedding banns being posted at every coffee shop in town, maybe we could hang out together?"

Obviously, those shared kisses meant nothing to him. I guess I was the one over-reacting. But even he couldn't ignore the family matchmaking.

"After what happened at dinner with Jack? Are you crazy?" I asked, glancing at him as I finished wrapping the vase.

"So what if your family takes it the wrong way? We'll know it's only friendship—that's what counts, right?"

There was a form of logic in there somewhere. I hesitated.

"C'mon, you've got to be as bored as I am on the weekend," he coaxed. "We'll drive up to Sturgeon Bay where fewer people know me if it'll make you feel better."

"After that big sale, it's hard to say no."

"Great. How about Sunday? I know you don't work on Monday, and I'm not on call. We'll have dinner and then a movie."

"I can do that. Actually, it sounds like fun." He was right. I needed to get out more. I was in danger of letting my obsession take over my life again.

"Will Lucy be all right for the evening?" Peter asked, his concern for his patient showing.

"She's been doing a whole lot better these past weeks, but just in case, I'll leave my cell phone number right by the phone and hide her car keys."

"See you then." He winked, and with a flash of his sexy grin and his packages under his arm, headed out the door.

My feelings ran up and down like I was on a roller coaster again as I watched him leave. Part of me was really looking forward to spending time with him and another part was hesitant. Would it be safe? When I'd looked into those deep blue eyes, I'd felt a familiar sexual stirring within only he seemed to bring to life.

Maybe the question should be would *he* be safe?

12

Driving into Sturgeon Bay that Sunday evening, traffic was light as the weekend tourists departed. Day-trippers wouldn't arrive in force until Tuesday when all the shops were sure to be open. Signs of summer were everywhere along the highway, from the intrepid dandelions poking up through the edge of the grassy shoulder to the shrill call of gulls piercing the quiet evening air. We crossed the bridge and turned along the lakeshore road.

"Want to see the latest yacht being built at the shipyard? I heard it's a real beauty—a one-hundred-fifty-footer with every possible luxury. It'll need a crew of ten to sail her." The boyish look on his face was dangerous to my emotional equilibrium. "It's set to launch soon," Peter continued. "Maybe they'll have it out of the construction shed, and we'll get a view of it in the lot."

As kids, this had been one of my brothers' favorite pastimes. I still found it hard to believe that this little town, nestled between the waters of Green Bay and Lake Michigan, housed the shipyards where luxury yachts were custom-built for a global clientele and large commercial vessels were manufactured and repaired.

As we got out of the car and walked up to the chain-link fence to gaze at whatever craft was there, many fantasies whipped through my brain. We were in luck and got a good view of the newly constructed sleek yacht. Watching Peter's expression as we walked around the perimeter of the enclosed shipyard was like watching a football fan after a winning game. His eyes lit with pride as if he'd designed and built it himself.

When we left the shipyard and turned down a familiar side street, I knew where we were headed. Mama Mia's was a small family-owned restaurant that been there forever, a favorite of the locals.

I hadn't been there in years but remembered the welcoming scent of garlic and rosemary as soon as I stepped through the door. I knew I was in for a culinary treat. I set my uneasiness aside, determined to enjoy every morsel. Gram and I hadn't exactly been very creative in the kitchen these past weeks.

A smiling waitress seated us at a cozy table for two. From the friendly "*Hi, Peter!*" greetings echoing across the room, I knew he was a regular. The low ceiling and soft lighting, starched white tablecloths and red candles sputtering in the tall glass chimneys made it even more intimate. After downing a glass of wine and a superb pasta dinner, my mood was relaxed and satisfied. I didn't even mind that I'd left my felting obsession for the evening. The conversation shifted from news of old acquaintances and former classmates to family. We had more to talk about than I'd imagined.

"So, what have you been doing to fill your evenings since you've been here? Other than taking care of Lucy?" Peter leaned back in his chair, looking more relaxed than I'd ever seen him.

"I've spent a lot of my time on felting lately." I ran my fork around the now empty plate. "I've actually become quite obsessed with it. I've already started on another wall hanging."

Now, why did that confession embarrass me? Was it because I had visions of Steve and his around-the-clock painting burned in my brain, and I was rethinking my life priorities? When would I come to terms with my life goals?

"It happens, doesn't it? I have the same problem—can't seem to get away from the clinic some days, emotionally or physically —even when I'm not on call." He paused. "Everyone has to make a choice sooner or later—family or career. Can't have both."

Wow. That was the statement of a disillusioned man. There

were deeper layers to this easygoing guy than I'd thought. Steve
and I had never had such a conversation. He'd just assumed his
art would always come first, and our relationship would work
around it. I'd gone along without question. I didn't even want to
speculate on my reasons.

"Why can't one have both?" I asked.

Peter finished off the last of his wine and set the empty glass
on the table with a soft thud. "Do you really have to ask me that?"

He shrugged and, after looking at his watch, pushed his chair
away from the table. "We'd better get a move on, or we'll miss the
beginning of the movie." He guided me out of the restaurant, his
hand warm and somehow familiar against the small of my back.

The movie had barely begun when Peter slipped an arm
across my shoulders. Was this simply a friendly gesture or a
replay of the night at Gram's? *Whatever.* I was tired of trying to
figure out the meaning behind his every move. There was just
something so secure about him, like I'd come home after a long
trip. I put aside my scruples and enjoyed the moment.

The movie turned out to be a family drama involving a
mother and son relationship. I sensed raw tension radiating
through Peter in waves during the family arguments and glanced
at his face, but he watched the screen with a fixed stare. It got me
to wondering again about his family life. I wished I'd paid closer
attention during our younger years.

After the movie, we drove back to Gram's and walked up the
steps, hand in hand. It seemed so natural to do so. As I turned to
face him before opening the door, he raised his hand, as if about
to caress my cheek, and I caught my breath. Being this close to
him brought on those familiar mixed signals. I knew I should
step back, out of reach. But my feet seemed to have grown roots.

"Would you like to come in for a drink?" I whispered. "Gram
must've gone to bed. I see she's put out most of the lights."

"Sure, why not," he whispered back, his breath like a soft
caress against my face.

My heart picked up several beats. I forced myself to turn and
open the door into the dimly lit foyer.

"Take off your coat. I'll make us something to drink. What

would you like?"

"Whatever you're having," he said, still whispering.

"I usually have a cup of herbal tea at this time of night. Will that do?"

"Sure, sounds good. I have an early day tomorrow," Peter said, finding a comfortable spot to sit down.

As I handed him a mug of tea, still puzzling over what he'd said at dinner, I settled beside him on the couch. I took a sip of my tea, the mug warm and comforting in my hand. "Peter, do you really believe it's either family or career? Why must they be mutually exclusive?"

"It's a lesson I learned from my father. A pillar of the community, right?" He turned his gaze away from me. "He was always there for everyone else but never had time for us." The planes of his face had hardened with tension when he looked back. "But I had to relearn that lesson—the hard way. So, I decided to do womankind a favor by staying single. Don't I deserve a medal for that?"

"Yeah, right. You're quite the hero," I said, giving him a playful punch in the arm. "Where's your mom now?" I knew his father had passed away.

"She left when Nancy and I were still in school. Didn't you know? Moved out east to be with family and friends. Seems to be enjoying life out there."

I'd forgotten about that. Wow, he'd lost both his parents in a way, and it sounded like he never had the attention of either. I moved a little closer. I wanted to hug the hurt little boy in him and assure him I'd always be here for him. I tightened my grip on the mug. *Wait a minute.* Hadn't I learned anything? Falling into that old caregiver role that got me into so much trouble first with my family and later with Steve would be a mistake.

An unsettling thought interrupted my musings. What if I'd found artistic success early in my career and then had a family? Would I be like Steve and Peter's father—expecting my family's life to revolve around my needs? Was Peter right? It would've been a recipe for disaster. At least the two of us were aware of our shortcomings and knew better than to get involved in a serious relationship. But that didn't necessarily mean we couldn't be close friends, did it?

I longed to ask him about the romantic affair Nancy'd alluded to but couldn't get up the nerve to invade his privacy. I moved even closer and rested my head on his shoulder. His arm slipped around my shoulder. I was doing it again, but I couldn't stop myself. It just felt so right to give him comfort. Or maybe I was comforting myself. Whatever. We were two misfits in the emotional landscape of love.

"What did you think of the movie?" I asked.

"Too much emotion for me. I prefer the shoot 'em up variety. Helps me get rid of all my inner aggression."

He tightened his embrace, kissing me softly on the top of my head. I finally gave up trying to convince myself these feelings I was having were sister-like. Since we both knew it could never be anything more than a light flirtation, why not go with it? We sat like that for some time, comfortable with the silence between us.

"I'd better go before I fall asleep," he whispered close to my ear. "Lucy would be surprised to find me here in the morning."

"Okay."

We walked to the door, and I started to say goodnight. But before I could get the words out, he pulled me into his arms, placing a searing kiss on my open lips. I stood transfixed, burning with unfulfilled desire, before gathering my wits and stepping back. When I finally tried to speak, he put an index finger softly to my lips.

"Ah, ah, no temper tantrum, Squir—Cara. Lucy might hear," he whispered and slipped silently out the door.

I watched him go down the porch steps, as confused as hell. This was not going according to my plan. I was supposed to remain emotionally untouched.

After watching his car drive away, I paced the living room floor for a few minutes. Was I in for another sleepless night?

I walked over to the phone, still in a state of frustration that was totally inappropriate, and checked the caller ID, just in case someone had called while I was out. I couldn't rely on Gram's memory.

Surprised to see she'd talked to both of my brothers, I smiled at the coincidence. How great was that, they'd checked on her the one evening I was out. I tiptoed up the stairs, not quite so alone with my concerns about Gram now.

GRAM WAS READING the small local phone book that Monday morning, putting faces and other memories to the names listed, one of her favorite mind exercises.

"I saw on the caller ID that both of my brothers called last night," I commented as I got out a cereal bowl. She looked at me blankly.

"Are you sure?" she asked.

Oh, no. I hadn't seen that look since her medication started taking effect. Her face flushed at the look of dismay I couldn't hide.

"That's okay, a minor detail. It was late at night. Don't worry about it." I walked over and patted her on the shoulder. Why bother questioning her about the conversations when it would just upset her if she didn't remember? She'd tell me if and when the memory returned.

"Did you have a good time with Peter last night?" Gram looked as relieved as I was at the change of subject.

"Yes, the movie was very good."

"That's not what I asked," she said with a raised eyebrow.

"Nothing happened between us, if that's what you want to know." Yet I couldn't stop the blush from creeping up my face. "We had a nice dinner and went to the movies. No big deal."

"Okay," she said. But the knowing gleam in her eyes made me uncomfortable.

Since it was Monday and the shop was closed, I decided it was a good time to organize the stock again.

"Are you sure you don't want to come to the shop today?" I asked.

"No, I'll just stay home. There's work to be done around the house and the yard."

.   .   .

COMING HOME after a long day at the shop, I found Gram out in the barn that evening, talking aloud as she fed the animals.

"It's for her own good, you know. Someone has to set those two straight. The boys were right." She turned toward the llama. "Don't go giving me that look," she said, looking for all the world like she expected Zeke to answer her back.

"Who are you talking about, Gram?" I asked, coming up behind her.

She turned and blinked in surprise, and I wondered where she'd been in that mind of hers. Visiting with old friends, I imagined.

"I didn't see you there. How were things at the shop today?"

"Pretty busy. The stock was in a mess. Maybe you should start coming in with me again. You haven't been in the shop for more than a week."

"Oh, I don't think so dear. I might muck things up again. Everything is so much better now that you've taken over the business for me. But if you're that busy, why don't you ask Nancy to come in and help. She likes working in the shop. Told me she's looking for another part-time job."

Could I do it? I really needed another pair of hands. Now that the weather had warmed up, more tourists were coming to the area and business had picked up. Nancy would be the logical person to hire. She knew her way around the shop—better than I did. The question was whether we could work together long-term. Remembering the past days I'd put in trying to handle all the sales by myself and still keep an eye on the customers, I decided it was worth a try.

"You're right. I'll call her."

"You know," Gram said, "I could almost thank that Steve person for getting you to come back here. Even if he didn't mean to do it."

"Please, Gram. I don't want to dwell on the reasons for my being here." Thank God, she still hadn't figured out why I came home in the first place.

13

Hiring Nancy turned out to be one of the best decisions I'd made since coming to Shoreview. We'd be at the height of the tourist season in early July, and the shop was already filled with customers most days. Working together, we actually developed a kind of camaraderie. I really appreciated her concern for Gram and decided one morning to confide in her about the return of Gram's memory lapses.

"Wow. I hadn't noticed. Are you sure you're not just worrying too much?" Nancy frowned, clearly surprised.

"No, things get worse when we're alone in the evening."

"Let's see how it goes at the Wool Gatherers tonight," she said. "Is she making a dish for you to bring?"

"Yeah, she's making my favorite tomato and fresh basil pasta salad. I've been thinking about it all day." My stomach had been rumbling since three o'clock, but I didn't want to ruin my appetite for what I'd learned would be a great smorgasbord of dishes.

"That should give you a clue as to where her mind is," Nancy said, looking confident.

Sure enough, when I got to the farm and asked about the dish, Gram stared at me with that blank expression. "What are you talking about, Cara? What pasta salad?"

"Never mind. I must have forgotten to mention it this morning when I left the house. I'll pick something up at the store on the way there."

"Really dear, you should tell me about these things before-hand. I can't just whip up a salad in five minutes." She tsk-tsked softly and went to the pantry. "I do have a pie here, however. We can take that."

I smiled over my frustration. "Sounds good."

BY THIS TIME, I was totally discouraged by Gram's behavior and decided to discuss things with Joan that night. She'd been a friend of Gram's for years and knew her as well as anyone did. They often talked on the phone, and Joan sometimes visited Gram at home.

When Gram stepped into the kitchen to speak to Martha, I set the felt purse I was working on down on my chair and went over to where Joan sat at her spinning wheel.

"Can I talk to you for a minute?" I asked, keeping my voice low.

"Of course, dear. What's up?"

"It's about Gram. I can't figure out what is going on with her."

"What do you mean?" She looked toward the kitchen where Gram was in animated conversation with Martha. "She seems a lot better to me."

"I'd love to believe that, but I've noticed a change in her lately. She'd been doing so well, Peter thought he'd found the answer to her problem, and now she's reverting back to her old behavior. I'm worried sick about her, Joan."

"Are you sure? I was just talking to her earlier, and she seemed perfectly lucid."

"Well, just as an example, she forgot to make the salad for tonight after telling me this morning she would. I thought we'd have to stop at the store and buy something to bring along."

"Really? I could swear she told me the other day that she was bringing apple pie."

"No, she definitely told me this morning she was making my favorite tomato and fresh basil pasta salad."

"Well, good thing she changed her mind because Lila already brought a pasta salad." She patted my hand. "You worry too much. She probably just had a senior moment—like most of us do at our age."

I closed my eyes briefly and took a deep breath before making my way back to my chair. She could be right, and I was finding problems where none existed. But just in case, I'd take Gram into the shop with me more often, even if she insisted she'd rather stay home and care for her animals. If only for my own peace of mind.

Martha came back in the room then and took the chair next to mine.

"Have you started a new painting?" She reached into her knitting basket as she asked the question.

"No," I said, much sharper than I intended. I was immediately contrite. How could she know what a painful subject it was? "I've been too busy with Gram and the shop," I amended.

"And yet you have time to do all this beautiful felt work."

What was she trying to say? And why was it any business of hers anyway? I had my reasons, and they were good ones. "Felting is different. I feel good when I finish a piece."

"And you don't feel that way about your painting?"

I shrugged. "No, not anymore."

"Did you ever feel that way about it?" she asked, her voice laced with curiosity.

"In the beginning—yes."

"Something or someone made you change. Think about it." Her penetrating look was unsettling. I wanted to sink into my chair or run away.

"It's really hard to paint while taking care of Gram," I mumbled.

"Are you sure you're not using Lucy as an excuse? One bad review from a critic doesn't mean you're a failure."

She didn't understand. None of them did. All the years of struggle I'd wasted to become a better artist, and now even *I* didn't like my work. How could I expect anyone else to appreciate it?

IT WASN'T EASY, but I coerced Gram into coming to work for the next few days. Having Nancy come into the shop on a regular basis relieved a lot of my pressure, giving me time to spend time with Gram. Nancy and I had actually formed a kind of wary friendship now. I still wasn't sure how it happened, but I was grateful for her help at the store.

While sitting in the back room Tuesday afternoon, enjoying a well-deserved break, I got up the nerve to broach our past.

"Nancy, why weren't we friends when we were kids? I can't figure it out."

"Our circumstances were different, I guess."

"What do you mean?" I asked.

"I don't want to go into it now. It was a long time ago."

"Well, I just have to tell you how much I appreciate all you've done for my Gram."

Nancy pushed a strand of hair behind her ear. "It works both ways. Lucy's been like a mother to me these past years when I needed one. With my mother gone and Peter away at school, I don't know what I would've done without her and Ina. They were my surrogate mothers. That's why I love working at the restaurant when Ina needs me and helping out here when I can."

"I had no idea you were left here alone." My heart went out to her.

"It's water under the bridge now. Peter's back here to stay, and I've made a lot of good friends." We smiled at each other, and I hoped I fell into that category now.

I could hear Gram puttering around in the store and got up to check on what she was doing. I sighed with relief when I saw her dusting glassware.

"Have you noticed a change in Gram this past week?" I asked, coming back to where Nancy was standing. "Things seem to be worse."

"In what way?" Nancy asked.

"She seems more forgetful and spaced out. I can't quite put my finger on it," I whispered.

"When it's just the two of us back here painting, she's perfectly lucid." Nancy frowned. "Do you think it's because she's busy doing what she loves?"

"Hmmm. I suppose that could be it."

"Have you asked Peter about it?"

"I didn't want to call until I had something specific to report. She has an appointment coming up soon."

"I'm sure you'll feel better after you talk to him. I've only noticed her getting better and better myself."

"Maybe it's that wild imagination Gram always accused me of owning. No one else seems to notice." I found myself pulling on my fingers in frustration again. *When had I developed that annoying habit?* "Peter did say it would take time for the medication to work. I suppose I just have to be patient." But inside, I couldn't shake this nagging feeling something was dreadfully wrong.

MARTHA'S WORDS from the previous Friday tumbled over and over through my brain like agates in a stone polisher. Was she right? Was I using Gram as an excuse to cop out?

Then there was that other emotional roller coaster I rode— my attraction to Peter. When we were together, it was a climb to the top, filled with exhilaration. Then when he left, my mood did a flip and a plunge downward until I hit rock bottom, realizing we had no future together and leaving me to wonder if I'd ever be upright again. Was this what they called love? If so, why would anyone in their right mind long for it? I sure didn't.

WHEN THE PHONE rang on Sunday evening, Gram managed to pick it up before I got there. It always made me nervous when she answered. I was never quite sure what would pop out of her mouth.

"Why, hello, Peter. It's so good to hear from you. Uh-huh. Uh-huh. That sounds wonderful." She scribbled a note on the telephone pad. "We'd be happy to come. Okay, see you then."

Looking exactly like the Gram I remembered from my youth, she handed me the note.

"Peter invited us to dinner tomorrow evening. He has some unexpected free time and wants to return our dinner invitation. Isn't that sweet of him?" It really wasn't a question, more like a statement of fact. "It'll be so good to get out again. I've never seen his new home, but I hear it's quite charming," Gram said, smiling to herself.

I looked at the note, studying the address she'd written, not quite comfortable with the glow I'd seen in her eyes. It was in a newly developed site along the lakefront. I'd never been in the area, only heard about it.

"Fancy neighborhood. Does Nancy live with him?"

"Oh, no, she lives in the family home. Her mother still keeps it, but I can't imagine why. I doubt she has fond memories of the place. But Nancy and Peter take good care of it for her. A lovely place, if you remember."

I remembered the place all right. A large, red-brick house with Georgian white pillars on a large lot with a winding brick walkway, set in the heart of Shoreview. I'd been there with my brothers and found the place intimidating. Everything was perfect, inside and out—from the formal furnishings in the living room to the distant expression on Peter's mother's face when she was introduced to us. I also remembered being relieved when we left.

Hopefully, Peter's home would be different, more welcoming. More like Peter.

THE NEXT EVENING, I took extra pains with my appearance and was about to ask Gram if she was ready to leave when she announced, "I'm not going."

"Don't be silly. Of course, you are." She caught me totally off guard, and I stopped dead in my tracks. "Peter's expecting us."

"No, I've changed my mind. I don't feel up to it, I'm too tired," she said, her voice suddenly flat.

"You were perfectly fine a few minutes ago." I looked at her closely. Would I have to cancel at the last minute? "C'mon, it'll be fun. You don't want to disappoint him. Maybe he's cooked a great meal."

"You go without me," she insisted.

"I can't do that. He invited both of us." A light flirtation at the movies was one thing, but I didn't look forward to an entire evening alone with Peter at his home. That was too dangerous on so many levels.

"Yes, you can. I'll call Peter and explain if you want me to. He's a doctor; he understands these things happen when you get old. Besides, Nancy will probably be there. She said something about cooking dinner this evening, I think." Gram had that vague air about her again.

I studied her closely. "You didn't seem to be suffering from old age when you chased Zeke out of the barn earlier."

"Well, maybe that's why I'm so tired now. My head's feeling all muddled. Guess it's time I started acting my age." She raised both eyebrows, daring me to contradict her. "You go on ahead. I'll call Peter and explain. We can't both bail on him, not after he's prepared things."

I huffed. "Fine, Gram. Go up and rest. I'll check on you when I get back."

I drove my Escort down the country roads toward the site of Peter's home and mumbled all the while under my breath about being such a pushover. What if Nancy wasn't there? Gram had remained vague on that score.

Putting more pressure on the gas pedal, I continued on up the winding gravel road leading to his lakeside home. *It wasn't fair. Gram was the one he wanted to thank.* My annoyance grew with each passing mile until I was ready to snap at anyone within striking range. I really, really didn't want to be alone with him all evening in his home. I expected the feeling would be mutual.

Thank God for Gram's explicit directions, which in itself was a miracle. I never would've found the house hidden way back in the woods. The isolation added to my panic. We would *really* be alone if Nancy was a no-show.

I was curious to see his place though. Would it be all warm and inviting, like the persona he showed his patients, or cool and detached, as he fought to keep his personal relationships?

But mostly, I wanted to know and understand more about the man. I knew now he wasn't the affable, easygoing jock I'd grown up believing him to be. He had layers of pain I never suspected. That burning curiosity to know exactly what made him into the man he'd become cooled my annoyance.

However, without Gram along to act as a buffer, I was entering into dangerous territory. Risky to me, anyway, because I was more attracted to Peter each time I saw him. That little bead of sweat popped out along my hairline. The trick would be to keep a physical distance from the man, no matter my feelings.

I pulled up to the front of the newly constructed house. It was a large clapboard one-story, painted a soft beige color that blended neatly into the surrounding trees as if it had always been there. The landscaping was sparse, missing the usual shrubs and flowerbeds that anchored a home to its surroundings.

The wind howled around me, and I could hear waves crashing against the rocky shoreline behind the house, probably built on a limestone bluff common to the area. I imagined there would be steps leading down to the beach below.

"Come in." Peter greeted me just as I reached the door, taking my gift of Gram's fresh-baked bread in his large, capable hand. "Kind of cold out there, isn't it?" He looked behind me. "Where's Lucy?" he asked, a tightness around his mouth when he noticed I was alone. I couldn't be sure, but I had the idea I was right about his feelings matching my own.

"She wasn't feeling well, said she had to get some rest," I managed, my heart doing that trip hammer thing. *Darn.* Gram must've forgotten to call. I pursed my lips. Wait a minute. What right did he have to be annoyed? It was all his doing. I didn't ask to be invited here.

"Oh, all right. Can I take your jacket?"

"Sure." I slipped out of it and handed it over to him.

The evening was unusually cool and damp for July. But then, that often happened along the lakeshore. I gravitated toward the low fire burning in the huge fieldstone fireplace that dominated the great room. Giving a little shiver, I already missed the jacket I'd worn over my light cotton pants and blouse and drew closer to its warmth.

"Let me get you a drink," he said and disappeared around the cabinets I presumed led into the kitchen. While he was gone, I checked out the room. It had all the warmth of a furniture warehouse—nothing like the Peter I knew, or thought I knew. Stark white walls, light hardwood flooring, a very modern, uncomfortable-looking leather couch and one ratty-looking recliner that had definitely seen better days. A holdout from his college years, I suspected. The chrome-edged coffee table had a striking blue glass vase plopped in the center, looking sadly out of place. I recognized it as Swedish glassware. Was it the one I'd sold him? It certainly looked like it, but I couldn't remember. Oh, that's right. He'd said that one was a gift for someone.

Stacks of medical magazines were piled on the floor around the recliner and the lone bookcase in the corner, stuffed to overflowing with well-used books and more magazines, the only sign that someone actually inhabited the place.

It was totally different from what I'd expected. Certainly not like the home of his mother nor the professionally decorated home of a successful physician. I'd expected it to be more like a man cave, I guess—with the mammoth TV, over-stuffed couch and chairs. This place belonged to a man without roots.

"You look disappointed." He'd walked up behind me, and I gave a little jump at the sound of his voice. "This is why I usually take guests out to dinner at a good restaurant."

That would be an understatement. Surprised, shocked. Either word would fit. Should I be insulted or honored that he thought of us as good enough friends that it didn't matter? "It's fine, Peter." I tried to cover up my disappointment.

"Nancy thought you and Lucy would be more comfortable here."

"Where is Nancy? I thought she'd be joining us."

"She was called away at the last minute. They needed help at the restaurant, but you're in luck. She did the cooking and set everything up in the kitchen before she left. So, don't worry. I didn't try to cook." He flashed that lethal grin, and my knees went weak.

He handed me a glass of wine, and our fingers briefly touched. I caught my breath as we locked eyes for a moment, the tenderness in his gaze surprising me. He blinked, and before I realized it, the moment was gone. With a light hand on my back, Peter directed me over to the back wall of windows facing the lake. Even on this bleak evening, the view was breathtaking. My eyes followed the path leading down to the shoreline. No steps here. Waves crashed against the rocks, obliterating the sandy beaches in the tide.

"You have a spectacular view," I said, thinking how much fun it would be to sit here and take picture after picture of the crashing waves.

"That's what attracted me to this place. It's either soothing or turbulent—depending on the mood of Lake Michigan. Everything changes with the seasons, even the ships passing by—from ice cutter to freighter to sailboat."

It was clear he loved the place—even as austere as the furnishings were. We stood in silence for a few moments, lost in our own thoughts. Mine centered on the man beside me and the warmth of his hand on my back that he'd never removed. Was he even aware it was there?

I stepped a few inches away. I couldn't seem to lose this feeling of a magnetic pull between us, and it made me uncomfortable. I felt his arm drop to his side.

"What do you say we eat while the food is still warm?" Peter asked, keeping his tone light but serious.

"Sounds good." Hopefully, I could get this meal over with and be back on the road to Gram's before I repeated my former stupid behavior. Being alone with him in his bachelor space was beginning to feel claustrophobic, like I was surrounded by everything Peter.

"I hope the kitchen's okay—haven't furnished the dining

room yet. I just moved in a few months ago." He struggled with his excuses. "I thought about hiring a decorating service but haven't had time. I really bought the place as an investment and for privacy, but it's become so much more. No one comes up this road unintentionally."

"That I can believe."

At least the kitchen was friendlier. Nancy had covered the square wooden table with a bright yellow cloth and set a bouquet of yellow and white daisies and creamy white candles in the center. At least I assumed it was Nancy, judging from what I'd seen of the house so far.

"What a lovely table." I'd expected generic paper plates after seeing the great room but was pleasantly surprised by the flower-patterned china and gleaming silverware. It was quite romantic. I looked up to see Peter studying my reaction. Was that a hopefulness I saw in his eyes? I was flattered that it would matter to him.

"Nancy said she wanted it special for Lucy—because she doesn't get out much "

"When did Nancy cancel out?" I asked, suddenly suspicious.

"Not long before you came. She'd come over early to set things up for the four of us when she got the call from the restaurant. Someone called in sick, and she had to fill in. She apologized so many times, said I had to make sure to give her apologies to you and Lucy."

"Funny how that worked out, isn't it?" I was beginning to get suspicious about the dinner arrangements.

He frowned. "What do you mean?"

"Well, doesn't it strike you as odd that Lucy and Nancy both canceled out at the last minute?"

"I'll be damned. Are you saying we were set up?" He crossed his arms and frowned.

Now I was sorry I'd brought it up. Most likely, it was my paranoia again, and Nancy would get blamed. "Never mind. Sometimes I let my concerns about Gram play with my head."

"Is Lucy having problems? If you're worried, I want you to bring her in to the clinic."

"No, she's okay. Her next appointment is coming up soon. I'm finding problems where none exist, at least according to her friends."

"Well, I'm always here if she or you need anything. Don't hesitate to call."

"Thanks." Knowing someone with a lot more expertise was available did a lot to ease my mind. "But let's enjoy our meal."

Now I felt petty, burdening him with my imagined problems. We'd had a great time that Sunday evening, and there wasn't any reason this one couldn't be just as pleasant. As long as I kept my guard up with a safe distance between us, I'd be okay. I also would keep track of my wine consumption.

"I didn't realize Nancy was such a great cook," I said between bites of the delicious casserole she'd prepared. "There's a spice in here that I'm not familiar with. But whatever it is, it sure is good."

"Don't ask me. I'm clueless when it comes to cooking. I lean more toward my mother's skill level and keep the phone book handy."

"I'm thinking your sister has a lot of hidden talents," I said, looking at him.

"She actually did most of the cooking in our house when we ate in. I'm not sure how. I guess she just read the cookbooks and figured it out. As I said, Mother preferred to order out and Dad was never around."

"Lucky you. Getting any type of take-out was a big treat at our house."

"Believe me, it can be a drag. I guess you don't remember how often I stayed for dinner at your place as a kid?"

I thought about that for a minute. "Actually, I never noticed." My nose didn't grow an inch, so I stuck with the untruth. "You were just another one of those pesky boys I had to put up with in those days."

"I figured as much. Well, you were nothing but a little squirt then." He laughed.

"Peter!" I glanced away, trying to get up my nerve. "Could I ask you something that has been bothering me for some time?"

"Shoot."

"How come you never brought Nancy with you when you

came to our house? She must've been pretty bored there alone with your mother all the time."

He rubbed his chin in thought. "Never thought to. She never asked to come along. Looking back now, she probably thought she wouldn't be welcome. I was a dumb kid, what can I say? Anyway, my mother would've been alone if she had come along. They did a lot of girly things together—shopping, movies, that kind of stuff. I don't think she would've liked to go fishing and play ball like you did."

"Hey, I had no choice. It was either that or stay home alone." I'd save the questions about the animosity that lay between Nancy and me once we reached high school for a later time. "I'm just glad that we've finally become friends after all those wasted years."

"Nancy isn't the easiest person to get close to—Mom's leaving affected her the most. But if you do, she'll be your friend for life." He stood up and reached for my empty plate.

"Let me help clean up. That's one thing I'm an expert at doing."

"No, we'll let that go for now. Let me show you the rest of the house," he said, stacking the plates in the sink. "Nancy tells me that women are interested in that sort of thing. As you've probably guessed, she tries to clue me in periodically. I admit, living this long as a bachelor, I sometimes forget about the little niceties. But I think I could've managed the dinner even if she hadn't made the offer."

"I'm sure you could've, Peter, and I'd love to see the house."

He led me down a hallway to the left of the great room. Again, plain white walls looking like an unhung gallery, with three empty bedrooms and adjoining baths.

"What's up with this? Was white paint the blue light special in the hardware store?"

"The builder thought he'd leave the colors up to the buyer."

I could only imagine what it would be like on a sunny day. Already I felt a headache coming on from the glare. "You know, you could've hung my felt piece somewhere in here. These bare walls are enough to make someone like me break out in hives. I have this uncontrollable urge to cover them with color."

"Well, if you'd like to come over some time and paint them, let me know." He grinned. "I put your hanging in the clinic because that's where I spend most of my time. It would be a waste to hang it here." He smiled that endearing grin, and I felt my guard slipping.

"The master suite is on the other side of the house."

At last, here was a room with a little color. Little being the operative word. A brown and turquoise quilt covered the king-size brass bed and sheer turquoise curtains framed the wall of windows facing the lake.

He flicked on a bedside lamp. Dusk was falling, and the light coming in the windows had turned a deep purple hue.

On my way to the windows, I passed his bedside table and noticed a framed picture. Intrigued, I picked it up, surprised to see it was one of him, my brothers, and me, taken when I was about ten years old. I stood in front of the boys, holding my "just caught" fish, my hair in pigtails, grinning with pride, my new front teeth too large for the rest of my mouth, and wearing cut-off jeans that one of my brothers had outgrown. How I'd treasured them.

"I had some of my best times with your brothers," he commented. "Do you remember that day?"

"Oh, yeah." I remembered as if it were yesterday. I'd begged my brothers to take me along fishing, but they wouldn't hear of it. Peter had stepped in and convinced them I wouldn't be any bother. That was the Peter I'd pushed from my thoughts during my teen years. Feeling uncomfortable with the memory, I set the picture down and walked over to the window and stared out at the dark lake.

"I see lights," I said

"It's a freighter crossing."

He clicked off the lamp. The room went dark and still with only occasional drifts of moonlight gleaming on the water between clouds. His step was as stealthy as a cat's when he walked up behind me and handed me a pair of binoculars.

"How's that—better?" he asked, resting his hands on my shoulders as he leaned down, his voice close to my ear.

"Yes-s-s," I stuttered, knowing he stood way too close in my comfort zone. I set the binoculars on the windowsill and turned around.

Big mistake.

Now, we faced each other. It would've been difficult to run a credit card between our bodies. And he wasn't moving.

"Sorry," I squeaked and backed up, only to hit the window frame. Too late. His arms were already wrapped around me in an attempt to steady me. As we stared into each other's eyes, all pretense of detachment disappeared.

I watched, mesmerized, as his full lips slowly descended onto mine. My lids fluttered shut, and I took a hiccough of a breath before reaching for him, all the while my mind kept telling me to stop and think.

What was this attraction between us? Peter was like a bottle rocket to my firecracker, each of us ready to explode into an atmosphere of danger. Was this what my mother warned me about when she said never to play with fire?

And yet here I was, unwilling to stop and take the chance of missing something momentous. My inner self refused to be cautious and follow the rules when it came to Peter.

As our kisses grew more heated, his warm fingers slipped between the buttons of my blouse.

"Wait," I whispered into his open mouth and his hand stilled.

"You're right," he said. I thrilled at the reluctance I heard in his voice. "You'd better leave now if you know what's good for you. I don't want your hot-headed brothers coming after me." He stepped back, and I could see by the upturned corners of his mouth that he was trying to make light of an awkward situation.

But that was not what I wanted to hear. I didn't need my brothers dictating my sex life. They'd done enough interfering already. Definitely the wrong thing to say if he really wanted me to leave. He should've known that. Or did he?

"Be quiet—you're ruining the moment," I snapped and started unbuttoning my blouse.

He stepped back even farther, looking uncertain now. "Cara, do you have any idea what you're doing?"

"Damn straight," I said as my blouse fell to the floor. His eyes homed like a laser onto my exposed flesh.

"You really *are* all grown up," he whispered, his voice soft and thick as cream. He stepped forward and reached to cup my breasts, only partially covered by the lacy demi-bra. And I let him.

Oh, you wicked girl, I chastised myself, realizing then why I'd been so careful in selecting undergarments that evening. This had been a cat-and-mouse game since our first reunion, and it was about to come to its inevitable conclusion. And now we both knew it.

I wrapped my arms around his neck and pressed my body against his. It felt so good to be wanted in this way by Peter. I was in the throes of a passion I hadn't even known existed in my soul. Where had it been hiding all these years? And was Peter the only man who could arouse it? His clever physician's hands left a trail of pleasure wherever he touched, and judging from his moans and sighs, it was an even match. We came up for air.

"I want to make love to you," he whispered, his voice husky with desire and the look in his eyes hot enough to melt my mascara. "If you only knew for how long..."

How long?

"Then do it," I whispered back, afraid if he waited much longer, I'd come to my senses and the moment would be lost.

But instead of kissing me hot and heavy like I wanted him to, he raised his hand slowly to the back of my neck, kneading the tight muscles there.

"I can't," he said in a tortured voice, backing away. He turned his head as though he couldn't bear to look at me.

"What do you mean, *you can't*?" I hated the pleading sound in my voice.

"It wouldn't be right—I care too much for you. You know how I feel about marriage—and you're a girl who deserves it all. Not some cheap one-night stand with me."

"What? Is that your excuse? Isn't that the quintessential break-up line? 'You're too good for me?'"

"It's not like that, Cara." He put his hand on my arm and squeezed it gently.

I grabbed for my blouse, my face flaming with shame. I was angry and confused. Peter wasn't making any sense.

"Let me help you," he said, reaching for a sleeve.

I jerked away from him and hurriedly did the buttons.

"Cara, please," His warm fingers touched the side of my face. "I didn't mean for it to go this far."

"Don't touch me," I said, my voice hoarse with emotion.

I don't remember leaving the house, but a few minutes later I was back in my car, driving through the woods like a maniac in a hurry to leave his house, a part of me filled with that now familiar frustration and another sobbing at my stupidity. I'd made a complete ass of myself. Peter didn't want forever; he'd told me that right up front. I thought I didn't want forever either, but things had changed.

My cell phone rang before I even reached Gram's.

"Listen, we have to talk." It was Peter.

"No, we don't," I said into the phone. "Let's just pretend the last hour never happened."

"I can't do that, and I don't think you can either. I'm off call tomorrow night. Meet me at the pub after you close the shop."

"No. Why? What's the point?"

"The point is that I want to try to make things right between us. Please. Just be there."

That was the last thing I wanted. I'd much rather hide my head under the blankets at Gram's and pretend I'd never gone to Peter's alone.

"I'll think about it," I said before clicking the phone shut.

THE MORE I thought about facing Peter this evening, the less appeal it had. He was tripping out if he thought we could just go on as usual, pretending to be old friends. I knew it would be impossible for me. But what did I know about what went on in his head? Maybe he'd been in a similar situation before.

Okay, drop it. It was too painful and humiliating. If I didn't face him now, the whole episode would fester and grow in my mind, making me just as crazy. I forced myself to get into my car and drive over to the pub. The sooner we got this over with, the better.

I saw him as soon as I walked through the door. He was seated at the dark mahogany bar, conversing with the bartender, a dark beer in his hand. Our glances met in the mirrored back bar, and he stepped down from the high stool immediately, hurrying toward me.

"Leaving already, Peter?" the bartender asked, and all heads turned in our direction, nodding in greeting when they recognized me. Once again, I realized how impossible it was to go unrecognized in this town.

"Not yet," he said. Taking my arm with his free hand, he directed me to a small table. "We'll have more privacy here."

I slumped onto the wooden chair, turning my back to the bar and those curious stares. He'd just sat down when the barmaid appeared, her eyes lit with curiosity and envy. No wonder he was so gun-shy about dating anyone local.

"What can I get you?" she asked.

"I'll have a Guinness," I said. It seemed appropriate.

As soon as she left, Peter pulled his cell phone from his shirt pocket, turned it off, and reached for my hand on the table.

"For once, I'm really going to take a night off and let Dan have his night on call all to himself."

"What does that have to do with me?" I wasn't happy to be there. I only wanted to get this meeting over with so that the next time we met at the clinic these awful feelings would be gone.

"C'mon, the world hasn't ended."

"Maybe not, but it sure has gotten a lot more complicated." I glanced around to see the barmaid had returned with my beer, and I took a quick sip.

"Why does it have to be complicated, Cara? We got carried away—it happens."

"Not to me, it doesn't." That penetrating glance of his told me it was the wrong thing to say. Pretty soon he'd connect the dots and realize how my feelings for him had changed.

"I made a big mistake. I'm sorry." Peter looked down at his own beer, peeling away the label while he talked.

This humiliating situation was getting more and more awkward by the moment. I had to do something.

"Listen, Peter. You've always treated me like a little sister. People don't treat their little sister like you treated me last night. Things are different now."

"You're not my little sister, and I haven't thought of you that way for a long time. Why can't we still be friends?" He raised his eyes, wearing an unreadable expression. "I know you have plans to return to Chicago, and I won't try to hold you back. I understand. There's not much here for a woman like you."

Well, that pretty much told me where I stood with him. I had to get out of there before he realized what a life-altering experience last night had been for me. I took a big swallow of beer.

"I have to leave," I said.

Before I could get up, the barmaid came back to the table. "They just called from the hospital. They've been looking for you, Doctor. You're supposed to turn on your phone. It's urgent."

Peter picked up his phone and turned it on. The color drained from his face as he listened to his messages. He put the phone back in his pocket and got up, his face a portrait of guilt.

"I'm sorry, Cara. My partner Dan's been in an accident on his way to a call. They need me." He was already walking toward the door. "Will you get home okay?" he asked as an afterthought.

"Don't worry about me, just go."

I decided to stay and finish my beer. Why not? He wouldn't be coming back.

14

"What was I supposed to do? You saw what happened to my plan of remaining cool, calm, and collected. One kiss and it evaporated," I said a day later.

I held onto Zeke's halter as I tried to explain the gravity of my situation to my captive audience of animals that Friday. I admit it. I was falling into Gram's pattern. It was easier than I thought.

"Don't look at me like that. If I'd admitted I was falling in love with him, it wouldn't have changed a thing. He'd have beat it out of the pub faster than you guys could scarf down a full bucket of grain."

The geese waddled their way out of the barn at that point, grousing their disgust in low tones before I'd even finished my tale of woe. "Oh, sure, desert a sinking ship. I'll remember this when you want extra grain," I yelled to their retreating backs.

"Argh!" I dropped the llama's halter and threw fresh straw around the barn like a mad woman. Now, every time Peter showed up at Gram's there'd be this giant bubble of uneasiness between us. The family was sure to pick up on it.

I heard a car drive up but ignored it. Gram could deal with any visitors. I didn't feel like talking to humans. Knowing I'd actually sunk low enough to turn to animals for advice proved it. At least they didn't talk back. Though judging from the disgusted looks I'd received as I told my story, even they agreed I'd blown it as far as maintaining a friendship with Peter and with my life in general.

Peter had given me an out of the situation that awful night before I'd thrown myself at him like a French poodle in heat. But instead of feeling grateful and backing out, I just continued to humiliate myself. Hadn't I always prided myself on not being "that kind of girl"?

Now, I'd learned how easy it was to remain in control when you've never really been tempted. He was an aphrodisiac for my body. I'd even choose him above chocolate. I pounded my knuckles against my head.

Damn it. It wasn't fair to feel this way about a man who had no interest in commitment. As if I didn't have enough with my worries about Gram and my future.

Looking out through the open top of the Dutch-style barn door, I saw the object of all my angst striding purposefully toward the barn and me. I swiveled my head around like a possessed woman—looking for a place to hide.

"You haven't returned my calls," he said with deadly softness after unlatching the door, the sparks from his dark eyes practically singeing my clothing.

"I was busy." I croaked the words out of my now-parched throat.

"I see," he said, moving closer. "So, now we can't even be friends?"

I grabbed the pitchfork leaning against the stall and held it in front of me like a shield. Where were those damn geese when I needed them? "Friendship isn't going to work between us—anyone with a brain can see that."

He crossed his arms over his chest. "What happened between us isn't going away because you decided to ignore it. It happened. Deal with it and we can get on with life."

"I don't want to *deal with it.* It shouldn't have happened, and it won't happen again because I plan to stay completely out of your orbit. You can bank on it."

"Oh, really?" he asked.

"Yes, really." I looked through the tongs of the pitchfork,

determined to keep my distance.

"I wish I could be as sure as you," he said.

His look of chagrin was endearing, even in the midst of my pain and anger. These mixed signals were driving me crazy.

"If you're so sure, what's to stop us from being friends?" He lifted an eyebrow over his penetrating stare.

"Are you naturally obtuse, or did you take a stupid pill before coming here?" I snapped.

He stepped closer, looking down at me with a frown.

"I've never met anyone else who could be so damn infuriating," he ground out between his clenched jaw. "You've been this way ever since you were a kid. I should've taken a cue from your brothers way back then."

I lifted the pitchfork closer to my face, and he sighed before stomping to the door, leaving me a puddled mess of confusion and longing.

"Call me when you grow up, Cara." He threw the words over his shoulder.

"Don't hold your breath," I whispered to myself.

Damn, but the man had a knack for driving me to adolescent clichés. I had to snap out of it.

I blinked back tears of regret and set the pitchfork aside. How I wished things could go back to when we were two old friends concerned about Gram. It wasn't my choice to get romantically involved with a man only interested in his career. Been there, done that, and by God, it wasn't going to happen again.

I heaved a deep breath before hearing his car drive away. Only then did I venture back into the house.

I WAS REARRANGING things on the shelves in the shop a few days later, mumbling to myself about the mess I'd made of my life, when the bell above the door announced a customer.

Steve.

I sat back on my heels with the unexpected shock of seeing him, finally standing in welcome like a zombie during the warmth of his prolonged kiss. Which, as far as I was concerned, had as much electricity as an Amish kitchen.

"I've missed you," he said against my ear before releasing me.

I watched like a brainless twit, still silent, as he wandered through the shop. Was there something in the water here that caused this slowing of my reaction time?

He picked up the corner of my latest felt creation, a wool jacket. "I just made that," I said proudly.

"Cute."

The short comment snapped me back to life.

The jacket was quite bohemian, the fabric made up of vibrant purple mohair and deep fuchsia wool swatches randomly placed and felted into the natural colored wool. I'd knit the sleeves with the same purple mohair—Martha had hand-spun some into a soft yarn for me—and then used it to trim the edging in a blanket stitch.

"*Cute?* That's it? That's all you can say?" Taking a deep calming breath, I ran my hand over the soft fabric I'd created. "It's handmade felt. I just learned the process from some local artists."

"Well, I guess if you're into it. I've never been one to appreciate crafts."

"It's referred to as wearable art," I said, trying to educate the dense man.

"Really?" He dropped the jacket and moved farther into the shop. "Is the glassware imported?"

"Most of it." I barely listened to the question, my mind reeling with his callous dismissal of my work. Had he always been such a jerk?

Okay, so maybe the jacket wouldn't win any design awards, but it was warm, vibrant, and unusual. At least I thought so. It'd only been in the shop a few days and had already garnered a lot of interest.

"I thought this place would be much larger—how provincial." Was that a slur or a compliment? I decided to go with the compliment. Otherwise, I'd be tempted to slug him.

"Is your grandmother actually able to make a living off this business in such a small town?"

"We're doing just fine." Now, I was beyond annoyed. "What brings you up here, anyway? I thought you were too busy to make the trip?"

"I had to see what my protégé was up to—didn't want all those years of mentoring to go to waste."

If that was his idea of humor, it fell flat. And why had I never noticed that weasel-like smile?

"I was also hoping you'd realized by now that you're wasting your time and talent here and would be ready to come back home."

"Home? How many times do I have to say it? Gram shouldn't be alone, and I won't leave her."

"I need you at the studio," he pouted. "Everything's a mess. I can't work the way I should. I have another big gallery show coming up and I'm way behind."

I had to hold myself back from smacking the petulant look off his face. "So that's really all that brought you up here?"

"No, something much more exciting. I'm in charge of what's in the show and I want a few of your pieces hung—as my protégé."

Either he was delusional about my work or desperate. I didn't know which, but I wasn't going to put myself in that god-awful position again. "That isn't going to happen. What you really need is a housekeeper."

"I'll pay for your grandmother's care, I already told you that. We'll find a nice place for her where she'll get round-the-clock care and be with people just like her."

"People just like her?" That familiar red cloud of anger rose up, leaving an acrid taste in my mouth that made it difficult to speak. How could he even contemplate putting my Gram in a home for his *convenience*?

The door of the kitchenette swung open and Gram came in, wearing her usual welcoming expression. Thank God she hadn't heard him. I swallowed the venom burning like acid in my throat and tried to recover my composure.

"Hello," she said, smiling at the man whom she assumed was a customer.

"Hi," Steve nodded, looking uncomfortable.

"Gram, this is Stefan, my artist *friend* from Chicago." The word stuck in my mouth like a dried saltine.

"Oh, yes, Steve. We've talked on the phone."

I gave her a questioning look. Had she called him "Steve" on purpose?

"Did you come to congratulate our Cara?" she asked.

He frowned and looked at me for an answer.

"Gram, what are you talking about?"

"About your upcoming marriage to Peter, of course." She gave a coy smile. "Or was that supposed to be a secret?" She beamed happily at Steve. "Oh, well, the cat's out of the bag now. An October wedding would be wonderful, don't you think? All the fall colors and crisp air. Such a perfect set-up for a cozy autumn together. You'll have to be sure to make the trip back up here for their special day."

Finally closing my mouth, I searched for words. I don't know who was more shocked, me or Steve. "Gram, I'm not marrying Peter. Wherever did you get that idea?"

"Who's Peter?" Steve asked.

I'd forgotten he was there for a moment. "He's Gram's doctor."

"You're right on one account," Steve said. "The woman needs help."

"I think you'd better leave. I need some time alone with my grandmother. Now."

"Can we meet later—maybe for dinner? I need an answer."

"I already gave you your answer. I'm not interested."

"You can't be serious! At least take some time to think it over, Cara."

"Goodbye, Steve." I dismissed him with a wave of my hand.

"I'll call you next week after you've had time to think. You can't just throw away the years we spent together like they meant nothing. You owe me, Cara."

"Those years didn't seem all that important to you when I asked you to come up here with me." I pulled my glance away from Gram for a moment. "Please, just leave. Whatever it was that we had is gone. Even you have to realize it."

As we walked back toward the kitchenette, I heard the bells

tinkle, signaling the door opening and then it slammed shut. I didn't glance back to make sure Steve was gone.

It couldn't be any clearer now that I'd been existing in a dream world, seeing only what I wanted to see, so enthralled with my fantasies of our being a famous couple in the art world that I shunned the reality of who Steve really was and where I fit in to his world. I'd dwell on that life blooper later.

Right now, I had Gram to worry about. I'd been fooling myself that the medication was doing its job. How could I have been so wrong? I had to make an appointment for her to see Peter as soon as possible, never mind that I'd rather jump into the freezing water of Lake Michigan than face him again.

"I'm going to make an appointment for you to see Peter at the clinic."

"Why? There's nothing wrong with me. I feel better than I have in ages."

The confidence in her voice sounded more like bravado. But I didn't want to repeat to her what she'd just said about my marrying Peter. It'd be better if that random thought didn't get fixated in her memory. Lord only knows whom she'd blab it to then.

THE NURSE USHERED Gram to the chair beside Peter's desk. "Have a seat while I check your blood pressure, Lucy." Thankfully, she didn't have to check mine. My stress level was so high at this point I should be on bed rest.

When she finished, Gram asked, "Is it high?"

"It's normal. Are you having any special problem you'd like to discuss with the doctor?"

"No, there's nothing wrong with me." She gestured toward me with her thumb. "She's the one with the problem."

Ever since I suggested that she see Peter, she'd been like this, denying the fact that her memory was slipping again. I gave the nurse one of those smiles that didn't reach my eyes, and she nodded in understanding.

"The doctor will be right with you," the nurse said.

Gram got up from the chair and started pacing, looking more like the agitated woman she'd been when I first arrived in Wisconsin.

"It'll be all right." I tried to reassure her. "Peter will know what to do." And surprisingly, I really did believe it. His abilities as a doctor had never been in question since that first day I brought Gram in to see him. I trusted him implicitly on that score.

The professional Peter strode in, hair slicked back, blue shirt and dark tie in place under his white medical jacket.

"Good morning, ladies. What brings you in today?" His broad and welcoming smile slipped a little when he looked at me. I felt myself flush. It would be tough to remain professional myself.

"She's got a problem—seeing things that aren't there." When I looked at Gram, she had a stubborn set to her jaw and that worried me.

"The meds don't seem to be working as well as they have been," I said carefully.

"In what way?" His brows knit together in concern. He was in strict physician mode now.

I hated saying these things in front of Gram, but I had to. What else could I do?

"She's made some ridiculous statements about things that only exist in her imagination. She sometimes forgets to tell me things—like phone calls I've received when I'm out. That kind of thing." It sounded pathetic as I said it, but I could no longer deny the episodic changes in her behavior. The thought of her slipping back into that person I found when I first arrived was too frightening to contemplate.

"What about numbers? Has she had problems at the shop with the cash register?"

"Actually, I've been handling the sales. She keeps the shop in order, helps me reorder stock, and so forth."

"Any problems there? Or with lost keys?" He jotted notes as I answered.

"Oh, don't mind me," Gram murmured. "Just pretend I'm a senile old woman who can't hear or understand what you're saying."

"Maybe a change in dosage is necessary." He looked at me and winked. "Why don't you wait in the other room while Lucy and I talk." It wasn't a question but an order. "I'll call you back in when we've finished."

I went out into the waiting area again, filled with misgivings. Was I making too much of this? Why did she seem so cognizant today when she'd been so confused a few days ago?

I looked around the room as I waited. My glance froze. There on the wall next to the reception desk was my wall hanging, just as Peter had said, in a place where everyone entering the office would see it. How had I missed it when we checked Gram in? Too upset about Gram, I guess.

At the risk of false pride, I had to admit it looked lovely hanging there. He'd had it framed with a dark mahogany wood that brought out the colors even more. I marveled that I'd been able to create such a thing of beauty, and a little of my self-confidence returned.

Peter really did like the wall hanging and wasn't just being kind. A small plaque beneath it gave my name and the name of Gram's store. My heart swelled with pride that he thought enough of my work to give us free advertising.

"You can go back in now," the nurse said. "The doctor is finished examining Mrs. Olson."

I followed the nurse into Peter's office where Gram sat waiting, a satisfied look on her face.

"We had a long discussion," Peter said. "Lucy doesn't feel she needs an increase in dosage. In fact, she's refused. After some verbal testing, I have to concur with her at this point. All I can tell you is to keep monitoring her condition and let me know if there are any further changes in her behavior. We have to give the medication a chance to work up to its fullest potential before I do a repeat of her blood studies."

I put my hand on his arm before he could leave the room.

"She's been telling people you and I are getting married—planning a fall wedding," I blurted.

"What?" He looked as shocked as I'd felt when she first dropped that bomb on Steve but quickly recovered.

"I only told that poor excuse for a man from Chicago," Gram said stubbornly. Instead of getting upset as I'd expected, it was laughter I saw dancing in Peter's eyes.

"I can understand why that would get you upset," he said, "but as long as she knows it isn't true, there isn't anything to be done medically. But please," he said, looking at Gram with raised eyebrows, "don't spread those rumors around here. I'd have to leave town to squelch them."

I looked from Gram to Peter. Neither one of them looked as concerned as I felt. I shook my head in disgust. If that medication didn't work up to its potential soon, my life could become a living hell.

I WAS STEWING over the clinic visit that evening when my mother called on my cell. Did Gram really know what she was doing when she told Steve I was getting married? Or was she covering up for herself in a moment of lucidity? I told the whole story to Mom.

"I think something's wrong. One minute she seems perfectly lucid, and then she goes off the deep end."

"What did Peter think?" Mom asked.

"He says we have to wait a bit and give the medication a chance to work."

"That sounds perfectly logical," Mom said with relief. "Doesn't it?"

"Yes, but she was doing so well earlier. What could've happened to change things?"

"Stop worrying so much. Things are going well." She paused a moment. "I hear you've gone out with Peter a few times."

"We're just friends, Mom. That's over. I was merely acting as a buffer between his patients and their eligible female relatives."

"That's not exactly the way I heard it. He'd be quite a catch—please don't mess it up."

I could feel my blood pressure rising. I wanted to scream. *It's too late. I already have.* But talking to her and everyone else in my family about Peter was as helpful as beating my head with my cell phone.

"I gotta go, Mom. I'll call you in a few days. I told Gram I'd feed her animals."

BY THE NEXT DAY, I'd worked myself into a fit of uncertainty. I watched Gram's every move and analyzed her every word. Was it me or was it her? One of us wasn't seeing reality. I knew I had to do something to shake off these feelings of foreboding. There was only one thing that would get my mind off of Gram and her problems for any length of time.

I dug out my paints and supplies. I couldn't hold back any longer. Just the smell of the oils and turpentine was like nectar to a bee.

It wasn't long before I was engrossed in the landscape I'd envisioned on that walk through the woods on the spring day I'd taken those first snapshots. I started with a small canvas. The tension that held me in its grip lessened with each stroke of the brush. The greens, the violet, the brown earth—colors soft and yet so alive, the way only nature could produce them. I had come alive myself, experiencing my own rebirth, I guess.

Gram came in so quietly to say goodnight that I never noticed her until she patted me softly on the back. Her wide smile and soft "ahhh" only added to my joy.

I couldn't stop until I'd finished, and I sighed in fulfillment as I put on the final stroke, hours past my usual bedtime. I was spent but exuberant. A picture of Steve, so engrossed in his work for hours on end, flashed through my mind unbidden. Had the joy that had been missing in my painting returned at last? It was too daunting to even contemplate right now. All I knew was that when I looked at the simple landscape, I felt a peace I hadn't felt in years.

Was Gram right? Was it time that I found my own style? And would I find it here?

15

"WHAT ARE YOU WORKING ON?" LILA ASKED WHEN I SAT IN THE caned rocker next to her that Friday evening. The Wool Gatherers were meeting at Gram's this time, and I got to play hostess. Which was a good thing because I needed the distraction from my worries about Gram.

"I'm not working on anything right now, too busy with the shop and all." Gram stood behind my chair, and I flicked my eyes in her direction.

"Ahhh." Lila nodded in understanding.

"She's finally back to painting," Gram said loud enough for everyone to hear.

"Really?" Lila asked. All eyes turned to me expectantly.

"Well, sort of," I mumbled. I wasn't quite ready to admit that felting had been replaced by an old love. I wanted to remain an active part of this group, working on my felt projects alongside this wonderful group of women. They had been so good to me, taking me under their wing and supporting me along with Gram. If it weren't for these women, I never would've found felting, the art that saw me through those bleak days after my humiliation in Chicago. Through them, I'd relearned the importance of friendship and small-town values, something I'd almost forgotten over the years. I even managed to regain some confidence in myself and in my artistic abilities.

The problem facing me now was I couldn't seem to focus on felting the way I had previously. My every free moment was consumed with painting. Everywhere I looked I saw scenery and faces just begging to be put on canvas. Glancing around the room, I saw possible studies. The face of Gram's friend, Joan, would be a perfect model of a Norwegian woman of the past if I could get her to dress in vintage clothes and model for me. And then there was Martha...

"Come on, don't be shy," Martha said, interrupting my thoughts, her face lit with anticipation. "Show us what you've been doing."

"Mostly landscapes," I said, "nothing spectacular, just scenes of the local woods, the town, and of course, the lake."

"I'm so glad you're back at it." The glimmer in Martha's eyes reminded me of her earlier accusation of using Gram as an excuse. "And I'm guessing from the look on your face you're really enjoying it."

"I am, Martha. To tell you the truth, I've been losing a lot of sleep lately—getting up early and going to bed late, all so I can paint. I haven't been this excited about painting since my student days."

"When do we get to see them?" Joan asked.

"They're not ready for prime time. Not yet."

"I'll show them to you," Gram said. "She's just gun-shy these days."

Nancy gave me a sympathetic look and started after Gram, ready to intervene. I put my hand on her arm. "It's okay. She's right. There's no point in hiding them."

Gram left the living room and returned a few minutes later with several small canvases she propped on the mantle. The women ohhed and ahhed and got up from their seats for a closer look.

"What a beautiful job you did of the harbor," Lila exclaimed. "I recognize Al's fishing boat."

"And look at the people on Main—they look so alive. How did you get them to pose?"

"I took a lot of photos and worked from them," I said.

"I didn't know you did watercolors, too." Cheryl turned to look at me. "Is this something new?"

"No, I did a lot of watercolor as a student—thought I'd try it again as something different—a way to stretch my skills. Watercolor just seemed to fit some of the scenes better."

"These are spectacular, Cara." Martha turned to me, hands on her hips. "You have a lot of emotion here. It's obvious to any observer that you love this place. Now—what are you going to do about marketing?"

Leave it to Martha. Sometimes she sounded as practical as my mom. "I haven't given it much thought. It's still so new."

"You've been hiding out here long enough. Time to get back on the horse, I'd say." Martha wasn't giving an inch.

I squirmed under her measuring look, even while my body glowed with the warmth of her praise.

After the ladies left for the evening, I picked up the canvases one at a time, preparing to put them back in my bedroom. I stopped and looked at them critically. Martha was right. It was time to put them out in public and see what the reaction would be.

"Leave them out. They add a freshness to the room." Gram glanced around as if seeing the room with new eyes. "We have to do some decorating. I think I've gotten too set in my ways and it shows." She turned back to me. "Are you upset that I brought out your work?"

"No, it's all right." She knew why I was hiding them in my room. My new friends' admiration did give me a needed boost.

I toyed with the idea of hanging a few in the shop. Someone local might appreciate them. But as far as being great wall art, I knew better. I'd learned a lot from all those years with Steve, even if some of it was hard to swallow.

Later that night, as I lay in bed thinking of Peter once again, I remembered the stark white walls in his home and envisioned my paintings hanging there, adding color and most importantly, warmth.

I recognized I'd been thinking of his home all the while I'd painted those scenes. The man needed love around him. Not adoration. He got plenty of that from his patients. Even if I couldn't be there personally, I could give him one of my paintings —as a thank-you gift for taking such good care of Gram.

"WHY THE LONG FACE?" Nancy asked me as we were rearranging new stock on the shelves before opening the shop the next morning.

"I'm really worried about Gram, and no one takes me seriously. Everyone says to wait and see what happens once she's been on the medication longer. I feel I should be doing something to help her before it's too late. This waiting is driving me crazy. I think I'll take her to see Peter again."

"Come in the back. There's something I have to tell you before you do that."

My heart dropped at the look on her face. Whatever it was, I wasn't going to like it. I trailed her into the kitchenette. When she motioned me to a chair and poured a cup of coffee from Gram's old pot, I guessed things were bad.

"First, you have to promise you won't kill the messenger." She sat down across from me, wearing a grave expression.

"Did Peter say something to you? Is Gram dying?"

"No, Cara. But you might want to kill her when I tell you what I overheard."

"*What?*" What could make me be angry at Gram?

"Your brother called yesterday while you were out getting office supplies. I couldn't help but overhear their conversation— you know how loud Lucy talks on the phone these days."

I nodded, waiting impatiently for her to continue. "So, what were they talking about?"

"I think Lucy's medication is working better than she lets on." Nancy played with the paper napkin under her cup, looking everywhere but at me. "They were talking about their plan to keep you here until you and Peter come to your senses."

"'Come to our senses?' About what?" I looked at her blankly.

"Come on, Cara, you can't be that dense. That little crack about the two of you getting married was well planned. They've done everything but dressed you in white and stood the two of you before Father Dan."

"Oh my God. What are you saying?" I covered my mouth in horror for a moment. "I know that's what they'd hoped for—but I had no idea they would go this far. So, this 'regression' of Gram's was all a ploy?" I crumpled back into my chair. "Does Peter know?"

"Are you kidding? He's clueless."

I hid my face in my hands. At least I could be grateful for that.

"I hope I didn't screw things up by telling you, but I couldn't stand to see you worry so much. I must confess I even had a hand in it myself, preparing that romantic dinner for the two of you and pretending to be called into the restaurant. If it's any consolation, I don't think they realize what you're going through here or they wouldn't have done it. They really love you that much, you know. And for what it's worth, I agree with them. You and Peter would make a great couple."

I couldn't move for a moment, trying to absorb the ramifications of what Gram and my brothers had done.

Did this mean that Gram was really okay—that her recent relapse was all a sham?

"I can't believe this is happening," I said, trying to absorb it all.

"I know. I have to admit, when you first came back here, it was Peter I worried about. I knew he'd carried a torch for you since you were kids, even if he didn't realize it, and thought for sure you'd break his heart. But now I know better. It almost looks like you'll break each other's heart. Think about it."

She left me there, still in shock, and went to care for the customers who'd just entered the shop.

Think about it? As if I could do anything else.

Focusing was impossible for the rest of the day, I was so consumed with anger and hurt at their betrayal. What had I ever done to my family to deserve this inexcusable treatment? I'd always been there for my brothers, even if they didn't realize it, caring for them like a second mother.

My first thought was to get away from here if Gram didn't really need me. It was just too humiliating.

But where could I go? I'd lost all my options when I gave up my Chicago job and my apartment. Things with Steve would never be the same. I could never look at him in the same way; my hero worship had disappeared. It wasn't that I no longer appreciated his art—I did. But it would never be my style, and I'd finally realized it. There was no going back. Things had changed for me.

I wanted to paint, yes, but I also wanted a family and a loving home where I could raise my children.

Dare I say it? I wanted Peter. I knew it wasn't an option; he'd made that abundantly clear. He wasn't interested in marriage and a family. I was stuck here until I found a new future for myself and for my art. Until that happened, I had to keep my feelings for him buried. But that was damn difficult when I was falling for him, more with every contact we had.

Just wait until he heard this story. I couldn't even guess at his reaction. But first I had to confront Gram and my brothers.

Gram met me at the door that evening and the look of shame on her face told me she'd talked to Nancy.

"I hear the jig is up," she said in a feeble attempt at humor. I couldn't laugh about it or even smile. It was hard to hold back my tears.

"Gram, how could you?" All my pent-up hurt came out in a shower of pain and betrayal.

"When I saw you and Peter kiss that night, I just knew it was the right thing to do, for so many reasons. You two are so blinded by pride and fear of rejection that you can't see your nose in front of your face." She stiffened her slim shoulders with resolve. "Besides, I was scared. You have no idea how frightening it is to know you're losing your mind. I wanted you both close by— together, if possible—before I lost my senses."

"Gram, no matter what you thought, you had no right to mess with our lives that way." I took a deep breath, barely able to get the words out.

"I had to do something." Her face crumpled, and she was

crying herself now. "I couldn't stand around and watch you waste your life trying to live my dream any longer."

"What are you talking about?" I asked.

"I'm the one who planted the idea of art school in your head years ago, aren't I? I saw you as a way of fulfilling the destiny I always wanted and couldn't have. It was my dream, not yours. I've watched you struggle for years, wasting your time with that Steve person, too blinded by your admiration of his work to see that you were getting nowhere with your own. I've lived with the guilt long enough. I had to try to fix it before it was too late."

"No, Gram. Thanks, but that was my decision, not yours." I put my arms around her, trying to comfort. "Shh, it'll be all right."

My righteous anger fizzled away like a Popsicle on a summer sidewalk. How could I be angry with her when she thought she was doing what was best for me? It was my brothers who deserved the tongue-lashing. They'd taken advantage of an old, confused woman, plotting to keep me here with her to assuage their own guilt.

I turned that anger into cold resolve. They wouldn't get away with their tricks this time. I knew once Peter learned of their scheming that any idea of our being together would be over and their plans squashed.

Peter.

I couldn't put off telling him. He was as concerned for Gram as I was. After calming Gram down and having her rest in the living room with her favorite TV show, I went to the phone and called him. I'd never sleep until he knew what was going on.

He picked up on the first ring.

"Peter, I have to see you, it's very important," I said into the phone.

"Has something happened to Lucy? I'll be right over."

"No, Gram is fine. We need to talk." Just the sound of that calming voice soothed my nerves a bit. God, but I missed him. "I'll meet you at the coffee shop in twenty minutes." A neutral place would be best. I didn't want Gram to see his reaction, whatever it would be.

. . .

I WAS the first to arrive and decided to take a booth in the rear for privacy. What I had to say would be fodder for the gossips for months if it got out. The lingering scent of frying bacon and sweet pancake syrup that always permeated the coffee shop, no matter what the time of day, gave a feeling of hominess to the place. Some of the tension I'd carried since Nancy dropped her bomb eased. Maybe things weren't as bad as they'd seemed at first.

I'd just ordered coffee for the two of us when Peter stepped through the door. I watched as he scanned the room, walking toward me with a decisive gait when he saw my waving arm. How different he looked in that moment from the carefree high school boy I'd pictured in my mind all these years, his brow furrowed, wearing a forced smile.

He slipped into the booth across from me. "So, what did you want to talk about? If it's about that night—"

"No, it's about my brothers and Gram. You'd better take a drink of your coffee first." Maybe this was a mistake and we should've met at the pub. I knew I could've used a strong drink before telling him and he'd probably need one afterward. I quickly explained what had been going on. His jaw muscle tightened, and there was an expression of pain in his eyes that wrenched my heart. Had I made a mistake in telling him? Would he hate my family forever?

The unflappable Peter looked ready to explode, and the coziness of the rear booth turned claustrophobic.

"They *did* that? This time things have gone too far—messing with the mind of my patient." His voice rose above the clanging of pots and pans coming from the kitchen, and I broke out in a sweat.

"Keep your voice down," I said, hoping the noise of rattling dishes would drown him out. "If it makes you feel any better, Gram was in on the plan from the beginning. She saw us kissing on the swing and decided we belonged together. For all we know, she may have been the instigator of the plot."

"I think it's time I turn Lucy's care over to a colleague. It would be better for her and for me."

"No, you can't do that." I looked at him, horrified. "She would be devastated if that happened. She'll never trust anyone like she trusts you."

"Well, maybe it would be best if I just moved out of the area. I've certainly thought about it. There are too many people messing with my personal life here. Now, they're even interfering with my practice."

"Peter, don't be stupid. The people in this town need you. They think you walk on water and you know it. Everyone would be devastated."

He shrugged. "They'd get used to it. It wouldn't take them long to learn to trust whoever took my place."

He might think that way, but I knew better. Peter had grown up here; he knew the local culture like no stranger could. These people trusted him because he was one of them.

If anyone should leave the area, it was me. I'd have to work on that.

"Listen, don't worry about it. I'm looking into some future plans of my own. If all goes as planned, I'll be out of here before too long and the heat will be off you." I patted his arm reassuringly.

Big mistake.

Merely touching him sent waves of heat through my traitorous body. I pulled my hand back like I'd touched fire.

"What do you mean?" he asked.

"Now that Gram's doing better, she won't need me with her all the time."

"I guess that means you'll be going back to the big city as soon as you can?"

"Hopefully." My voice faltered as I tried to be upbeat. "Finish your coffee. I have to get back to Gram's." My own had turned lukewarm now, much like my life would be without Peter. I turned to get out of the booth.

"Well, it didn't take you long to decide on that, did it?" The sarcastic bite in his words didn't sound like the affable man I'd come to expect.

"What do you mean?"

"Going back to the city—and the old boyfriend."

I decided not to answer and gave him a backhanded wave. If only I did have an excuse to return to Chicago. Let him think what he liked, at least it gave me a little of my pride back.

I paid for the coffee at the counter and walked out. The moist evening air hung heavy around me as I made my way to my parked car. As I glanced into the coffee shop, Peter still sat in the booth. It was going to be another long night.

MY BROTHER JACK called later that evening.

"Hey, Squirt. How ya doin'?" he asked.

"I'm not speaking to you. If you're smart, you'll hang up the phone before I tell you how I really feel."

"Don't bother. I just got off the phone with Peter, and believe me, he said anything that needed saying." His voice softened. "Listen, I'm really sorry and so is Joe. We just wanted to help you two blockheads see reality."

"That doesn't sound very apologetic to me."

"It's just that we love you both and want the best for you. Peter's been in love with you since you were a teenager and don't bother to deny you don't feel the same towards him."

What the hell was he saying? Was my brother nuts? "What are you talking about? He never. . ."

"Let me finish, please." I could hear Jack take a breath before he went.

"We thought we'd help the two of you along, that's all. Neither of you was seeing clearly. Okay, I know it wasn't too smart, but when Gram suggested it, it sounded like a good idea. But Peter explained how much Gram depended on you and what you've been going through with worrying over her needlessly. I realize now that Gram had an excuse for not thinking clearly—we didn't. Can you forgive us?"

"Not at this point, Jack. I have to cool down a bit."

"Don't take too long, kid." I'd never heard that crack in Jack's voice before. I guess even he realized he'd gone too far. "I just hope we haven't messed things up between you and Peter even more than they were.'

"I'm going to hang up now, before you say anything more." Just when I'd begun to feel sorry for him, he'd spoiled it.

I hung up the phone and looked out the window at the now dreary landscape where a cool mist fell. I didn't know how to tell him just how hopeless things were without showing my true feelings.

It wasn't until later I remembered what Jack had said about the teenaged Peter. Could he really have had feelings for me then? If so, why had he been such a jerk the night of my prom? He'd had a strange way of showing those feelings, that's for sure. Was there a chance he was doing the same thing now? Was it possible if I stuck around long enough, I'd find out? Could Peter and I actually have a future together?

16

THE SKY CLOUDED OVER, AND LIGHT WAS FADING FAST FROM THE early evening sky. It had been almost a week since the fiasco with my family, and August was approaching. I hurried to finish the section of the painting I'd been working on for several hours, holding my right arm steady with my left hand as I flicked small splashes of sunlight onto the tips of the grass shoots I'd created.

Standing back and squinting at it, I could almost feel the somnolent mood of the warm summer landscape. Gram would like it.

"Hey, Gram. Come and see how far I've gotten." No answer. "Gram?" Still no answer. I got up and walked to the kitchen, certain I'd find her there, preparing a late supper. No sight of her and no scent of food warming in the oven. I called up the stairs and down the hallway but still no answer.

An uneasy feeling crawled up my spine like a thousand tiny ants. I glanced at my watch. I'd been lost in my painting longer than I realized.

She must be in the barn, feeding the animals. I dashed out to look for her. Zeke's long neck stretched out the open top of the barn's Dutch door.

"Where's Gram?" I asked him, as though he could actually give me an answer. Pushing him gently aside, I carefully locked the lower door after entering the barn. I didn't need to be chasing him around, too.

The interior was semi-dark, and I flicked on the overhead light. Florence watched me with beady eyes, her white wings spread out protectively over the eggs she nested on. Fritz flapped his wings and honked softly, while strutting like a proud father back and forth in front of his mate.

"Gram, where are you?" I yelled into the empty space, hoping she'd peek her head around the corner of the open door leading out to the pasture. No answer. I went out the door and scanned the field. Nothing. The land was hilly, so I hurried up to the highest point but all I saw was tall grass waving in the breeze.

A cool mist fell softly now. There was a definite chill to the air. I looked at my watch. Gram should be headed back from wherever she'd wandered off to by now. I said a quick prayer to her guardian angel and scanned the area once more, calling her name.

After waiting a few more minutes, I ran back inside the barn and then out the door I'd come in, hurrying toward the front of the house, my eyes searching the highway in both directions. A car whizzed past, and my heart leapt in my throat. If Gram walked along the highway in a daze in this dim light, she'd be almost invisible.

I jumped into my car and drove a mile down the highway in both directions, searching along both sides of the road. No sign of her, so I parked the car back in the drive. Maybe she'd returned in my absence.

Calling her name, I walked around the yard, my arms crossed in a self-hug, my hands tucked into my armpits. When she didn't answer, I raced into the house, grabbed my cell phone off the kitchen counter, and dialed Peter's number.

"Doctor Andresen." He answered on the first ring, as usual.

"Peter, I've lost Gram," I whimpered, my voice laced with a fear I couldn't disguise.

"Cara?" His voice was unusually soft. "Is that you?"

"Yes." I forced myself to take a deep calming breath. "Gram

isn't in the house or the barn or anywhere on the property that I can see."

"Don't panic. She probably went for a walk and got turned around. It happens to people in her condition."

"It's all my fault. I've been busy painting and lost track of time. I know this is the worst time of day for her. How could I be so careless? Can you come over and help me search?"

"I'm at the emergency room with a patient. I can't leave. I'm sorry, Cara."

"Of course, I should've realized." I felt like a fool. Why had my first instinct been to call him?

"Call Nancy. She'll come over and help. If you don't find her within the hour, you'll have to call 911."

"Sure, thanks." I hung up and went back outside. Maybe he was right, and Gram had taken her favorite path in the woods and gotten confused when dusk fell. All those deer trails looked alike if you weren't paying close attention. Especially in the fading light.

I walked around the field toward the woods, calling her name. We'd had rain recently, and the lowlands would be wet and full of mosquitos. Had she even put on a sweater?

By the time I reached the woods, I realized I needed a flashlight. Night was falling fast. As much as I hated to, I had to go back and call for help. Wandering through the woods alone in the dark wasn't going to accomplish anything.

I took Peter's advice and called Nancy.

"Nancy, Gram's wandered off. Can you come and help me search the woods?" I asked, trying to keep my voice steady.

"I'll be right there. Don't leave the yard without me. It'll be easier if we work together."

I paced up and down the driveway and around the yard, still calling Gram, but afraid to leave the area. Twenty minutes later, a car pulled into the drive, followed closely by several others.

"I called the group. We'll find her, don't worry." Nancy took control and soon had all the Wool Gatherers divided into groups of two. We took off into the woods with our flashlights, calling her name loudly.

I was right about the patches of wet earth and mosquitos. What if Gram had fallen and been knocked unconscious? She was too frail to spend a night in the woods. I was too upset to even talk to Nancy, who'd partnered with me.

It seemed forever before I heard the joyous shout. "We found her."

Running toward the sound, I found Gram sitting on a tree stump in a small clearing, deeper in the woods than I ever thought she'd wander. Martha stood next to her, wearing a broad smile of relief. I couldn't speak so I just threw my arms around Gram, my shoulders shaking with emotion. Several others had joined us now, all chattering with relief.

"It's all right." Gram patted my hand. "I just got a little turned around and decided to wait here for you to find me. Didn't think it would take so long or so many of you, though."

"You scared me to death, Gram. Don't ever go for a walk without telling me first. It's a miracle we found you in the dark."

"Don't treat me like a child," she softly admonished.

I threw my arms around her narrow shoulders again. "I'm sorry, Gram. I don't mean to, but I've been beyond worried. I don't know what I'd do without you."

"What do you say we all go into the house and warm up," Nancy said.

Twenty minutes later, we were in the kitchen drinking coffee. I'd managed to scrounge up a few snacks, realizing we'd never had dinner. Looking around the group gathered there, I wondered how Gram and I would ever get along without these wonderful women.

"How can I thank you?" I said to them. "I don't know how long it would've taken me to find…" My voice cracked.

"None of that now," Joan interrupted. "It's over. Lucy's safe and sound in her own home. That's all the thanks we need. I'd say it was time we left and let her get to bed."

Joan walked over to Gram, using her cane now. "It's been quite a day for you, my friend." I saw a glimmer of understanding in her eyes only two old friends could share.

We said our goodbyes, and I helped Gram up to bed after she assured me that the snacks had been enough to satisfy her hunger.

"I love you, Gram," I whispered as I tucked the quilt around her like she'd done for me a thousand times in my youth.

"Love you back," she said, already half asleep.

Remembering the exchange between Gram and Joan, I felt so alone and vulnerable. Leaving here would mean leaving all my friends, too. Who could I call on in Chicago when I needed help? Steve? He was too self-involved. I would always play second fiddle to his career. If I stayed here in Shoreview, it would be the same with Peter. His work would always have to come first. But at least I'd have friends to help fill the void.

Who are you to complain about Steve and Peter? A little voice in my head scoffed. *Didn't you once again put your painting first, almost losing Gram in the process?* The truth had a habit of stinging.

I was preparing for bed after eating a quick sandwich when the phone rang later that night.

"Nancy tells me you found Lucy. Is she all right?" It was Peter.

"Yes, she's fine."

"I want to check her out. Is it all right if I come over?"

"She's already in bed, Peter."

"It doesn't matter. I want to see for myself that there are no residual effects." Peter sounded more like a concerned friend than a doctor at this point.

A part of me wanted to refuse. Leaning on him for help and comfort could only bring pain in the end. But I couldn't take the chance that there was a problem with Gram I'd missed.

"Well, hurry up then. We want to get some sleep. It's been a bad night."

After hanging up the phone, I went up to check on Gram again. She was resting quietly, not quite asleep.

"Peter just called. He's coming over to check up on you— make sure you're all right," I said quietly.

"That's not necessary." She turned her back to me. "I'm going to sleep."

"I told him that, but he wouldn't take no for an answer."

"Humph. Well, he'd better get here quick."

We'd barely finished our conversation when I heard a knock at the door.

"OKAY, LUCY, EVERYTHING CHECKS OUT." Peter folded up his stethoscope and put it back into the bag he carried. We were up in Gram's bedroom, and he'd given her a short exam. "Your blood pressure and pulse are normal, and you're breathing without any problem. No elevated temp either."

"I told you I was fine. Honestly, all this fuss for nothing, it's downright embarrassing. If I could just get some sleep, I'll be right as rain in the morning." She pulled the covers up to her neck. "However, you could stay and visit with Cara for a while. She got herself all shook up."

"All right, Lucy. Sweet dreams," Peter said.

"Goodnight, Gram," I muttered before shutting her door. Would the woman ever give up?

"So, is everything really all right?" I asked when we got downstairs.

"Yes, I didn't see any problems." He ran his hand through his hair and sighed in relief. "I'm really sorry I couldn't come when you needed me."

"Don't apologize I shouldn't have bothered you in the first place. You gave me fair warning, didn't you?"

He shook his head. "This is exactly what I expected to happen." He caught me by the shoulders and stared into my eyes. "You couldn't count on me to be there in a time of trouble and now you're blaming me. Your family was there when I needed them most, and I'd hoped to do the same for them, always."

Looking into those dark blue eyes, I had to harden my heart. "It was no big deal."

"Cara, you know how I feel about you...all of you. Please, can't we still be friends?"

"I think it would be better if we kept our distance for a while." Being with him and feeling so vulnerable just reaffirmed the danger. I escorted him to the door even though he seemed reluctant to leave. "And I'm not blaming you for anything. We know you'll always do the best you can for us."

"You can bet on it," he said, still lingering in the doorway.

"Good night, Peter," I said firmly, closing the door while I still could. I sunk into the closest chair as I heard him walk away.

IT WAS a few days later that Steve showed up again, looking very retro in a Nehru jacket and spiked hair. A tall, sharply dressed man followed him into the shop.

"Cara, I missed you." Steve walked up to me, arms outstretched for a hug. I backed up in panic. He stumbled midstride and dropped his arms at his sides, his smile slipping. The older man standing behind him watched the scenario between us with obvious embarrassment.

"I brought someone I want you to meet," he said in much cooler tones. "Cara Olson, Gustave Weintraub. Gustave is the owner of a new art gallery in the Lincoln Park area. He's heard amazing things about the art colony in Door County and wanted to see it for himself. Personally, I wasn't that impressed."

"Hi." I offered my hand, hoping for a way to get the two of them out the door before they started insulting the area and my work. I was not in a mood to placate, especially since they weren't customers.

"Call me Gus," the man insisted, shaking my hand and looking askance at Steve. "I have to disagree with Stefan in this case. I saw some very promising work. If you don't mind, I'll just look around the shop while you two visit."

My impression of him changed immediately. "Of course, look all you like."

"Have you come to your senses yet, or are you still determined to let your talent wither in this little backwater town?"

"We've had this discussion before, Steve. Let it go." Even though I had to leave Shoreview, going back to my old life held no appeal. I'd burned all those bridges when I left the last time. I knew without a doubt that whatever the relationship between Steve and I had been, it was over.

"Stefan, come here." Gus's voice called from the other room. "You've got to see this."

Steve reluctantly turned and walked into the room. The man stood in front of my latest landscape, staring intently, his hands folded together, steeple-like.

"Is that your signature?" he asked me.

"Cara doesn't do bucolic scenes," Steve said, disdain rich in his voice.

"Yes, it's mine. I've changed my style."

Steve gaped at me as if I'd just sprouted a second head. "*What?* Why would you do that?" He was aghast, and I could see he took it as a personal affront.

I shrugged. "Maybe I've grown in a different direction?"

"I would be very interested in showing work like this in my gallery. The colors have a quality of softness and warmth that evokes another time—a more soothing lifestyle. I have a few clients who would be very interested in this piece. Do you have any others?"

"I have a few more in the back—unframed."

"Could I see them?"

"Sure. I have something else that might interest you—if you're in the market for something unusual for your gallery."

Was it possible fate was giving me another chance? Damn, but I had to grab it, even though the taste of terror lay like glue on my tongue. Would I be setting myself up for failure?

Never mind. Somewhere, I'd find the guts to show him my felt pieces. I'd moved way beyond false pride.

I led them into the kitchenette/storage room, my heart beating so rapidly I thought it would jump through my chest. I had a newly completed felt piece. Since it wasn't framed, I hadn't hung it in the shop. I had misgivings about displaying it anyway, not sure anyone would want it. I had a lot of emotion attached to the piece and didn't want to see it criticized.

The colors in the work ranged from a deep cerulean blue wool to an icy silver thread, my interpretation of the lakeshore in the depth of a cold January morning, a scene I'd often witnessed growing up here. I'd managed to portray the rising sun shining through the starkness of frosted trees, using various shadings and almost translucent wool.

As I showed the hanging to the two men, I had an epiphany of my own. Their opinion didn't matter one whit. No matter what they said, this was a part of me, and I loved it. The piece was a symbol of my new freedom, the freedom to express myself in any way I needed. Selling wasn't the deciding factor in my success.

Neither one of them spoke for a moment.

"Amazing," Gus said in a half-whispered tone, his hands lifted like a preacher praising the Lord.

"It certainly is different," Steve said grudgingly.

Gus folded his hands together again and turned to me. "Okay, how soon can you have enough pieces ready for a show of your own?" he asked, his voice laced with excitement. "We'll do a mixed medium portrayal of your work."

It took me a few moments to absorb what I was hearing. Things were moving too fast.

"I'd need some time," I managed. Who would mind the shop and keep an eye on Gram while I worked on my art? I couldn't do both and produce enough. Certainly not the amount required for a showing of my own.

"You'll have to come back to Chicago." Steve had a triumphant gleam in his eye. "There's no way you'll get enough done here."

"Impossible." I'd lost my flat and my job, and with no visible means of support, that wasn't an option. And most importantly, there was Gram to consider. Even though in the heat of my anger I'd said I could leave her, there was no way I could do it. When I hesitated, Steve quickly filled in the silence.

"You can stay with me and work in my studio." He looked at Gus. "Doesn't that sound like a logical solution to you?"

"No, that won't work," I said. A sense of deja vu swept over me. Hadn't we already covered this territory?

As tempting as the offer of the use of his studio was, I knew I couldn't go back to a life with Steve. I didn't want to get trapped there. My mind sifted through ideas as rapidly as I could. "I'd have to sell a few things first to make enough money to rent my own place. But I will take you up on your offer of using your studio, if things work out at some point. I'd pay rent, of course."

That look of triumph crossed Steve's face again and he nodded. He was in for a surprise if he thought the naïve little girl who'd hero-worshipped him would be coming back.

"I could take a few pieces with me and frame them." Gus spoke up. "I think they'll sell fairly quickly. That would give you some quick cash. Or I could buy them myself for that matter. As I said, I have a few clients looking for just this type of art." Gus's mind appeared to be working as fast as mine.

With the decision made, we packed up the pieces. Steve and Gus left after a promise that I would let them know when and if I could come to Chicago. It had all happened so quickly that I was still in a daze when Gram and Nancy came in from an extended lunch.

"What's the matter with you? You look like you've seen a ghost." Gram came over and felt my forehead, a familiar gesture I remembered from childhood. "Are you ill?"

"No. The most wonderful thing just happened." I walked to the kitchenette and plopped in a chair. "I may have just found the path to my future."

"Was Peter here?" Gram asked. The look of anticipation on their faces was almost comical.

"No." I smiled.

"Then what are you talking about?" Gram's lined face grew even more wrinkled with perplexity.

"Steve was here. And he had a Chicago gallery owner with him."

"So?" Nancy asked guardedly.

"Get on with it, girl." Gram was impatient.

"He wants to put my new work in his gallery, even the felt hangings. I'm to have a show of my own." Saying the words out loud made them real, and I squealed in delight.

"That's great, Cara," Nancy said. "Congratulations."

Gram didn't seem as happy, though she still congratulated me.

IT TOOK some time for the euphoria of having my work actually appreciated to wear off and be supplanted by reality. The cold hard fact was that going to Chicago would mean leaving Gram and this new life I'd managed to create behind. She was handling things so well now that I'd never be able to talk her into going with me, no matter how successful I became. She'd want to stay here, among the people who knew and loved her and who would watch out for her. But she still couldn't be left to fend for herself, and I would never let that happen again.

Then there was Peter. Leaving him would be one of the hardest things I've ever had to do, even if he only wanted to remain friends. I would always harbor the dream that there could be more in the future. But his threat to leave the area still hung heavy over my heart. I could look at this as the answer to several problems.

It all came down to making the choice between my career and my personal life. Someone had finally heard my prayers and given me this golden opportunity. I'd be a fool not to take it. My mind jumped from one alternative to the other. Chicago or Shoreview. How could I make this work for Gram *and* for me?

Dare I ask Nancy to take over running the shop? She'd keep a close eye on Gram, I knew that. At least until my family could work something else out. The bond between the three of us kept growing.

Moving would also mean putting up with Steve on a daily basis. Would he try to influence my work again? Would I have the strength to keep my own style? I wouldn't have the beauty of the countryside and my friends and neighbors for inspiration either. And I'd lose the easy access to material for my felting projects and to the women who shared my enthusiasm for working with fiber. Who was I kidding? I didn't want to leave my new life in Shoreview and Peter, even if it was a great opportunity.

Enough of the negative thoughts. I could do it for a short time—

a year at most. By then, I would either be an established artist who could work from anywhere or I'd have given up the dream for good. The gossip about Peter and me would've disappeared and I'd be there for Gram as her illness progressed. This was the best solution to our problem. I had better put on my big girl pants and accept it.

WHEN JACK CALLED a few nights later, I was still wrestling with the decision.

"I hear you're leaving for Chicago soon," Jack said.

"Who told you that? I haven't made up my mind. There are a lot of things to settle first."

"Listen, Squirt, we can take care of that for you. This is your big chance, and we don't want you to lose it. Gram explained everything to us, and we've worked it out already. I spoke to Nancy just a few minutes ago, and she's willing to stay with Gram and run the shop until you see how things go."

"Are you trying to run my life again? I said I haven't made up my mind whether this is a good idea or not." I clenched my fists.

"Of course, it's a good idea. Are you crazy?"

"Listen, I appreciate the effort, but I'm not so sure."

"Why do you always have to make everything so difficult?" he sighed. "You've been this way ever since we were kids. No one could ever do anything for you."

"I don't know what you're talking about, Jack. The fact of the matter is that Nancy is a wonderful person and gets along great with Gram, but she's not family."

"Joe and I are going to take turns coming up for our vacations and for weekends in the fall. No more excuses. You're going."

"We'll see."

"Please, let us do this, Squirt. It's time you gave up the family reins. We want to help, but we can't if you won't let us."

"I'll think about it, Jack."

"CAN YOU MEET US FOR COFFEE?" I was surprised to hear it was

Martha on the phone the following evening. "We want to talk to you before you do anything stupid."

"What do you mean?" I asked.

"Lucy called me this morning and told me about what she and your brothers have been up to." I could hear her tongue click in exasperation. "I still can't believe it. Honestly, Cara, what was she thinking?" She took a deep breath. "Oh, right, I guess we have to cut her a little slack but still…. Do you have time to get together?"

"Sure. Where do you want to meet?" Getting out of the house for a short time would probably be good for me and for Gram. More than a week had passed, but as much as I'd tried, I couldn't forget how she and my brothers had tried to manipulate me.

"At the Cuppa' Joe café. We'll be there in thirty minutes."

I was surprised to see the round table at the back filled with the Wool Gatherers when I arrived. The noise of the café slowed to a dull murmur as soon as I entered the place and all eyes were on me as I walked to the back of the room. I gave a wry smile. News sure traveled fast in this area.

"Sit down, kiddo," Martha said. "We need to talk." I didn't like the look of concern on their faces. Did they think I was about to abandon Gram?

"Nancy tells us you're moving back to Chicago."

"Nothing is definite, but it's looking that way," I said.

"Why? Is it because of the fiasco with Peter and your family?"

"That's only part of it. The good news is that I have the chance for my own showing in a Lincoln Park gallery. Being from Chicago, you should appreciate that." The last comment was directed at Martha.

I wanted them to be happy and excited for me, not sitting around looking at me like I was in need of therapy.

"But why do you have to move there?" Lila asked. "Couldn't you still live here and sell your work in the gallery? I know a woman up in Ephriam who's a nationally known artist. She sells her work all over the country, even out of a gallery in San Francisco."

I nodded. "It would be a lot easier for me to work out of my friend Steve's studio, no distractions. At least to start. Now that Gram's condition is under control for the time being, I'm not really needed here twenty-four/seven." After I said the words out loud, they even made sense to me.

"Well, it seems to me you had to get away from that Steve person and move back here before your real painting style had a chance to blossom," Cheryl said in a huff.

"Are you sure you're not just running away from your feelings for Peter?" Lila asked.

Busted. I should've known I couldn't fool these women. Sometimes, it seemed they knew me better than I knew myself, but I'd keep trying.

"There is nothing going on between me and Peter. I've explained that ad nauseum. He has no desire to commit; he's made that perfectly clear."

"Maybe it's because at the first chance you got, you made plans to hotfoot it back to the city with your old boyfriend. Could it be just what he expected to happen?" Martha gave me a penetrating stare.

"No, that's not the case. You don't know all the facts." I sounded desperate.

"Well, tell us then," Lila said.

I stared at them for a moment. How could I tell these ladies I was leaving town because there was a possibility Peter would leave if I didn't? I had to do it for Peter and everyone in this community who loved and trusted him as their physician. But I knew if I told them the details, I would sound like a martyr, giving up my happiness for them. And it wasn't that way at all. This was the best thing for me and for Peter. I couldn't be around him all the time without those old feelings bubbling up to the surface. He was too much a part of my love for these people and this area. They were just all jumbled together with a longing for part of a girlish dream. A year away should take care of those feelings once and for all.

"I can't explain," I said instead. "Just take my word for it, please."

Regret shining in her eyes, Martha said, "We'll miss you." The others nodded in agreement.

Nancy had been unusually quiet, not saying a word during the discussion. We were the last ones at the table, and she stopped me as I started to leave.

"Can I talk to you alone?" Nancy asked.

"I have to get back to Gram. Can it wait?"

"No."

"We can talk tomorrow."

"This is very important," Nancy repeated, her hand on my shoulder holding me back. How could I leave without hearing her out? What kind of a friend would that make me?

"What's wrong?" I asked. The look on her face spelled trouble, and I slumped back into the booth. "Has something happened to change your mind about staying with Gram?"

"No, it isn't that." She sat across from me, nervously twisting her hair, something I'd noticed her doing whenever she was stressed. "It's about you and Peter."

"What about us? And by the way, I hate it when you link our names that way."

"I know it's none of my business, Cara, but I have to get this off my chest before you leave here and start a new life."

I shrugged. "Okay, spill it."

"Peter's in love with you—always has been," Nancy said seriously.

I shook my head as I listened in dismay. It was the second time I'd heard it. Why were these people so delusional?

"I don't know where you got that idea, but it isn't true," I said, my throat clogged with pain. "I gave him every opportunity to ask me to stay, but he didn't. Instead, he practically pushed me out the door and out of his life."

"Of course, he'd never *ask* you to stay. He's too afraid you'd end up like our mother, hating him and everything about your life. He would never do that to you."

I looked down into the empty coffee cup sitting in front of me, wishing with all my heart that her words were true, but I knew better. I shook my head again.

"Let me tell you a little bit about our background," Nancy continued. "My mother comes from a very wealthy family back East. She married a socially unacceptable man as far as her family was concerned. I don't know exactly what happened; I never met my grandparents. But every time there was a family argument—and there were a lot of them—she threw it in Dad's face.

"Dad was a workaholic, mostly to get away from her nagging, I suspect. When Mother's parents died, they left her a good sum of money. She decided to leave Dad and move back home. It was the summer before I started junior high, but she insisted I go along. I barely made it through that summer. I didn't fit in with her friends or their families and had no desire to. I missed Shoreview and Peter terribly, something she couldn't understand.

"I was so miserable she finally gave up in disgust and let me come home. Dad hired Ina as our housekeeper, and she was the one who got me through my teen years—she and Peter. I'll always love Ina for that. Now that Ina runs the restaurant, I help her there every chance I get. She's more like a mother to me than my own ever was. Dad didn't change when Mom left; he still lived for his work. That was just him."

She took a deep breath before continuing, and I just sat there and listened.

"I've always wanted to explain why I was so jealous of you in high school. You had everything—a normal family, even my brother was crazy about you. And you seemed to take it all for granted. I'm afraid I let my love for my brother color my opinion. I figured you'd turned him down because you thought he wasn't good enough, being a small-town guy, when you were only interested in art school and the big city. I was very wrong. I see that now.

"My brother carries a lot of baggage. But I really believe the only reason he came back here after his residency was because he hoped you'd return someday. Even if he still doesn't realize it."

I glanced up at her, and she had a tear in her eye.

"Nancy, I'm sorry, but I think he's made up his mind about me. No one is going to change it. There isn't anything more to be done. He's at the end of his rope with people interfering in his life. He even threatened to leave town over it. The truth is, my leaving now is best for both of us. I've got to go...check on Gram."

I couldn't take any more of her wishful thinking. I rushed out of the coffee shop before she could see just how much I wanted her words to be true.

17

I WOKE UP DURING THE NIGHT, WET WITH SWEAT, IN THE MIDST OF A terrible nightmare where I was being swept away by a fast river current. I tried to grab for tree branches, anything to stop the swift flow from carrying me away, but everything was just out of my reach.

It didn't take a rocket scientist to figure out what that was all about. I was losing control of my life again, letting others push me into making decisions when I wasn't ready. I had to talk to Peter even though my gut told me it was hopeless. How else could I be sure it was what he wanted? Nancy had convinced me to try one more time.

I lay there in bed until dawn arrived and then dressed for the day. I called the clinic as soon as it was open and made an appointment. That way I could keep things on a professional basis until I could gauge his feelings.

As I waited for Peter to come into the small exam room that Monday, my hands got clammy.

He knocked before he entered. "Cara. What can I do for you? Are you ill?" The little knot of worry in his forehead gave away his concern. It was the same way he looked at Gram.

"No, I'm fine. I came to talk about Gram."

"You didn't need to make a clinic appointment for that. A phone call would've been okay. Is she having problems?"

"No." He wasn't making this any easier. "My brother Jack called and said the family has made arrangements for Nancy to stay with Gram and run the shop. They plan to spend a lot of their time here in Shoreview—weekends and vacations in the next few months."

I took a deep breath and plunged on. "I was offered this amazing opportunity for a one-woman show in Chicago, but it means I'll have to produce a lot of work to hang in the gallery. I need to go there to do it. I don't seem to get much done here, between running the shop and caring for Gram."

"So I heard." His voice was carefully neutral.

"Anyway, in order to produce enough work, I should move back to Chicago where I can work in Steve's studio."

"Ahh, Steve. That's the boyfriend, right?"

"Former boyfriend."

The look he gave me was very skeptical. "Uh-huh. What does all this have to do with your visit here?" He'd retreated into a cool and distant professional persona.

"I wanted to know your feelings."

"About what?" Peter said.

How could he be so dense? Did I have to remind him of that night at his home and how it had changed me forever? I tried to read his thoughts, but those dark eyes wouldn't meet mine. He was a master at hiding his feelings, and I'd just begun to realize it.

"Do *you* think I should go?" I finally blurted out, demanding an answer.

"It seems like you've got everything worked out. I don't see why you shouldn't, if that's what you want to know. I'll check in on Lucy from time to time."

We were talking on two different levels here, and I couldn't tell if he was getting the meaning behind my question or not.

"Peter. Do you *want* me to go?"

"I want you to do whatever you want to do, Cara. If that's what will make you happy, then you should do it." It was sincere but still distant.

"Okay," I whispered. "Thanks for your help."

"Listen, I told you. Lucy might stay the same for years or she could gradually slip deeper into dementia. Each person is different. We don't know."

I nodded, too upset to speak. He walked toward the door, and I got up from my chair. So, this was it. The end. No flowers, no unicorn standing in front of a rainbow. Just me, another sucker in love with a man who couldn't commit.

Just before he turned the handle, he reached for me, pulling me into a warm embrace, resting his forehead against mine. "Goodbye, Cara. Have a good life."

Before I could gather my wits and respond, he was out the door and on to the next patient. It was clear to me now how Peter felt.

And wow, that had sounded final. Didn't he plan on *ever* seeing me again? I went home and called Steve and made arrangements to work out of his studio. I left for Chicago the following Monday, when Gram and Nancy wouldn't be working, my latest artwork and a few personal items stuffed into the trunk and back seat of my Escort.

As I waved goodbye, I refused to even think about why I'd left everything of real importance back at Gram's, just as I'd left my artwork at Steve's when I first left Chicago. It seemed I always needed to keep one foot in each place.

I'd called my former landlord to inquire about available rentals in the area and found that another furnished apartment in my old neighborhood had recently opened up. He was eager to help out. Guilt, I suspected. But I grabbed it, sight unseen. The rent was doable, especially since Gus had sold two of my paintings already and there was interest in another. And no lease required. I would be free to leave at any time should Gram need me or if my sales turned out to be just a fluke. I couldn't ask for more than that.

The ride down was uneventful. The weather was clear. Arriving in the city, I found the apartment pretty much the same as the last one: non-descript, early seventies décor, and minimal kitchenware. After carrying in my few personal effects, I called Steve on my cell and made arrangements to drive over and drop my artwork and supplies at his studio.

Later, as I looked around the large space of his studio, filled with his easels and modern paintings, I wondered how I'd ever felt at home here. If I didn't know better, I'd swear that the same empty pizza boxes and Chinese take-out cartons littered the counters.

Maybe it was the familiar smell of linseed oil and paints that had attracted me here originally and made me feel at home. After happy years spent painting with Gram and then all my time at art school, the odor of fresh paints turned me on like cinnamon and spice baking in the oven to a hungry kid.

"You can keep all your equipment on this side of the studio. I cleared space," Steve said after helping me carry in my things. This new enthusiastic voice of his made me a little uneasy.

"I'd like to pay my rent before I get started." That feeling of unease sent needles up my spine.

"That can wait. Why don't we have some dinner first? I'll order Chinese."

"No, I want to take care of it now. I won't feel right until I do." My uneasiness rapidly turned to distrust.

"Well, here's an idea I wanted to float. How about instead of paying rent, you help out around here. You know, like you used to."

"That's not the deal we made. Why don't you hire a cleaning woman if that's what you need?" My hands shook with suppressed anger. "It's either strictly a business arrangement or nothing. I won't be your gopher around here again."

"Hey, don't go all 'I am Woman' on me. You know I can't work with strangers messing around with my stuff." He raised his hands as though warding off a madman. "We'll do it your way, by all means. I only wanted to help."

"Thank you," I managed to grind out. "I'd like my own key, as well." Before he had a chance to react, I continued. "In case I want to start work early in the morning—when you've been working all night. My working hours have changed. I find I'm much more productive in the early morning—better light."

I wasn't about to tell him I wouldn't be caught in this studio anywhere near dinnertime if I could help it. I'd learned a little more about myself during my time in Shoreview. It would be too easy to fall back in the old habit of making Steve's art a priority because he was the one selling and getting the publicity. At least for the time being. I intended to change that.

"Fine. I'll go find your old key. I like to sleep in." He winked at me, and my stomach rolled with disgust. Sleeping with Steve had become so far off the realm of possibilities that I shivered with repulsiveness.

MY NERVES WERE a little shaky as I began my new adventure in the world of the working artist. For the first time ever, this was my full-time job. No more excuses like The Daily Grind or Gram or running her shop to distract me. This was my big break. Was I up to it? Sweet Jesus, I hoped so.

Steve had cleaned up the studio, finally taking the hint that I wouldn't be around to pick up after him. It looked more like a professional studio now with our easels set up to catch the light, my still-life arrangement on a small table next to my chair and Steve's bright collage of colors on the wall. No empty pizza boxes or food cartons littered the hardwood floors, without my even commenting. I gave myself an imaginary pat on the back.

As the days wore on, Steve and I were like two ships silently passing in the night—barely taking the time to greet each other as I left the studio in late afternoon when he was just beginning his work. I'd never paid much attention to the fact that he'd slept all day while I worked at the coffee shop.

"Why don't we have dinner together?" Steve asked for the umpteenth time.

"Not tonight." Sheesh, you'd think he'd take the hint after so many refusals. I'd finally given up and didn't bother with excuses. I was determined not to fall into bad habits again.

I spent the days painting like a mad woman while berating myself for the quick decision I'd made about the gallery show. *What was I thinking?* The words played repeatedly through my head. Whatever possessed me to think I could produce enough quality art for a gallery showing of my own? Gus had been in to check my progress several times, and so far, he seemed pleased.

"Let's set a date so I can begin the publicity," he said. "I want to get this info into all the papers and have posters made to hang in the affluent areas of the city. It has to be done in a timely manner so people can plan ahead. The clients we want to interest have a busy social life," Gus explained, looking over my shoulder at my work. "I think early October would be a good time."

"Be careful, Gus. Every time Cara's under pressure to produce, she finds a reason to run home to her family." Steve kept his back to us as he continued painting, his bitterness coming across loud and clear.

"That's about the dumbest thing I've ever heard you say." I could feel my face flushing with anger.

"Oh, really? Let's see." He turned and tapped a finger on his chin. "One time it was your mother coming to visit in Wisconsin." Looking at Gus, he continued. "Like she couldn't come here to see you. And then there was your nephew's first communion. And let's not forget all the birthdays."

"This really is none of your business," I huffed, trying to stay professional.

"Facts are facts, Cara."

I longed to wipe the now familiar smirk off Steve's face.

"You're a great artist," Gus said, patting my shoulder. "It's time you realized your own potential and ignored the criticism of others." He flicked his glance toward Steve.

"If you say so." I ran a hand across the back of my neck to relieve some of the tension. "It won't be easy."

My hands began to tremble as that awful evening at the gallery came back to haunt me. Could I really face those critics again? I swallowed the panic and asked, "Is it absolutely necessary that I be at the opening?" The squeak in my voice gave me away.

Gus lifted an eyebrow. "Why wouldn't you want to be there? You're the one who created all this wonderful work. You should be proud."

"Yes, well, everyone might not think it's as great as you do." I cleared my throat, embarrassed at the neediness I heard in my voice.

"So now you're telling me I don't know my stuff?"

"No, no, of course not." The twinkle in his eye calmed my embarrassment. I breathed a heavy sigh. Gus was on my side. I had to believe that.

18

IT WAS EARLY SEPTEMBER NOW. I SLOGGED AWAY AT MY WORK FOR days, desperate to produce enough quality work in time. The painting that had been such a joy was becoming a chore. I missed the inspiration of the people and scenery around Shoreview. Looking out the studio window early one evening when my only view was one of rooftops surrounded by a yellowish-green cloud of smog drifting in from the factories, claustrophobia overwhelmed me. I had to get out.

I'd worked later than usual again, messing up my plans to be gone before Steve's dinnertime.

"I'm leaving, Steve. Have a nice night," I called out to him.

"Are you sure you don't want to stay and have dinner with me?"

"No, I have to call my grandmother and check on her."

His sarcastic, "Of course, you do," only spurred me on.

"Don't even start," I warned. I picked up my jacket and cell phone and headed down the street toward the lake. Maybe I could put more enthusiasm into my voice when I talked to Gram if I was close to the water and the sandy shore, knowing it was the same lake that touched the shores of Shoreview. The thought made Gram seem a lot closer. It was a trick from my early student days when the city had seemed so cold and foreign.

I hadn't yet reached the lake when my cell rang. It was Martha.

"Cara, hello! I have some exciting news and a great big favor to ask," she said. "The Wool Gatherers came up with the most wonderful idea. We've decided to have a fundraiser to help establish a center specifically for Alzheimer's patients. As you of all people know, this disease is affecting many in the community, and it's only going to get worse.

"So, we've decided on an auction. There are a lot of other organizations working with us, thanks to Peter. He agrees there's a great need for a respite place in this community. Right now, people have to admit their relatives to facilities in other towns when they can no longer care for them at home. What do you think?"

"It's a wonderful idea." I smiled for the first time that day.

"Here's where you come in." Martha cleared her throat. "I know you're terribly busy with your show, but could you possibly donate a painting for the auction? It would be a great addition to the fundraiser. A local scene done by one of our own would garner a lot of bidding, I'll bet."

"I'd be honored to, Martha." I felt the tears rising. I hadn't fully realized how badly I wanted to return home until that very moment. "What's the date of the auction?"

"October fourteenth. Will that give you enough time?"

Only one week after my opening. That gave me very little time to get a painting worthy of an auction completed. My enthusiasm deflated like a day-old balloon. *Were the heavens sending me a message here?*

"I'll make time. I'll come up next weekend to take a few pictures. I need to be there to get some fresh ideas. It'll give me a chance to see Gram. I still worry about her, no matter how much she assures me everything is fine."

By this time, I'd reached the lakefront, and as I walked along the beach listening to the soothing sounds of the waves lapping against the sandy shore, I asked a few more questions about my friends before disconnecting. Imagining them working together to organize the event left me feeling lonely. *The important thing to remember is that I'm living my dream*, I repeated over and over.

I took the cell phone out of my pocket again and called Gram, anxious now to tell her that I'd be home next weekend. I knew she'd be pleased, even more so when I told her about the painting I planned to donate.

"That's nice." The vagueness in her voice sent chills of dread up my spine. "Where are you, dear?"

"I'm at the lakefront, walking along the beach," I said.

"Will you be home for dinner? It's almost time to eat."

"I'm in Chicago, Gram, remember?"

"Yes, of course, I remember. How silly of me."

"Where's Nancy? Isn't she staying with you?" I asked.

"She must be out feeding the animals. I don't need a babysitter every minute, you know." There was that hint of irritation in her voice that I hadn't heard in some time.

"I'll be up next weekend, Gram. Write it down on that tablet I put next to the phone so you don't forget."

After I disconnected, I sat on a bench near the water, trying to assimilate what I'd just heard. Gram seemed so much better when I'd talked to her last. What was going on? Was it because I'd been calling her in the morning when her cognitive skills were at their peak?

The lapping water lost its soothing sound, instead reminding me of the relentless passing of time, wearing down on us like beating waves wore the rocky shore to fine grains of sand. Gram was aging, and there wasn't anything her medication or I could do to stop it. When I lost her, I'd have nothing. Peter would be a distant memory of a love that wasn't in the cards. But I'd have my art.

And as much as I loved it, it wouldn't be enough. Not for me. I wasn't like Steve. I wanted a family of my own. I wanted children, and I wanted Gram to know them before she lost her personality to this dreaded disease.

I had to go home and see what options life had in store for me.

. . .

I PULLED into the parking space behind the shop that next week-end, my heart filled with a weird mix of happiness to be home and fear of what I might find. The last hour of the drive had been horrific. I'd forgotten all about the annual Fall Festival and wasn't prepared for the huge influx of tourists. It was bumper-to-bumper traffic with unhappy tourists unused to driving on narrow country roads with a lot of no-passing zones. It gave me too much time to stew over my last conversation with Gram. Could my family be protecting me from Gram's failing condition while I pursued my dream? The thought nagged like a persistent toothache.

Gram stood in the open doorway of the shop when I drove up, smiling a welcome. I breathed a sigh of relief. She looked happy. Things couldn't be as bad as I'd feared.

"Did you have a good trip?" she asked when I approached, wrapping her so thin arms around me in a tight embrace. I let out the breath I'd been unconsciously holding, so grateful she recognized me.

"It was uneventful," I said. "I forgot all about the weekend festival though. Is it my imagination or are there more people here than usual? Have you been busy?"

"Lordy, there've been so many people in and out of here like bees in a honeycomb all day." She led the way toward the kitch-enette. "We've had the coffee pot on for hours, and we picked up our favorite cheesecake from the bakery."

My conscience pricked. She'd missed me more than she'd let on in our phone calls.

"Come on in back, and tell us what you've been working on these past weeks."

Nancy, who'd been standing quietly behind Gram, hugged me in greeting. Never in my wildest imagination would I have thought we could become this close. It was the one bright spot in this terrible mess of my life.

"I have to talk to you," I whispered in her ear. She nodded in response.

We trooped into the kitchenette, Gram leading the way. She poured coffee into the three waiting mugs, and we sat around the chrome yellow table, facing into the front of the shop so we'd see any entering customers immediately.

"Okay, let's hear it. What's been going on?" Gram sent me that sharp look so familiar from my childhood. I wanted desperately to pour all my unhappiness into her sympathetic ear, knowing it would all seem trivial after sharing it with her. But it was no longer an option. I was now the caretaker and should be listening to her problems.

I took a big gulp of my coffee, forgetting where I was for a moment. It came back to me with a jolt. Starbucks' strongest brew had nothing on a pot of boiled Scandinavian coffee. After two cups, one's ears could start ringing, unless, of course, you were like Gram, immune after years of drinking the potent brew.

"Do you have cream and sugar?" I managed to choke out.

"Don't change the subject. Is it that Steve person who's causing those circles under your eyes?"

Dark circles? I hadn't noticed. "No, Gram. We're only friends and barely see each other. We've both been working non-stop."

"Humph." She broke a piece of her cheesecake off with a fork without taking her eyes off me.

"So, what have you been working on? C'mon, tell us," Nancy said.

"Mostly I've been doing scenes from around this area. That seems to be my strong point." I sent Nancy a grateful look when she set the sugar and creamer on the table.

"Of course, it is, dear. This is your home, where you belong." Gram picked up her coffee cup but kept watching me over the brim. The door chimed.

"Oops, a customer." Nancy started up from her chair.

"You stay here. Maybe you can find out what's bugging this girl. She sure doesn't look any happier since leaving."

We sat silent until we heard Gram conversing with the customer.

"She sounded very confused when I talked to her a few evenings ago." I knew the fear showed on my face. I'd had a difficult time hiding it from Gram, but I didn't bother now with Nancy.

"She is slipping a little, especially in the evening. But the rest of the day she seems to do all right," Nancy said, twisting her hair around an index finger.

"Why didn't you call me?" I asked.

"Your brothers told me not to," she said, her expression defensive. "They were afraid you'd come home."

"But if Gram needs me..."

"We're getting along fine. Don't worry," she said, putting her hand over mine on the table. "Your brothers have been very supportive, coming on the weekends and even spending their vacations here."

"But what about you? Hasn't this been hard, staying with her all the time, running the shop and all?"

"Actually, it's been great. Lucy and I get along very well, and I enjoy running the shop. It gives me a chance to not only meet new people but to actually converse with them. Not like the restaurant where we're so busy I never have the chance to talk to the customers. Lucy goes to bed early, and I have the evenings to myself. It isn't as if I'm missing out on some great social life. Besides, like I told you, your brothers have been helpful and so have her friends." She rolled her eyes. "If they don't stop calling to offer help, I swear I'll start flinging glassware at the wall." She laughed.

"Okay, I'll take your word for it. But you will call me, won't you? If she continues to slide?"

"Of course, I will. But you know, according to Peter, she could go on like this for years." She squeezed my hand again. "I'd better get out there. I like to be within hearing distance when Lucy's handling customers.'

The shop was so busy the rest of the afternoon that Gram and I stayed to help Nancy. I watched Gram as she interacted with the customers. Things weren't as bad as I feared, but there wasn't the miracle cure I'd been hoping for either.

When Gram and I got home there was still light in the sky, so we went for a walk in the woods and I snapped pictures like crazy. The landscape had changed to early fall now, the trees just beginning to turn their awesome colors. Leaves crinkled beneath our feet as we walked, and the familiar scent of burning leaf piles wafted through the air, a scent no longer familiar in the city.

Everywhere along the road I'd seen stands selling shiny red apples, bright orange pumpkins, and multicolored gourds. Fall had arrived with its mix of emotions, appreciation for the awesome beauty and a deep ache for something lost.

"What did we do before digital cameras, Gram?" The whir of my camera was almost constant. "It's so great being able to snap all the pictures I want and vetting them before printing."

Gram looked around, deep in her own thoughts. Evening was falling, and I guessed her mind was wandering. But when she turned toward me, my Gram was still there in her eyes.

"This land was a part of your grandfather, like it'd been passed down into his bones. He thought your father would be here to take over the farm when he was gone, but God had his own plan. Your brothers never felt that connection," she said, a deep wistfulness in her voice. Turning away from me, she looked out toward the field, golden now in the setting sun. "I hoped it would be you who'd live on the place. You always were more attuned to the land than anyone else in the family."

She paused, her voice cracking. "It scares me to think that I might forget all this someday. Take lots of pictures and show them to me often, will you?"

"Oh, Gram, please. Don't think the worst." I stopped walking and held her in my arms, trying to comfort her like she'd always comforted me. She relaxed against me for a moment and then pulled back. I could see her resolve hardening as she straightened those bony shoulders.

"Never mind me. I'm just an old woman letting her fears get the best of her." Picking up her pace, she asked, "Now, what was that you were saying about your camera?"

"It wasn't important. Let's just enjoy our time together." Watching her from behind, I could see she'd become even frailer. "Hey, if you're not careful, I'm gonna be taller than you. Are you drinking your milk?"

"Don't you go throwing my advice back in my face, girl."

I snapped a picture of her face at that moment, capturing the mischievous look I knew so well.

"So, what do you think I should use as the subject for my auction painting?" We'd talked about it earlier, and she was just as excited about the entry as I was.

"I don't know—guess you're the one who has to decide. You'll know when you see it. That's what a good painting is all about. It'll come from your heart."

"What about you? Are you going to do a piece of rosemaling?" She looked at me, surprise lighting her face.

"Are you serious?" she asked.

"Of course, I'm serious. Did you think you'd get off scot-free while the rest of us slave away?"

"I don't know if anyone thinks I'm capable anymore. Even I don't know if I am."

"Enough of that now. Tomorrow you can get started while we're at the shop. I know Nancy will be happy to work along with you after I leave."

THE NEXT MORNING, we were off to the shop bright and early. I'd told Nancy to take the day off as I'd be working. There was a parade planned for that morning, so we were able to close for a time. We heard the music approaching and stepped out into the street to watch the parade. I managed to snap a few pictures of the high school band and local farmers, so proud on their shiny tractors. I also snapped a few of the volunteer firemen in bright red trucks. Even the local animals were part of the parade, pulling antique carts and buggies. The children ran in between the floats in a frenzy scooping up the candy thrown toward them with abandon.

When we returned to the shop, Gram set up her rosemaling supplies in the kitchenette, and I helped her choose a basket to decorate. I could hear her humming while I opened the cash register again and prepared for the onslaught of customers.

Gram worked intently the rest of the morning. Customers

came in and out, and I was able to handle things with ease. By lunchtime, signs of fatigue lined her face.

"Why don't you put your paints away for the day. You've got several weeks to finish."

Her body sagged in relief. I figured it was best if she only worked in the morning anyway, when her cognitive skills were at their highest. I'd have to remind Nancy of that.

"Wait a minute. I want to take your picture, Gram."

She gave me a look but relented.

I ended up taking several. Gram and her rosemaling was such a dear subject to me. I knew I would treasure these pictures forever.

As much as I hated to, I had to call Peter that evening after Gram went to bed, hoping to catch him at home. There wasn't any opportunity for me to make an appointment at the clinic as I'd be leaving for Chicago the next day. I needed his reassurance that Gram wasn't regressing, no matter what Nancy had said.

"I heard you were in town for the weekend. How're things going in Chicago?" he asked.

"Things are moving along." Talking to him was so difficult now when I had to constantly keep my guard up so he wouldn't guess my feelings. "Do you have a few minutes? I want to talk to you about Gram."

"Who are you talking to?" Gram called. She was halfway down the steps, already in her nightgown. "Is it Jack? I'm too tired to talk tonight. Tell him to call back tomorrow."

"I'll tell him. You go on to bed." I waited for her to start back up the stairs before whispering into the phone, "I can't talk right now."

"I'm coming over."

"Tonight?" This was not going as I'd planned. All I wanted was a little reassurance that I was doing the right thing by staying in Chicago. Seeing Peter in the flesh was not going to help.

"I'll be there shortly." The phone clicked in my ear before I had a chance to tell him not to come.

I checked on Gram to make sure she'd fallen asleep and then

spent the next fifteen minutes pacing, hurrying to the door as soon as I heard his car drive up.

"You didn't have to come out tonight."

He stood in the doorway, wearing jeans and smelling of fresh air and spicy aftershave. Oh, God, he looked good enough to eat. I wanted to throw myself in his arms and beg him to spend the night.

"I wasn't busy." He took off the light windbreaker he was wearing before I even invited him to stay and threw it on the back of a chair, like it belonged there. I sometimes forgot all the time he'd spent here with my brothers and now again that his sister was staying with Gram. "What's the problem? I could tell by your voice something is wrong."

He was once again the affable friend, and it ticked me off. My worries about Gram weren't the only things wrong with my life. *He* was a big part of my problems. How could he pretend that nothing had happened between us? Had it meant so little to him?

"It's Gram. Have you seen her lately?" I stuffed down my frustration.

"Nancy brought her into the clinic a few weeks ago. Has something else happened?"

"Did Nancy tell you that Gram's been getting confused in the evenings?" I asked, coming to the point.

"She did, but that's not unusual. It happens."

"You don't think Gram's slipping then?"

We'd wandered into the living room by this time and stood near the sofa. "Not necessarily." He picked up my hand and started to rub the back in a comforting gesture, but the minute we touched, it was like a strike of lightning and he quickly drew back, muttering, "Sorry."

I knew then I wasn't the only one feeling the electricity between us. I had to admit it gave me a sense of satisfaction.

"It's like I explained earlier," Peter said. "She's going to have these ups and downs and may slowly progress into Alzheimer's disease. I can't give you a definitive timeline. All we can do is keep her on medication and hope to slow the progression. Nancy assured me she's following all the guidelines—making sure she walks every day and takes her vitamins. That's about all we can do."

"So, she really doesn't need me here?" Disappointment lay thick in my voice.

"Not at this point. Why? Were you thinking about moving back home?" He studied my face. I thought I saw a glimmer of hope in those dark eyes before the familiar shutters came down.

"Yes, I've thought about it." I looked away, afraid he'd see the need in my eyes. "I want to be here for her when she needs me."

"I don't think she'd want you to give up your career. You'd get bored here pretty fast."

"Will you please stop telling me what I want and feel? *This is my home.*"

"Oh, c'mon, you didn't waste any time running back to the city at the first opportunity. Not that I blame you," he added with haste.

"If you think it's so boring here, why do you stay?" *Let's hear your answer to that one, buster.*

"It's not boring for me. I have my work." His brows drew together in a perplexed look.

"And all the women chasing after you, right?" I couldn't resist the taunt.

"That's not a plus," Peter said with assurance.

"Yeah, right. Do you expect me to believe that?"

"What's your problem? I'm just telling the truth."

"The truth as you want to see it." I couldn't stop the impatient snort that escaped.

"What's that supposed to mean?"

"Just face it. You've got your life all planned out, nice and tidy, the way you want it, and to hell with anyone who tries to change things." The words came out snarkier than I'd planned.

"You don't get it, do you? I can't change who I am." He stepped closer, getting way too far into my comfort zone.

"What are you, Peter? Permanently stupid?" I egged him on.

"I'll show you who's stupid." He grabbed my shoulders, drawing me deep into a punishing kiss. Before I knew it, I had wrapped my arms around him, and the kiss turned soft and coaxing.

When he finally lifted his lips, he tenderly brushed away the hair that had fallen against my cheeks, slowly sliding his fingertips over each of my features, as if trying to commit them to memory.

"Now *that* was stupid. Go back to Chicago and find a normal life, will you?" he said softly before picking up his jacket and walking back out the door. "You deserve better than what I can give you, no matter how you feel now," he threw over his shoulder.

I wiped the kiss off my lips with the back of my hand. "I'm not your mother," I yelled after him, my heart pounding in my ears. "Isn't that your real problem?"

I slammed the door after him, forgetting Gram was upstairs sleeping. *Forget him.*

19

I'D BEEN BACK IN CHICAGO FOR DAYS, WORKING HALFHEARTEDLY IN the studio on an autumn still life involving pumpkins, gourds, and branches of bittersweet. Each stroke of the brush was a chore. Ever since that last scene with Peter, I'd lost my focus.

I planned to spend this morning in my apartment, catching up on all the little housekeeping chores I'd neglected for weeks and getting into the photos I'd taken in Shoreview. I'd downloaded several, even printed them out and done a quick study on a few the day before. Maybe if I finished downloading them, I'd find something promising, something to help me get my mojo back.

I'd flung the windows open to let in fresh air, but now that the workday was in full swing, only the suffocating scent from the nearby paint factory drifted in. Mixed with the screeching sounds of traffic, it was enough to pull my concentration from thoughts of the pristine beauty I'd left behind. I rushed back and slammed the windows shut.

Back at my computer, I flipped through the images, a feeling of desperation driving me. I needed to get my enthusiasm back or I'd never be ready for one of the most important nights of my life. Working on a new project could only help.

As I sat going through the photos, I realized just how good they were, even inspiring, but nothing gave me that special feeling, the feeling that made me want to stop everything and pick up a paintbrush. Then I saw the last picture to download. It was one of Gram, rosemaling on the wooden box in the back of the shop.

My heart stopped for a moment and then began beating erratically. *This is it.* The subject for my auction painting. It was perfect. I'd do it in watercolor. What better for that auction than a portrait of a woman suffering from MCI? Only Gram's friends would know, of course. But that didn't matter. I knew it would be fantastic—if I could capture that intense look on her face, along with her proud Scandinavian bearing. I printed out a copy and held it with shaking fingers.

I drove to the studio and began sketching that afternoon. My other work would have to wait. I wouldn't be able to think of anything else until it was finished. Some of Steve's work habits had rubbed off on me after all.

I worked on it for two days, barely stopping to eat. So what if I'd have to scramble like a mad woman to finish the other works in time for my show. I could do it.

Gus came into the studio the afternoon I completed it. I could feel him looking over my shoulder and I flushed in guilt.

"Wow, that's breathtaking. I knew you were good, but there's even more feeling in this piece than in your others. I wouldn't have thought it possible. It'll sell, no doubt about it."

"It's not for sale."

"I see." He stepped back and looked at the portrait again. "Is it for your grandmother?"

"Yes and no."

He studied me over the top of his black-rimmed spectacles.

"It's for an auction to help pay for a new treatment center for Alzheimer patients. They're in desperate need of one in my hometown."

"When is the auction?"

"The week after my opening. That's why I have to finish this and get it shipped to them as soon as possible."

"How's your other work progressing?" he asked, sympathy gleaming in his dark eyes.

"I only have two more pieces to complete. I did the studies already."

I pulled the small canvases out for him to review.

"Excellent. These are a little different from your other works. I really like this one." He pointed at the one on the left.

"I took the photos when I was home last week. There was a Fall Harvest parade that day. I haven't added much detail yet, but I know exactly what feelings I want the painting to portray."

"I'm sure you do, Cara. It already evokes small town America. I like the high school band leading the parade."

"Thanks. It's kind of personal to me—I was in the high school band, played flute." How did I ever get so lucky as the day Steve brought Gus into Gram's shop? I promised myself I'd never fail him.

"You only have one week left to prepare," he warned. "Everything has to be dry, framed, and hung in less than two weeks."

"I know. I'll be ready, I promise."

That only left a few days to frame and ship Gram's portrait. I chewed nervously on my lip. Was it my best work? Would it sell for a decent amount? I'd know soon enough.

THE NIGHT OF MY OPENING, I paced back and forth in my small apartment, willing the clock to move and yet dreading the night ahead. What if no one showed up? What if they hated my work? Who would eat all the canapés? I wasn't too worried about the wine; I could take care of a good portion of that if the evening was a failure. The thing was, I had to get through this night without disappointing Gus and everyone else who believed in me.

I looked down at my watch again. Finally. It was time to leave. I smoothed down the skirt of my new dress, a little uncomfortable in the dramatic black sheath and matching suede heels—so much more sophisticated than what I usually wore to art openings. The silver chandelier earrings jangled softly every time I turned my head, reminding me of the contrast between this and other openings I'd attended. I murmured a little prayer for strength to get through the evening, no matter the outcome.

Steve called again. "Are you sure you don't want me to pick you up?"

"No, I'd rather drive myself, honest."

"Okay. I guess you know what you want. You always do." What I didn't want was to be stuck in close quarters with him if the show was a failure. I don't know which would be worse; his "I told you so" or fake sympathy.

ARRIVING A LITTLE LATE, I spotted Gus across the room, a slight frown of concern on his face. I grabbed a glass of wine for fortification and made my way through the crowd to him.

"Something wrong?" I asked.

"No, just more traffic in here than I expected so early in the evening. I was afraid you'd miss out on some important introductions." He grabbed my arm in a death grip and began squiring me around.

"I won't run away," I whispered. "I promise."

"Sorry." He laughed and loosened his grip.

The gallery was crowded, and my stomach did its usual flip-flop as we circled. Was the crowd due to a slow night on the Chicago social scene or from Gus's reputation? *Whatever*. People were here and enjoying themselves. They seemed eager to meet me, or was it Gus who caused their animation?

"Let me introduce you to the artist," he said to the very same critic who had trashed my former work. This time, I was the one with the death grip on Gus. But instead of the sneer I half-expected, the critic's face lit with excitement.

"Your work is fabulous," he gushed. "I would count you as an emerging new star. Can I ask you a few questions?"

"Yes, of course," I answered. I was dying to remind him of our earlier meeting, but he obviously didn't recognize my name or me. "But we've met before." *The devil made me do it.*

"We have?" His questioning look confirmed what little of an impression I'd made on him.

"Yes. I had a painting in Stefan's show at the Lincoln Gallery."

"That was you?" His face flushed. "Well, I never would have

guessed." He put his hands on his hips and looked again at one of the paintings. "You've certainly improved."

"I'll take that as a compliment," I said.

"Gustave tells me you're from Wisconsin and get your inspiration there."

"Yes, that's true." The more he questioned me about Shoreview and my life there, the more it sunk in how much I missed it. Whatever the outcome of this show, I realized I couldn't possibly stay here in Chicago.

I had to go home.

We continued to circle the room and receive praise. It was a long and wonderful evening, and for the first time in my life, I felt my talent validated.

When the evening was over, Gus, Steve, and I celebrated at a fancy restaurant with champagne and cheesecake. I should've had more faith in Gus, and I told him so. Steve was very subdued and congratulatory. I think he was even more surprised than I at the reception of my style.

I returned to my apartment, filled with a wish that I could share the moment with Gram and, dare I say it, Peter.

My answering machine blinked in the dark as I opened the apartment door. I half-heartedly made my way across the room, assuming it was Steve, making sure I got home safely. He'd become uncharacteristically concerned about my welfare lately. Go figure. I hit the play button as I took off my coat.

"Just wanted to let you know that your painting arrived safe and sound." Martha's voice echoed through the apartment, warm and friendly. "I don't know how you could bear to part with it. It brought tears to my eyes."

I slumped down on my narrow bed, strangely depressed. *What was wrong with me?* I should be jumping up and down with excitement. All my dreams were coming true. Why then, did they have the perverseness of changing now?

I TOOK my first sip of coffee the next morning just as my cell phone started the William Tell overture. I loved my new ring tone.

"How does it feel to be the new artistic discovery in the city?" Gus's voice rang with an excitement I wished I could feel. I had tossed and turned all night, wondering how I'd make things right in my life. I had finally reached my goal—my work was recognized and I should be walking on air.

Instead, all I could think about was how much I wanted to be home among the people I'd grown to love.

"Good morning." I yawned to cover my lack of enthusiasm.

"Did you see the art section of the *Trib*? The critic must have phoned in his review late last night. You made it, kid."

"That's wonderful. We both know it wouldn't have happened without you." I finally got some enthusiasm back. If not for me, for Gus. It was his hard work and belief in me that made this happen. "How can I ever thank you?"

"By producing more work."

"Will do, but it'll have to wait. I'm leaving town as soon as I can get things organized here. The auction is next weekend, and I want to be there."

"Just get back as soon as you can. You have to strike while the iron is hot, as they say. We have to keep up the buzz. I'll be setting up more publicity, and you have to keep producing. Do what you have to do, and then get back here. Don't make the mistake of thinking you can rest on your laurels."

I knew he was right. But leaving Shoreview again would be tough. We talked for a few more minutes about my future plans, and after thanking him again for all his help, I hung up.

I called the shop right away to tell Gram I'd be home in a few days. I wasn't going to miss the auction, no matter how difficult seeing Peter would be. Nancy answered. "Scandinavian Gifts."

"Hey, just calling to tell you guys that I'll be there for the auction. How're things going?"

"It's pretty hectic around here. Peter is driving us all crazy. I've never seen him so enthusiastic about a project. He's putting his all into getting this new center started."

"That's great," I said, pushing down my envy. I wanted so badly to be part of it.

"I don't know what happened, but that weekend you were home seemed to light a fire under him. He's even been having lengthy phone conversations with my mother."

"That's great," I repeated. The enthusiasm in my voice sounded phony even to me. "Well, anyway, I'll see you and Gram soon."

THINGS WERE ALREADY in full swing when I arrived. I'd stopped at Gram's first and changed clothes. I wore the same dress that I'd worn for my opening, figuring it had brought me good luck that night. I needed all I could get to see me through the auction and a possible meeting with Peter.

The place was crowded with hospital staff, auxiliary members, and volunteers. Surprisingly, I was on a first name basis with a lot more people here than I'd realized. I looked around for Peter but didn't see him in the crowd and felt that now familiar mix of relief and disappointment. After the pre-dinner cocktails, I found my place at the table with Gram and a few of the Wool Gatherers.

After the dinner dishes were cleared, we stayed at our table. Everyone seemed in a mood of eager anticipation, and a lot of it centered on my portrait of Gram. If my churning stomach wasn't telling me different, I'd say Martha and Lila were as nervous as I was. I didn't know how much Gram would grasp of the evening activities, but I knew she'd seen the portrait earlier. Martha had passed on Gram's pleasure at seeing the portrait and her saying, "That's my girl," with pride. That was most important, I told myself as I tried to calm my jitters.

"Ladies and gentlemen, could I have your attention, please." The female president of the auxiliary stood up on the dais, mic in hand. "We're ready to start the bidding on these fantastic items donated to our worthy cause. First on our list is this wonderful week-long getaway to Mexico. Tell me who wouldn't want that next January when we're buried up to our eyeballs in snow here?"

She looked over the crowd expectantly. "Do we have an opening bid?"

I watched for what seemed like endless hours as she gradually made her way across the stage, stopping to elicit bids on each item displayed. It looked like my painting would be last. Finally, a gentleman stepped up and helped her hold it up to the crowd.

"I think some of us recognize the beautiful lady in this portrait, done by our very own Cara Olson. Am I right? Who'll start the bid?"

"Two hundred," someone yelled out behind me.

"Five hundred."

"I'll raise the bid to one thousand."

I began to hyperventilate and decided to get out of there before I made a fool of myself. "I'll be back in a few minutes," I whispered to Gram. "Stay with your friends."

"Is something wrong?" Martha caught up with me just as I reached the open doorway.

"No, just nerves. Come and find me when the bidding's over."

I paced the empty hallway. There was a lot of enthusiastic shouting coming from that room. Was that Peter's voice? I couldn't be sure. Good Lord, when would this be over? My nerves weren't this frazzled on my opening night at the gallery.

Well, maybe that was a slight exaggeration.

Loud clapping and shouting drifted out into the hall, and then Martha broke through the door.

"It's over, and you'll never guess how much the painting went for! I can't believe it myself."

I swallowed hard. "How much?"

"Ten thousand."

"You're bluffing. What fool would pay that much for a painting of mine?"

"Someone who thought it was worth it?" Martha said.

"More likely someone who really wants to help the new Alzheimer wing."

"Whatever you want to believe, it's done. Let me be the first to congratulate you." She gave me a brief hug before turning back toward the room. "Are you coming? Lucy's looking tired."

"Wait, you didn't tell me who bought the painting."

"Take a guess." With those words, she left me alone in the hallway. The crowd began streaming out of the banquet room, pushing through the doors towards me. Several people called out congratulations and compliments on the painting. I saw Peter come through the far door, a tall blonde on his arm.

Our glance met across the crowd, and he nodded in greeting before his gaze traveled slowly up and down my body. The intensity of his look caught me by surprise. I nodded back and quickly turned away, afraid he'd be able to read the raw hurt in my eyes. But not before I'd seen how good he looked in his tux.

Who was the woman with him?

I don't want to know.

I hurried through the crowd toward Gram. I shouldn't have left her as long as I did, even if she was with friends. But there she was, still waiting for me.

"Come on, Gram. Let's go."

Later, when we were in the car heading home, I asked Gram, "Who made the winning bid on the painting?"

"What?" She gave me that vacant look, and I knew it would have to wait until tomorrow, no matter how frustrating. "I'm afraid I can't remember."

Gram really was slipping. I couldn't deny it any longer. I didn't want to go back to Chicago and leave her again. The time I had left with her was too precious to waste. My brothers had done the best they could and so had Nancy. But I also knew staying here just wasn't possible now. According to Gus, I had to be in Chicago if I really wanted to succeed.

The problem was that I longed to be the one to care for Gram. Family was the most important thing in the world to me. Always had been and always would be. How could I have forgotten that? Replacing their need for me with Steve's had been my answer to missing them. It no longer worked. I was a little slow, but I finally grasped it. The emptiness of my success at the showing was proof.

I'd always been the family caretaker, true enough, but now I realized it was because I wanted the responsibility. It was a source of satisfaction for me. My family had depended on me because I'd trained them that way.

"C'mon, Gram, let's go to bed." I helped her into the house and led her upstairs.

"It was a good day, wasn't it?" she asked, looking unsure but hopeful.

"It was a very good day, Gram. Sleep tight, and I'll see you in the morning."

Since I couldn't call anyone this late, I was left alone to ponder who had made the winning bid. It had to be someone who knew Gram or had a vested interest in the new center. The more I thought about it, the more baffled I became. Martha made it sound like it was someone I knew. For the life of me, I couldn't think of who. No one in my family had that much cash to spare.

Could Gus have sent someone to purchase it for him? Not very likely. Oh, well. Nancy would be in the shop sometime tomorrow. I'd just have to wait it out.

I poured myself a glass of wine, intending to settle my nerves and restlessness. Too late. I couldn't get the image of Peter and the svelte blonde clinging to his arm out of my mind. There wasn't enough wine in the bottle to kill that image.

20

"PLEASE, YOU HAVE TO SAVE ME." A WOMAN'S VOICE WHISPERED over the phone.

"Nancy?" My heart fell into my shoes. "What's wrong? I can barely hear you."

"My mother's here," she said, as if that explained everything. "Call me right back, and say you need me at the shop. *Now*."

"Okay, but you're gonna have to explain this one." I disconnected and punched in her number. She answered immediately, speaking in an unnaturally loud voice.

"Of course, I can. Mother will understand. Peter will be happy to entertain her and Tiffany today. I'll be right in."

"Well, that was weird," I said to Gram. "It sounds like Nancy wants to come into the shop early. I thought she was taking time off while I'm here for the weekend."

Fifteen minutes later, Nancy arrived, flustered and red-faced. "I had to escape." She looked like she'd spent the morning in a 5K race. "I owe you big time," she said, hanging her coat in the back. "My mother and Tiffany are staying at the house. My self-esteem is in shreds, and I feel like curling up in a ball in the closet. Peter can darn well deal with them today."

"Who's Tiffany, and when did your mother arrive?"

"Tiffany is Mother's godchild, and she came along on Mother's annual visit. The story is she's never been to the Midwest—

only flown over on trips between coasts. At least, that's the line Mother gave me. What I suspect is she's really here to get her claws into Peter. She's a little long in the tooth to still be single among her set, and Mother's been after Peter to relocate for years. A good way for Mother to get what she wants on both fronts."

"That's a bit cynical, don't you think?" Gram frowned in disbelief.

"You obviously haven't met them," Nancy said.

"Is Tiffany the blonde Peter escorted to the auction?"

"Yup. That was her all right," Nancy said, lacing her voice with disgust. "I called Peter, and he said he'd go over to the house and entertain them—after I bribed him by putting a breakfast casserole in the oven, of course. She's probably hanging all over him as we speak, with Mother smiling on benevolently."

A fire began burning in my belly, and I tried to put it out with logic. "Peter won't do anything he doesn't want to do."

"You have no idea how badly Peter has always wanted Mother's approval. He'd go to any lengths to please her when we were kids."

"Well, he's a big boy now and should know what he's doing." I had my own news to stew over and couldn't wait any longer. "Who was the big spender who bought the painting of Gram?"

"Didn't anyone tell you?" Nancy looked at me in shock. "It was Peter."

"*Peter?* Are you kidding me? Why would he do that?"

"I can think of several reasons, but the one he's giving officially is that he's going to donate the portrait to the new center when it's finished. In the meantime, it'll hang in the clinic. What better portrait to hang there than that of a long-time member of this community suffering with a similar problem?"

All kinds of emotions coursed through my body. Relief that Gram would get to enjoy the painting whenever she visited the clinic, pride that Peter had thought enough of the painting to buy it.

And then reality dropped like an anvil. Did this mean I was now beholden to Peter? The thought soured my gut, especially after hearing the news about the gorgeous Tiffany and him being romantically linked. I didn't know what to say. I bit my tongue to keep from making a snarky remark. It was a done deal, and I had to live with it.

The three of us worked together the rest of the morning, Gram and Nancy spending most of their time in the back planning a new project. Gram's decorated box had done so well in the auction she wanted to do another.

I was determined to be happy at how things had worked out. Just because Peter was the one who paid that exorbitant price for my painting didn't mean it wasn't worth it. Others must have helped bid it up that high. I'd helped raise more money for the new center than I'd ever thought possible, and I would be proud of it, damn it.

We'd just returned to the shop after lunch at the café—my treat to celebrate—when the door chime announced a customer. I hurried from the back room where I'd been hanging our jackets, still buoyed by all the congratulations and praise from the locals at the café.

I had to put Peter and his problems out of my mind for now and enjoy the accolades. Soon enough I'd be back in the city—all alone with my work and wondering what the hell I was doing with my life.

"So, this is the little shop where you spend your time." I picked up on the demeaning tone before I saw the woman but guessed who it was immediately. From way back in my memory that voice came to me, reminding me of the day my brothers took me to Peter's house. I didn't remember her looks, but I'd never forget the voice.

She stood with hands resting on ample hips encased in a beige tweed suit, its pink trim matching the square-heeled leather pumps and Coach purse. But it was the Margaret Thatcher hairdo and narrow nose that really caught my attention. It all rushed back to me then—the feeling of being unimportant—like a bug to be squished on the pavement. Oh, God, did Nancy have to put up with this all her life? No wonder she'd been so bitter in high school.

The woman turned to the blonde at her side. "Isn't this

quaint? So provincial, just like the rest of the town. Now you can understand why I had to leave or go mad."

Gram was standing behind Nancy, and I could see her face flushing. Uh-oh. I'd better get over there right quick. Since Gram had lost her social filter, I never knew what could pop out of her mouth.

"And you must be the poor woman with mental problems Nancy has to help," she continued, smiling with false benevolence at Gram. Nancy's face flushed, and her mouth hung open in shock. She clearly was at a loss for words.

"And you must be the b—" I reached Gram and put my arm around her shoulders, giving her a squeeze in warning. This was bad enough for Nancy. No use in our sinking to her mother's level.

"Hi, I'm Cara Olson." I interrupted her. "I believe we met, a very long time ago."

"Oh, yes. You're the artist sister to those boys Peter insisted on hanging out with during his childhood." She turned to the younger woman, who I assumed must be Tiffany. "No matter how I tried, I couldn't get him to go to a good boarding school. And his father was no help whatsoever."

"Where is Peter?" Nancy finally found her voice. "I thought he was spending the afternoon with you?" Desperation lent an edge to her voice.

"Can you believe he was called in on some emergency—on his day off yet!" Mrs. Andresen sniffed regally. "That sort of thing won't happen when he comes to his senses and moves near us. Much more civilized there where good doctors are in abundance."

"Who gave you the idea Peter is leaving?" Gram was in a feisty mode, and I didn't blame her.

"We never said we were leaving for sure, Mother. Only that we'd think about it," Nancy quietly interrupted.

"I know my son; he'll come to his senses. Not like some people." She sniffed again, looking down her narrow nose at Nancy. "He has a future—why waste it in this backwater town? There's nothing to hold him here." She turned to Tiffany. "You saw his house." She shuddered delicately. "All white walls and open windows—and the lack of furnishings is telling."

Tiffany nodded.

"You don't understand, Mother. People here love him. We have good friends who care about us here," Nancy said.

"I'm sure you do, dear, but they'll love a new doctor just as much." She dismissed Nancy with a flick of her wrist and turned to me.

"Now, I'm sure your friend here—Cara is it?—will understand. Peter tells me you live and work in Chicago." Turning back to Nancy, she continued. "See—she was smart enough to leave, just as I told Peter she would. What could possibly hold an ambitious woman here?"

She put her hand on my arm. "I'm sorry. You'll have to find someone else to run the shop and care for this woman." Flicking a glance at Gram, she went on. "I want my children to come back with me. I'm getting on in years—it's time I see them suitably married with children."

"Mother, please."

I admit it. For the first time in my life, I could actually say I was speechless. I looked first at Nancy, who appeared on the verge of tears, and then at Gram who looked as shocked as I felt.

"You're leaving?" I asked her. Like Nancy, it took me a moment to regain my voice.

"I'd planned to talk to you about it later. Nothing is decided." She looked angrily at her mother. "No matter what she says."

"Why don't we leave now? I'd like to see more of the town." Tiffany must have had more behind that vacuous expression than I'd given her credit for. She herded Mrs. Andresen out the door, leaving the three of us behind, shell-shocked. "Pleased to have met you," Tiffany said before closing the door.

"I'm going to move back here as soon as I can," I said without hesitation and meant it. Nancy and Gram both looked at me in surprise.

"I'm so sorry," Nancy said, her face a picture of regret. "I didn't want to spoil your weekend, not when you've had such tremendous success. And I know how hard you've worked for it."

"So, you really are leaving?"

"I don't know what to do, Cara." She closed her eyes momentarily. "She's guilting me into it. As you can see, she's good at it. I'd planned to stay until we find someone else to run the shop and stay with Lucy. Maybe one of the boys—or their wives?"

"Nancy, it's not your problem. My family will work it out."

Gram walked to the back room and sat at the table, her head in her hands. "It's all my fault. If it weren't for this addled brain of mine, none of you would be having this problem. I feel so old—so helpless. I hate it."

"Hey, none of that now. We'll find a solution." I put a hand on her shoulder, the only way I knew to comfort her these days.

"How? Even Peter is leaving me. I don't want any other doctor. They'll put me in a home."

"Gram, stop it right now. I'll be here for you always. Just like you were always there for me." I looked helplessly to Nancy who had paled with misery.

"What has Peter decided?" I asked.

"I don't know. From what I gathered, he said he'd consider it. Mother wants him to go back with her for a few weeks and check things out."

"How serious do you think he is?" I couldn't control my curiosity.

"I have a bad feeling that getting the new center built will be his last hurrah. It would be kind of a legacy for him to leave behind when he leaves town," she said, her voice rich with regret.

"He told me he planned on staying here forever." *How dare he.* After all he'd said about not having room in his life for both a career and marriage. Had all that changed since the lovely Tiffany appeared on the scene? I had visions of wrapping my hands around his throat.

Nancy shrugged. "I'm just not sure any more about Peter."

AFTER GRAM and I got home that evening, I left her to feed her animals and prepare dinner, promising I wouldn't be gone long. I had to catch Peter and find out exactly what his plans were.

Nancy had left soon after her mother, and I didn't expect her back that evening, so I knew I only had a short window to leave Gram alone.

Remembering the look of Gram with her head in her hands in despair when she heard Peter was leaving drove me on. It was a picture that would live forever in my memory.

I got into the car and backed out of the driveway. Gravel flew under the tires as I squealed onto the county highway. Common sense finally prevailed, and I put my foot gently on the brakes. Either I slowed down or got killed myself before I had the chance to do Peter in.

I spotted his little sports car in the parking lot at the café and squeezed in next to it, so close that the only thing separating the driver's side of his car and my car was the new coat of paint I'd put on the Ford last month after receiving another check from Gus. Peter wasn't escaping until I finished with him.

The café door slammed behind me as I stalked over to his favorite booth. A hush fell over the room, and I could almost see the ears expanding and stretching in our direction.

"I need to talk to you," I said in a serious tone.

He was alone in the booth having dinner. He set his corned beef sandwich back on his plate, right next to the big dill pickle I remembered he favored.

"Hello to you, too," he said in greeting.

"Don't even try to be friendly, buster."

"You're upset?" He raised his eyebrows in surprise. "Is it about the painting?"

"Oh, you would bring that up now, wouldn't you?"

"Okaaay. What has you in a tear this time?" A frown crossed his handsome face.

I sat down across from him. "I heard you're planning on leaving the area for good."

"Quiet down, will you?" He looked around the room, staring back at the faces watching us.

"Mother." With closed eyes, he asked, "I take it she showed up at Lucy's?" At my nod, he gave a soft expletive. "That information isn't for general knowledge. I haven't made any definite plans."

"How could you even think about leaving—after what you told me about your life being here in Shoreview?"

"So I changed my mind, Cara. Women aren't the only ones with that right. I don't know why you're so shocked. It didn't take you long to decide to leave. As soon as the old boyfriend crooked his finger, you were out the door like a bat outta hell."

"What? My leaving had nothing to do with Steve."

"Oh, come on. You left just a few days after he visited."

"It wasn't because of him; it was because of Gus."

"Oh, I see. So now you've got two of them on a string?" He pushed his hand through the lock of hair falling over his forehead.

"No, you idiot. Gus is the art dealer who gave me a one-woman show in his art gallery. That's why I went back. Besides, you told me that if I didn't leave, you would—because of all the gossip."

He threw a twenty on the table, got up, and pulled me toward the door.

"Let's get out of here."

"Hey, slow down." I tried to smile at the gaping faces following us, but it was difficult when Peter had me in a tight grip. "Where the hell do you think you're taking me?"

"To my place."

"Not a good idea." Was he crazy? Or had he already forgotten what happened the last time I'd visited his man cave?

"It's a damn good idea." When we reached the parking lot, he stopped next to my car. "Give me your keys."

A part of me wanted to refuse, but the look in his eyes didn't bode well for a quiet discussion in the parking lot. I had never seen Peter this angry and had a vision of customers coming out to form a ring around us for the show. He moved my car and opened the door of his little sports car. "Get in."

"Listen, you're not my brother. You don't get to boss me around."

"You're damn right I'm not your brother. Just get in."

After I was in and buckled, he tossed my keys over. "I'll drive you back here after we talk privately."

"Well, it better be a short discussion because I left Gram home alone."

"I'm sure she'll be all right for an hour."

We barely got inside his house when the door slammed behind him and he slipped his hand behind my neck, tipping my face up to meet his. His touch was so potent that I felt my knees give out.

Whatever he saw in my eyes gave him the answer he sought because the next thing I knew, our lips were locked in a passionate kiss. All the anger between us melted into an insatiable need, and we clung to each other like long-lost lovers. I could feel our hearts beating in unison, a familiarity between them that had nothing to do with our reality.

He finally lifted his head, resting his forehead against mine. "Squirt, what the hell am I supposed to do about this? I tell myself we're no good for each other, but my body has its own opinion."

"Don't call me that."

"I have to—don't you get it? Otherwise, you're not Jack's little sister but a very desirable woman."

"Peter, is that you?" His mother's voice rang out from the kitchen, and I heard footsteps. She gasped when she saw us together.

"Mother, what are you doing here? Where's Nancy?"

"Ah, right here." Nancy slinked sheepishly out from behind her mother. "Mother wanted to wait here to talk to you."

His mother turned a steely-eyed look from me to Peter. "What is *she* doing here?"

"That's none of your business, Mother. What did you want to talk about?" he asked in a stern voice.

"Well, darling, I want to know when you'll be ready to leave."

"I told you I haven't made a decision about leaving."

"Oh, but you have to come with me. Can't you see how much I miss you?"

"Why should you miss us now?" Nancy asked in her old belligerent tone. "You're the one who left us when we needed you most."

"You don't understand. *How could you*? I didn't want to say this, but it's because of the two of you that my life was ruined. Do you think I would ever have married a man like your father and moved to this backwater place if I hadn't been pregnant?" She waved her hand at Peter. "Your father took advantage of me when I was young and stupid, fighting against everything my parents stood for. I've regretted it every day of my life since. I gave up my youth for the two of you."

Her face crumpled, and I was afraid she'd actually manage to shed a few tears. I held my breath in horror, looking from her to Peter. All the color had left his face.

"For God's sakes, Mother, it was the eighties. You didn't have to get married if you weren't in love." Nancy's face flushed with anger and resentment. "It wasn't as if you were some poor girl without any family to support you."

"Hush, girl, you don't know what you're talking about. You never knew my family. In their eyes, I had shamed them, and they didn't want any part of my low-class children or me. They'd had great plans for their only child, and I'd let them down. I was as good as dead to my parents."

"I'm sure you understand," she directed at me. "You're a woman who knows there's more to life than what this little town can offer. All I ever wanted was for my children to have the life I so stupidly threw aside. I knew they'd never find it here."

I stared at her in dismay, speechless for the second time in my life, all because of this woman.

Finally, Peter spoke in a voice devoid of its usual warmth and humor. "My father was a good man who worked himself into an early grave trying to please you." He continued in that same cold, deadly voice. "Thank you for finally helping me understand that." He walked out of the house, leaving us to stare at the closed door.

"C'mon, I'll give you a ride home." Nancy propelled me out to her car.

"What about your mother and Tiffany?"

"I'll come back to get them after I cool off."

We were silent on our way to the café, neither of us able to find the words to explain away what had just happened. I got out and unlocked my car. Before she drove away, Nancy shouted through her lowered window, "Don't worry about Lucy. I'm not leaving town. Not now, not ever."

I watched her car speed away, my heart bleeding for her and Peter. Where had he gone? Who would console him? After the passion he had just shown me, I wanted desperately to be that person.

NANCY CAME into the shop the next morning, surprising both Gram and me. It was Sunday, so we'd opened later as we usually did on that day, giving everyone the chance for church services and a leisurely breakfast.

"Hi," I said softly, feeling totally inadequate. I didn't know what to say to her. *I'm sorry your mother is such a selfish bitch* didn't sound right, even if it was true. If there was a way to make yesterday go away like a bad memory, I didn't know it. The pain and horror I'd seen on her face, echoed by Peter's expression, had haunted my dreams all night. I would never forget it or forgive the woman for her total selfishness.

Peter and I had been on the verge of an important discovery in our relationship before she had interfered. Would our feelings for each other ever be resolved now? I needed to see him and make things right.

Gram clasped Nancy in a fierce bear hug, letting her know our feelings immediately. Yesterday's scene totally trivialized my family problems. I, at least, knew my family loved me, as annoying as they were at times.

"I wish I could make up for my mother's behavior yesterday, but I don't know where to begin," Nancy said softly, her eyes moist with unshed tears.

"It's not necessary," I said. "The important thing is, are you okay?"

"Oh, yeah. I suppose I could say I'm used to it, but I don't think that'll ever happen. She still catches me by surprise, and this one was a whopper. Tiffany got a little shook up though." She gave a watery smile. "I think she left here realizing she'd dodged a bullet when she found out what Mother would be like as a mother-in-law."

"How is Peter?" I had to ask. The coldness in his voice and expression still haunted me.

"I don't know. I haven't seen him since he left the house yesterday. He won't pick up the phone or answer any of my texts. He doesn't even know Mother and Tiffany are planning to leave soon."

"They're going back East then?" Gram asked.

"I certainly hope so."

"Time heals all wounds," Gram murmured and directed Nancy to the back room. "Let's have a cup of coffee." That was Gram's answer to most of life's problems, but I knew this time it would take more than coffee and a cookie to fix things.

"That was a lot to throw at Peter, especially in front of you," Nancy said when we sat at the table. Pain still glimmered fresh in her eyes. "He must be so ashamed of her behavior and what she blurted out." Heaving a heavy sigh, her words followed softly. "We didn't know she felt that way, you see."

"What we think doesn't matter one whit. It's the two of you who matter." Gram poured us each a cup of her potent brew. She was right; we'd need it to get through the day.

"I think of you two more as family than she ever was," Nancy said.

"Oh, Nancy, no. She loves you in her own way," Gram said. "Cut her some slack. It sounds as though her family never showed her any love or compassion. Empathy is taught, you know." Only Gram could find forgiveness so soon after yesterday's verbal attack.

"Someday I may be able to understand and forgive her, I hope. She *is* the only mother I'll ever have. I don't know about Peter though. I've never seen him like that before." Nancy raised her eyes from the coffee mug as she took a sip.

"As I said, time will help." Gram put a comforting hand on Nancy's shoulder.

"I hope you'll still keep me on here. I told Mother I wouldn't be leaving, and I really would like to go back to our old arrangement, if that's possible."

"Of course, it is," Gram answered. "I can tell Cara's dying to get back to her work."

"You know it," I said with as much enthusiasm as I could muster.

The truth was, leaving everyone I loved behind again would just about kill me. Seeing Peter became even more crucial. I had to find a way to let him know I would be emotionally available whenever he needed me. He'd looked so devastated when he left. How would he ever recover from that emotional assault alone?

I tried calling him several times, but he wouldn't answer my calls. I called the clinic even though I knew it was closed, but all I got was a recording, asking if it was an emergency. I didn't bother leaving my number. What was the point? He'd recognize it anyway. There was nothing for me to do but pack up and leave.

21

DURING THE NEXT FEW WEEKS, I THREW MYSELF INTO MY WORK, once again trying to recapture enthusiasm for my projects. My love of painting had saved me after my last disaster, and it would again. Quitting was not an option. I owed this to myself and to Gram. And now to Gus, who'd stuck his neck out for me with nothing to go on but confidence in my work and my commitment to succeed.

Nancy reported on one of my frequent calls home that her mother and Tiffany had left. When I inquired about Peter, her answers were vague. "He's changed," was the only reply I got to my questions.

"In what way?" I asked. "Is he okay?"

"I don't know how to explain it, Cara. You'll notice the next time you see him."

Since I had no idea when that would be, I tried to put it out of my mind. *Oh, yeah, like that was gonna work.*

He had his work, and that was all he needed. Hadn't he told me so repeatedly? But that kiss in his house still lingered in my mind.

Steve and I had formed an understanding of sorts. He didn't critique my work, and I certainly would never even dream of commenting on his, except to admire his use of color. I paid my rent, and he accepted it reluctantly. He never mentioned sharing meals again. I worked on doggedly, trying to finish as much work as possible.

The weather turned cool, and I caught a cold. I figured it was mainly due to lack of sleep. Going to bed early didn't help; I simply tossed and turned even longer. So, I spent most of the day and night at the studio, working halfheartedly on several new paintings. I couldn't shake my melancholy mood even using my full arsenal of positive self-talk. Was this depression going to be my new reality? Watching the blustery clouds of November rolling in from the lake only darkened my mood further.

Gus came into the studio one Saturday morning to see what I was working on. My throat ached, and I knew my nose was as red as a cherry Popsicle. I'd tried covering it with makeup but had long since wiped it off with all the blowing. A pile of used tissues littered the floor around me. I didn't even have the energy to scrounge up a wastepaper basket.

"What's the matter with you? You look awful," Gus said.

"Just a cold." I croaked out the words. He looked at the canvases I'd stacked along the wall with a critical eye.

"Maybe you've been working too hard. Why don't you go home and get some rest?"

"No, I'd rather stay here and work."

"Cara, I'm going to be honest with you. These paintings are not up to your usual standards. It's obvious you need to get well before you can produce anything of value. You're pushing yourself too hard."

Was he right? I looked at the canvases again. Of course, he was. But I didn't want to return to that dingy apartment and the never-ending silence. If I did, I'd only lie in bed and think about the mess I'd made of my life. *What was wrong with me?* I asked myself for the thousandth time. I should be the happiest woman in the world. My dreams of success were coming true at last, Gram was being well taken care of, and all I could dwell on was what I had to give up to make it happen.

"You'd better see a doctor. I think you've got more than a cold," Gus insisted.

"No, I'll be fine. I'll make a cup of herbal tea and swallow a couple of aspirin, and I'll be good to go by morning. Don't make such a big deal out of it."

He didn't look convinced, so I smiled reassuringly. "I'll even go home early, just to make you feel better."

I DIDN'T FEEL any better the next day. If possible, I felt even worse and literally dragged myself into the studio. Gus called not too long after I'd arrived.

"Stefan said you don't look any better today. It's Sunday. Why don't you take the day off?" Gus said.

"I'm going to leave soon," I rasped.

"Is there anyone I can call for you? I think you need looking after."

"I'll be fine, stop worrying." I found some strength and pushed on.

An hour later, I had to set my brush down and grab onto the easel for support, overcome with an unfamiliar weakness and lightheadedness. Attempting to drive in traffic the way I felt was not an option.

"Steve, is it all right if I crash in your room for a bit?"

"Go ahead." He barely turned his head from the canvas he worked on. I stumbled to his room and flopped onto the mattress, too weak to even pull back the covers.

I must've fallen asleep because I awoke to someone pounding on the studio door. *Make them go away*, I prayed. Why wasn't Steve answering? My body felt on fire, and my head ached. The raised voices now coming from the studio didn't help.

"Go away, she doesn't want to see you. She's not feeling well as it is," Steve said.

"Step aside or I'll rearrange your pretty face." The surly voice had a familiar ring to it.

Peter?

No, he was in Shoreview where he belonged. Now I was having hallucinations. Heavy footsteps on the hardwood floor stomped closer, each one resounding painfully in my pounding head.

"Cara, are you in there? Open the door." This was accompanied by a heavy knock.

"Go away," I managed to croak. My mind was playing tricks on me. I'd swear it was Peter's voice.

"If you don't open up, I'll break down the door," he threatened.

"Just leave me alone. I don't feel well." My voice came out in a raspy whisper.

Whoever it was pounding didn't hear me or ignored my pleas because the pounding only got louder.

"Hold on." I managed to lift my head and looked at the bedside clock. It was five o'clock. I must've slept the day away. I'd barely turned the knob of the bedroom door when it flew open, and Peter pushed his way into the room.

If I hadn't felt so weak, I suppose I would've been shocked. But at the moment, everything was so fuzzy in my head, it took a minute to remember where I was.

"What are you doing here?" I rasped.

"Your friend Gus called the shop, said you were sick, and needed help. Nancy called me."

"And you drove all the way down here because I have a cold? Are you nuts?" Relief at seeing him turned to frustration.

"You look like hell. I doubt you just have a cold." He put his hand on my forehead. "You're burning up. What did your doctor say?"

"I don't have a doctor. I don't have health insurance, and they cost money."

"Well, did you go to the ER then?" Peter's tone was all concern.

"Oh, yeah, that's what I felt like doing, sitting for hours in a room crowded with really sick people so I could spread my germs around. Besides, the last time I went, it cost hundreds of dollars for them to tell me I had a bladder infection. Which is why I went there in the first place, to get an antibiotic for a bladder infection." I was babbling but couldn't seem to stop.

He lifted his black medical bag off the floor. I recognized it from his visits to Gram's. After pulling out his stethoscope, he pushed me back onto the bed. "Take deep breaths," he ordered, placing the instrument on my chest and then on my back. "Again," he said.

"It hurts to breath deep," I whined.

"That's because your lungs are congested. I wouldn't be surprised if you had pneumonia." He helped me up. "Get your things together. You're coming home with me."

"I can't do that. I have work to do."

"It'll keep. Right now, you need to get well," he said in a firm tone.

"Where are you taking her?" Steve demanded from the doorway.

"Where someone can look after her. She's ill."

He hustled me out of the studio and into his car. I directed him to my apartment, and he helped me up the steps. "Pack some things. I'm getting you home as soon as possible."

I was feeling too weak to argue and truth be told, the thought of being in my own bed at Gram's sounded heavenly.

"What did you have for lunch?" he asked.

"I didn't. I slept through it."

It sounded like curse words he muttered, but I really didn't care. I could hear him moving around in the tiny kitchen while I tried to wash my face and comb my hair. One look in the mirror had scared the heck out of even me. When I came back into the kitchen, he set a bowl of steaming chicken noodle soup on the table. One of the few staples in my limited pantry.

"Eat this soup before we leave. You're looking dehydrated on top of everything else. Do you have any bottled water?"

"In the fridge."

"Put a couple of bottles in your purse."

"Are you always this bossy with sick people?" I asked, trying to concentrate.

"Only when they're too stupid to take care of themselves."

"Listen, I appreciate your coming here and everything, but can't you just give me a prescription for an antibiotic and be on your way? There are sick people in Shoreview who really need you."

What little sense I could muster told me it would be too easy to fall into the trap of needing him and what would that get me? I'd wanted to help him in his time of need, but he'd brushed me aside like yesterday's news. Now, when I was too weak to resist, he came riding in like a knight on a white steed, or in this case, a do-gooder in a sports car. Was I supposed to fall all over him in gratitude? Not going to happen.

"I don't have time to play games." He grabbed the blanket I'd thrown on the couch. "Lucy is very worried, and it's not good for her."

He knew my weak spot better than I did.

Before I knew it, I was bundled up in a blanket and sitting in his car, speeding down the Illinois toll road toward Wisconsin, too weak to protest.

I slept fitfully most of the way to Shoreview, just waking as we pulled into the parking lot of the twenty-four-hour clinic. Why had Peter stopped here? I thought we were going to Gram's.

After weeks of hanging over my head, the dark cloud I'd been fighting opened into a torrent of emotion. I wanted to cry my heart out, but it would have to wait until I was alone again. How had I let myself get into another mess? I was a self-sufficient woman who'd always taken care of others, not the other way around. I needed to take control.

I opened the car door and stepped out before Peter got to my side. My legs gave way, and I grabbed for the door handle. Peter was there immediately and swooped me up in his arms like a rag doll, blanket and all, and carried me into the clinic.

"We need a wheelchair," he shouted out, and a nurse appeared instantaneously. "I'm taking her to X-ray," he said. "Order a chest x-ray, stat."

"Yes, Doctor." The nurse flew out ahead of us.

"For God's sake, what is this, an episode of *ER*? Are you going to find some weird substance in my lungs? Gold dust maybe? Oh, I hope it's gold dust—I could use the cash."

"Your temperature must be going up again," he said with a frown. "Do you have any allergies?"

"Just to bossy men," I croaked.

He muttered something under his breath before asking, "To any medications?"

"No."

"Okay. After the x-ray, I'm going to order some lab work and fluids with medication, depending on the outcome of the tests."

"Great," I muttered, too weak to protest any louder.

Several hours later, I was back in Peter's car, feeling exhausted but not quite as weak. His diagnosis was correct. I had pneumonia.

"Is there a chance that Gram will catch my bug?"

"I'm taking you to my house for a few days to recover. I need to keep an eye on you."

"No, absolutely not." I shuddered at the thought of those stark white walls. "I want to be in my own room, at Gram's."

"She can't take care of you, Cara."

"You forget, Nancy's there. She'll help out, I'm sure. Besides, after a few days of antibiotics, I'll be just fine."

"This isn't a simple cold we're dealing with here. If you don't take proper care of yourself, you'll be in deeper trouble."

Even feeling the way I did, just being near him brought out all those longings I'd repressed for weeks. It would be hell to be so close and yet so far away emotionally. As far as I was concerned, I was already in deep trouble.

"No, I insist. I'm going to Gram's. I can recuperate there. Besides, you'll be busy with other patients most of the day. Gram or Nancy will be around all the time."

"Alright, it's your decision. You're going to do what you want no matter what I say, as usual." His face tightened in disapproval.

I kept my thoughts to myself for the rest of the drive.

It was the middle of the night when we pulled up to the old farmhouse. Peter had called before we left the clinic. Nancy and Gram stood on the porch in their pajamas, looking anxious.

"How are you?" Gram clasped me to her breast, and I could

see tears in her pale blue eyes. I felt awful. She'd been worried about me when I was supposed to be caring for her at this stage of her life.

"I'm feeling better already, just being here." Laying my palm against her cheek, I gave her the strongest smile I could muster.

"Well, you don't look it," she said.

Nancy put her arm around my shoulders and guided me toward the stairs. "C'mon, let's get you to bed. We have everything ready and waiting."

"I don't have to go right to bed..."

"Yes, you do. And if you give these ladies any grief, you're going to the hospital," Peter said. The threat in his voice finally got to me.

"Don't worry, Peter. We'll make sure she follows orders."

And they did.

"Drink this before you go to sleep. Peter said you've been dehydrated."

I was propped up in my own bed, drinking broth with the two of them fussing about like mother hens before I had a chance to protest.

THE NEXT DAY WAS A MONDAY, so Gram and Nancy were able to stay home from the shop. I slept soundly for the first time in weeks and barely woke for meals that day.

On Tuesday morning, Nancy came into my room.

"I'm leaving for the shop now. Lucy is going to stay here with you. Is that all right?" she asked, a small frown puckering her brow.

"We'll be just fine, stop worrying," I said.

The words were barely out of my mouth when the doorbell rang. Nancy looked at me in surprise.

"Could that be Peter? Usually, he's at the hospital making his rounds at this time of day," she said.

We heard Gram's voice, followed by light footsteps on the stairs.

"What's this I hear about you working yourself to a frazzle, woman?" Martha stood in the doorway, carrying a pile of magazines, books, and her knitting bag.

I should have known the story of my homecoming would've spread by now and been prepared for visitors.

"I'm here to keep you company and help Lucy keep you in bed. We'll use rope if we have to. Doctor's orders," Martha said.

And so it went for the rest of the week. Every morning, one of the Wool Gatherers showed up at the door just as Nancy left for the shop. They brought soup, casseroles, books, and lots of conversation.

Cheryl pulled a gorgeous felt vest from her bag the morning she came to sit with me. I looked at it with envy.

"It's beautiful," I said, running my hand over the soft violet fabric.

"Thank you. It's a gift for my sister. The color matches her eyes. I only have to sew on these handmade buttons I found in a little shop in Fish Creek and it's finished."

"I'm sure she'll love it."

"Do you think you'll ever get back into felt making?" she asked.

"I'd like to, but it'd be impossible where I'm living now. No raw material at hand and not the space I'd need."

"Maybe you'll decide to move back here someday?" Cheryl asked.

"Who knows? Maybe." I couldn't admit it was my dream.

So ONCE AGAIN, Peter was right. I had to admit it. Walking from the bedroom to the kitchen had drained all my strength for several days. But as soon as my lungs cleared up and my breathing returned to normal, my strength returned. By the second week, I was feeling like myself and ready to return to Chicago.

Peter had been to visit several times to check on my progress but remained professional and distant. I waited for him on

Saturday morning, expecting a clean bill of health so I could get ready to leave. Gram and Nancy were at the shop when he arrived with his familiar black bag.

"Everything looks good. Your lungs are clear," he said.

"Listen, I need to thank you for all your help. You went way beyond the duties of family physician, and I appreciate it."

"No problem. So, does this mean you're off to Chicago?"

"Yes. I thought I'd fly out tomorrow. Gus promised to pick me up at O'Hare."

An awkward silence followed. During all this time together, he'd treated me with a strict doctor/patient relationship. We'd never discussed that scene with his mother, and it sat like the proverbial elephant in the room whenever we were alone. I couldn't take it any longer.

"Peter—"

"Cara—"

"You first," I said.

"We haven't really talked personally since that day at my home, and I'd like to straighten things out, if that's possible. You've probably figured out by now that I've decided against leaving."

"Yes, Nancy said you'd changed your mind."

"I'm sorry you had to witness our family's dirty laundry being aired that day. I don't know what to say about my mother's behavior." He looked off into the distance as he talked, his face stiff and cold. Was this what Nancy meant when she said he'd changed?

"Peter, it wasn't your fault—none of it was," I said softly. "Your mother is who she is, and you can't change her. You have to let the past go and look toward the future."

"Really? What future is that?" His bleak expression was so different from the man I thought I knew that I caught my breath in alarm.

"Peter, please..." I reached out to touch him, but he walked away.

"Have a safe trip," he called over his shoulder from the doorway. "And don't overwork yourself like that again."

So, that was it? There'd be no discussion about the mistakes of the past or a possible future for the two of us? That door closed again. I'd have to put aside my stupid daydreams and just accept it.

22

NOTHING HAD CHANGED WHEN I GOT BACK TO THE STUDIO. AT least on the surface. My work was exactly where I had left it. I picked up the canvases and looked at them in disgust. Boy, when Gus was right, he was really right. I'd gone back to my old habit of putting paint on canvas without any feeling for the subject matter. The last time it had taken a move to Shoreview to get me going in the right direction. What would save me now?

Steve came into the studio several hours later, a lighthearted bounce to his step I hadn't seen for ages.

"Hey, welcome back." He walked over and gave me a hug. I had to hold back from cringing. "There's someone I want you to meet. I'm mentoring a new grad—she'll be right up."

The studio door opened, and a young woman stepped through, her auburn curls bouncing and her pixie face lit with excitement. I could've cried at the eager and worshipful look she gave Steve. Oh, God, it was like looking in the mirror five years ago.

"Cara, meet Marcie. Marcie will be working here with us."

After the intros, the three of us discussed Marcie's art and what she hoped to learn by working in the studio with Steve. She was quite vocal about her plans for the future, and I caught a mesmerized look on Steve's face. What was he thinking?

As the days wore on, I realized Marcie was much more dedi-

cated to her art than I had been at the beginning. It became
obvious that Steve was just a means to an end for her. All his
hints about missing dinner or the mess in the studio, et cetera,
fell on deaf ears. I assumed it was because she came from the
same type of background. There'd be no job at a coffee shop for
her. She was here to learn all she could about art and determined
to succeed. I'd been wrong in my first assessment. In other words,
she wasn't the naïve country girl with stars in her eyes that I'd
been.

Their relationship couldn't have been more different from the
one Steve and I had shared during those first years. While I had
been all wrapped up in hero worship and blind to his inflated
ego, Marcie never even noticed his subtle hints for help with
everyday living. I realized then he'd found his alter ego.

"I'm starving," Steve moaned one evening. "I could go for a
pizza right about now."

"Me, too," Marcie answered, staring critically at the canvas
propped on the easel in front of her. "Make sure my half has
pepperoni, will you?"

Steve turned to me, his surprised look turning to pleading.
"What about you, Cara? Do you want to get a pizza?"

"No, thank you. I'm leaving soon." I bent down to get a clean
brush, trying to hide my grin. Oh, yeah, this would be fun to
watch.

But even the antics of Steve and Marcie couldn't heal the emptiness in my soul. After another week of watching them, so
engrossed in their work, I knew I'd never be like them—going
without sleep, skipping meals, all to finish their latest project.

I loved my art, always would, but staying in Chicago no longer
took precedence in my life. I could have my success in Shoreview
just as well. To hell with what Peter wanted.

The sun shone through the large windows on this beautiful
day, and I took it as a sign that this was my opportunity to have
the complete dream. Taking care of Gram was part of it.

My family and Gram would always come first, and I recognized I didn't have to apologize to anyone for those feelings. Just accepting them gave me a freedom I hadn't had before. I set down my brush and turned around to face Steve and Marcie.

"I'm going home," I said to no one in particular. Marcie and Steve never lifted their heads, so engrossed in their work that I could've said my hair was on fire and they wouldn't have paid the slightest attention. Well, Steve might have directed me to the fire extinguisher in the corner.

This time, I packed everything into the Ford before calling Gus.

"I'm going home." I almost sang the words. "And I'm not coming back to stay."

"You sound very happy, so I'll assume nothing happened to your grandmother?" Gus asked.

"No, I just realized that's where I belong."

"If it's any consolation, I think you're making the right choice. That's where your heart is and where you'll find your art. I was wrong to assume you'd work better here."

"Thanks, Gus."

"Call me when you have some work ready for the gallery— and I know you will." He hesitated. "By the way, is that friend of yours, Nancy I think was her name, single?"

"She is." My matchmaking antennae shot up. What was this? I couldn't help but smile. I thought I'd noticed sparks between Nancy and Gus when they'd first met.

I HAD a smile on my face all the way from Chicago to Shoreview, singing loudly along with the radio. Some of my dreams really were coming true after all. The sun was just beginning to set as I pulled into Gram's driveway.

She was standing in the doorway, watching for me. I'd called her just before I left, not wanting to give her too big of a surprise when I arrived with all of my belongings

"Did you come home because of me?" were Gram's first words when I walked in the door.

"No, Gram, I came home because of me." My heart was still singing. "And I'm staying, no matter what you say."

"Well then, I'm very happy." She gripped my hands and squeezed. "It's good to have you home, girl."

We hugged, both of us smiling broadly through our happy tears.

"Come into the kitchen. Dinner's ready."

THE WOOL GATHERERS meeting was especially festive that week. Everyone seemed to take special care with their food, making it almost a gourmet feast. I was welcomed back so warmly that I was on the verge of tears most of the night.

"We're going to have so much fun this winter," Carol said. "I can hardly wait to see what projects you come up with for the shop."

"It'll be good to see the place decorated again," Gram agreed.

It had been a long time since I'd spent the Christmas season in Shoreview. I'd always come for a few days, of course. Whenever I could get off work. But being able to spend the entire season here would be wonderful. Especially spending these busy days with Gram. The specter of her illness hung heavy over my head some days, and I didn't want to miss a moment of being with her while she was still aware of my presence.

The three of us fell into a routine in the days that followed. Gram and Nancy went off to work in the shop early mornings, and I stayed home—my most productive time for painting.

In the afternoon after preparing dinner, I went into the shop, giving Nancy a break so she could enjoy a life of her own, even though she was quick to explain she really didn't have one. I never mentioned Gus, just smiled to myself. I had a feeling...

I'd been home more than a week and still hadn't seen or heard from Peter. It wasn't much of a stretch to figure out he was avoiding me. Every time the shop bell chimed, I felt a little flutter, expecting it to be him and then that familiar depression when it turned out to be a customer. I told myself to face facts. There wouldn't be any grand re-awakening of his feelings for me.

It was on Saturday afternoon that he showed up at Gram's, just as I was getting dinner together before leaving for the shop.

"I just heard you were home," he said as I opened the door. "You're not sick again, are you?"

"I've been here over a week. Don't tell me Nancy or the local grapevine hasn't spread the news?" He followed me into the kitchen.

"I haven't seen much of Nancy lately. The last time we spoke, she called me a stupid ass." He looked sheepish. "Turns out she was right. And as for the local grapevine, I've been keeping pretty much to myself lately."

That sentence spoke volumes.

"How long are you staying?" he asked, not quite meeting my glance.

"Well, let's see." I mentally calculated my age and the normal life expectancy of a woman nowadays. "I'd say about fifty-five years, give or take a few." That caught him by surprise, judging from his puzzled look.

"Is it because of Lucy? Her condition really hasn't changed much and may not for some time."

"No. As I told Gram, I came back because it was what I wanted."

Peter folded his arms across his chest and looked away before asking, "What about your work—and Gus?"

"I learned something about myself this past year. My work is here, with my family and friends," I said, daring him to disagree.

He was quiet for a moment and then turned back to me.

"I've learned something myself these past weeks," he confessed. "I'm not the person I thought I was."

Our eyes met, and I saw a gleam in his that had been missing for a long time. Ever since that last fateful night at his home, actually.

"In what way?" I whispered, hopeful and apprehensive at the same time.

He reached for my hands and pulled me toward him.

"I've been so dense," he said, shaking his head. "How do I explain?" His hands were cold, but his look determined. "I've been screwed up all my life and am just now realizing it. It took that scene with my mother and a lot of soul searching to get things straight in my head. I figured by that time, I'd lost you forever." He squeezed my hands, looking for understanding before continuing.

"All my life, I thought I'd done something to cause my mother's coldness toward me. I didn't grasp that my just being born was the cause. It was easy to blame my father for always working, but now I understand why he worked constantly."

His dark blue eyes bored into mine with an intensity that made every cell in my body stop and listen.

"There wasn't anything my father or I could've done to change things. My father being a workaholic had nothing to do with mother's unhappiness. It was all about her family and status and small-town living. Yet, I've spent my life fighting these demons of self-doubt and unworthiness because of her mistake."

"Why didn't you ever confide these feelings to anyone...to me?" I asked.

He looked at me with haunted eyes and dropped my hands. "You wouldn't have understood, how could you?"

I couldn't think of another sentence quite as painful to me. I would've given anything to be the person he turned to for love and understanding.

"It was as if your family existed in a different universe from mine." Putting his hands in his pockets, he rocked back on his heels. "It's hard to explain the logic behind my actions. I'm just beginning to understand myself."

"Try me." I knew his next words would be important. Something about the real Peter that I needed to know.

"I thought when I came back here, things would be the same, only better, because I had made it in medicine and could be a contributing member of the town. But it didn't take me long to realize it wasn't just Shoreview I'd been longing for. As much as I love it here, it hasn't brought me the fulfillment I expected. When you blew into town and then left again, I knew what I'd been missing. It was you, Cara. That's what's been missing in my life."

My breath caught in my throat, and I stared at him, not

moving a muscle. He lifted a hand to my cheek, caressing it softly and looked searchingly into my eyes. That broke the spell, and I reached up and covered his strong hand with my own, hoping he'd know my feelings by that gesture.

I both heard and felt his intake of breath. "I also know how dedicated you are to your work, and I don't even know what kind of a husband and father I'd make—but will you give me a chance? Give us a chance?"

"Do you really need to ask after the way I practically threw myself at you that night at your house?"

"Cara, can you promise you'll stay with me forever? The thought of a life without you has become unbearable."

I'd never seen him look so vulnerable, and my heart melted at the thought it could be because of his love for me. Our lips met in a searing kiss. A kiss I wanted to last forever. "Just try to get rid of me now."

His eyes lit with humor and a desire that I knew reflected in my own. "Do you remember the picture sitting on my dresser? The one taken the day we went fishing with your brothers?"

"Of course. I looked so ridiculous in my brother's old jeans. I can't believe you saved it."

"I think I fell in love with you that day."

"Funny you should say that. I think that's when I fell in love with you. You were so much nicer than my brothers."

"I think I may have had ulterior motives for letting you tag along even then. I always enjoyed having you near. Do you remember the night of your prom?"

"How could I ever forget it? The trauma still haunts me."

"What do you mean, trauma? It was the most frustrating night of my life. You were so beautiful and so innocent, and I knew you had a crush on me. Do you have any idea how tempted I was? I wanted to sweep you into my arms and take you away from everyone, but I'd promised your brothers I'd look after you. Talk about letting the wolf guard the sheep."

"But you ignored me all night, chasing after the older girls like I didn't exist."

"Ha. Shows how much you know. I knew where you were and who you were talking to every minute."

"You didn't even kiss me goodnight. I'll bet I was the only girl at the dance who didn't get a goodnight kiss. I'm still mad about that."

"Believe me, if I'd kissed you the way I wanted to, your brothers would've beat the tar out of me. And speaking of your brothers, I can hardly wait to tell them the news."

"Does this mean I have to admit my family was right all along?" I groaned in mortification. "They will be so self-righteous. I wouldn't do it for anyone but you, Peter."

EPILOGUE

Six months later

I'D SET UP MY EASEL IN GRAM'S BACKYARD AFTER DINNER, INTENT on capturing the beauty and serenity of the bucolic scene and how it related to my own sense of contentment these past months. Would I ever be the famous artist I'd envisioned when I was part of Stefan's world? Very doubtful. Would I find fulfillment in the life I'd chosen? A resounding *yes*. I'd learned that success has many definitions.

Zeke came running out of the barn just then, an angry goose hot on his heels. Gram was close behind, waving her arms madly. I watched their antics with a smile on my lips and in my heart. What did the future hold for my beloved Gram? I didn't know the answer to that question, but the one thing I did know for sure was that Peter and I would be here to share it with her, for better or worse. We'd moved into the farmhouse after our wedding and used Peter's lake home as our getaway, knowing it would be much easier on Gram to stay in familiar surroundings.

I knew I couldn't cure Gram, no matter how hard I tried, just as she couldn't always give me the confidence in my work I'd needed. But I would always be there for her when she needed me, like she'd always been there for me. We'd take it one day at a time. Our time together was a gift from God. What more could I ask?

THE END

Thank you for taking time to read *It Never Felt so Good*. If you enjoyed it, please consider telling your friends or writing a short review. Word of mouth is an author's best friend and much appreciated.

BONUS EXCERPT

Weaving a Life
For the Love of Fiber ~ Book Three

An Irish Tale

Off the western coast of Ireland lies a small mountainous island, Oileán na mist, rising emerald green out of the Atlantic in the sunshine or shrouded in mist in the morning and evening fog. It was here, many generations ago, that Fergus the Leprechaun was changed into human form and lost his ability to find hidden treasure. Only the fairies can return his gift and only they know by what means it must happen.

"Nathan has changed so much. I just wish I could reach him," his teacher said, her eyes filled with sympathy. "I don't want to alarm you, but I've heard rumors that he's hanging out with a bad crowd —drop-outs who are older than he is."

My ex-husband Sam and I were sitting in a Shoreview, Wisconsin, high school classroom on this early April evening, in an attitude of mutual agreement to put our own feelings aside for our son. Or so I thought.

I heard the teacher's words, but they didn't compute. *How had this happened?* This was my bright, funny boy she talked about—

the one who had sat on my lap while I read to him, the same boy who later loved to draw and paint pictures of animals and scenery while concocting his own stories. I sank deeper into the cold plastic of the student chair, overwhelmed with a sense of failure.

What had started out as the teacher's laundry list of Nathan's faults, from indifference to laziness to downright surliness, had turned into a sympathetic set of suggestions after listening to his father drone on about his having nothing to do with Nathan's problems. According to Sam, Nathan had been a model student while Sam was in charge of our household.

"It all comes down to a lack of discipline in the home, doesn't it?" Sam turned to me with that "I told you so" smile that would cause my sainted grandmother to grind her teeth. "I've been telling Carol, uh…his mother, for the past year that it's time to stop babying the boy and make him grow up and face the consequences of his actions. If he lived with me, you can believe things would be different." He puffed up like a cartoon drawing of a self-righteous preacher.

Since I was the custodial parent, it followed that Nathan's behavior was my fault. As angry with Nathan as I was myself, listening to Sam's criticism made me more protective. I felt a niggle of fear wash down my back. What was he hinting at?

At least I could thank my ex's abrasive personality for the teacher's understanding. She tightened her lips at that last harangue and asked, "Was it around the time of the divorce that Nathan's attitude changed?" She looked from Sam to me for confirmation. "That's not an uncommon occurrence."

I managed a smile in return, knowing the awkward position she was in. Been there, done that myself as a fourth-grade teacher.

"Could you possibly get him away for the summer to a different environment—some place where he'd meet new people and be challenged intellectually? He's a very bright boy. It could change his attitude on life." Ms. Graham raised her eyebrows in a questioning look and gathered up her papers. "I'm sure you can work this out," she said before fleeing on to the next set of waiting parents.

"I want Nathan to spend the summer with Misty and me," Sam said. "The teacher's right. Who are these losers he's been hanging with this past year, anyway? I never heard him mention them before. He needs a change."

And there it was.

We now stood in the nearly empty classroom of Shoreview High School, in what should have been friendly territory for me. Student paintings of spring, eagerly awaited after a long cold winter, hung around the room, and a small vase of red paper tulips stood on the desk, all showing promise of sunshine and freedom.

"Sam, that's not going to happen." I struggled to keep my voice calm. "You know how he feels about Misty. And you're dreaming if you think a pregnant woman, busy with a three-year-old, wants to be saddled with an unhappy teenager for the summer."

God help me, the thought brought a momentary lift to my spirits.

"She's all right with the idea. He can be a help around the house—spend some time bonding with Delilah."

So, my ex remained clueless. Why should that surprise me? He'd never been around while his older sons suffered the throes of puberty. Supposedly, he'd been too busy at work. *But now I knew better. The rat was too busy all right—having an affair with Misty.*

"I don't think babysitting is what Nathan has in mind for his summer vacation," I said.

"That's the problem, isn't it? You're not capable of giving him any responsibility."

"Now just a minute—"

"He's been totally irresponsible for the past year. His grades are falling, he dresses like a heroin addict, and now he's in trouble with the law."

"Oh, for God's sake. Being caught out after the town curfew is hardly a criminal offense."

"Sure, take his side like you always do. If he had more discipline in his life, this wouldn't be happening." He threw the final zinger. "Do you want him to turn out like your loser brother?"

The man had become an expert at pushing my buttons. My brother Jim had been a hellion in his teen years, that was true, but thankfully that was all in the past and had nothing to do with Nathan and his problems.

I ran my tongue over my lips. Did I taste blood? If not, I should. There were so many accusations I longed to throw in his face. But this was not the time or the place. Besides, been there, done that. The past was over and done with. Now, I had to maintain my dignity for the boys. I breathed in deeply like the yoga instructor taught me I would not let him drag me into a pointless argument. Nathan was my son, and for better or worse, I'd take responsibility for him. There had to be a way to change his attitude, and by God, I'd find it.

I had one major card in my favor—I had custodial care. Sam had been only too happy to relinquish all responsibility for his three sons at the time of the divorce. He was totally focused on his new wife and the impending birth of his daughter.

"I've already made plans for Nathan's summer," I said, managing to hide my face as I reached for my sweater that hung over the back of the chair.

"What are they, Carol?"

"I'll let you know as soon as they're finalized."

"I'll bet," he said, his derisive tone setting my teeth on edge.

"I'll let you know," I repeated. It was a lie, of course. I had no idea of what I could do to save my son from the self-destructive path he'd chosen. But I'd find one. Ms. Graham and Sam were both right. Nathan definitely needed a change of environment and more discipline. Maybe I'd transferred my own feelings of self-pity on him.

I glanced up at the large school clock hanging above the world maps at the front of the classroom. Nathan should be home.

Sam left before I even managed to get my arms in the sleeves of my sweater. The air was still chilly on this early April evening, and I buttoned up the heavy knit cardigan before following him out of the nearly deserted school building. By the time I reached the parking lot, only the taillights of his minivan were visible. Anxious to get home to his wife and daughter, I assumed.

The March-like wind ran cold fingers through the cable stitches of my sweater now, and my muscles tensed in a shiver. I stared across the near-empty parking lot, watching listlessly as abandoned school papers and candy wrappers blew about. A damp drizzle began to fall. My shoulders slumped. No one waited anxiously at home for me. That ship had sailed long ago.

Wait a minute. Why did I let Sam get to me this way? I'd lived through a cheating spouse, a bitter divorce, and survived breast cancer while raising three sons. I didn't need a man complicating my life. I straightened my shoulders and got behind the wheel of my ancient van. The engine sputtered but finally caught and I sighed in relief.

That weight of failure still hung heavy over my shoulders as I drove into the darkening night. Where had things gone so wrong? I couldn't put all the blame on the divorce. Plenty of kids lived through a divorce without falling off the deep end.

My older sons managed to take it in stride, eventually. But then, their lives hadn't been impacted like Nathan's. They were already looking forward to college and an independent lifestyle at the time.

Was it simply teenage rebellion on Nathan's part as I hoped or was I kidding myself? Hadn't I given him enough attention—or did I give him too much? If only his brothers were home from college, maybe they could give me some insight. He'd always looked up to them. But John and Dave wouldn't be coming back to Shoreview anytime soon. They both had jobs at the university that carried over for the summer. And let's face it; they were more interested in the college scene than spending a summer in small-town Wisconsin.

Nathan was in his usual semi-prone position on the worn plaid loveseat when I walked in, couch-sized shoes resting on the scarred coffee table, a bowl of Cheese-nips in his lap, looking like he hadn't a care in the world. But I saw the haunted look he tried to hide in his sky-blue eyes. The same look had crossed his face when I had to tell him about my cancer diagnosis and the divorce. We'd already shared too much fear during his young life, and I wanted to spare him anymore. In his mind, he'd lost his father because of the divorce and almost lost his mother when I had the bout with breast cancer. He wrapped his free arm around Skip, our old golden retriever who'd been his best friend forever.

"So? What's the verdict? Am I grounded for life?" He threw a Cheese-nip up in the air and caught it deftly in his open mouth. A trick he learned from his new friends?

"Nathan, this is serious."

He grabbed another handful of nips and stared at the television.

"Turn that off—now." I raised my teaching voice, and he shrugged, reaching for the remote.

"Is this where I get the lecture?"

That was enough to get my back up. It was past time to get tough. "Don't be a smart aleck. We need to talk."

"Talk about what? Was Dad there? Did he have any suggestions about what to do with his *bad* son?"

"He's very worried about you."

"Yeah, right. Worried I might cost him some money?"

"He and Misty want you to spend the summer at their place. It would give you a chance to get closer to them, to know your stepmom and sister better."

His wild expression was the answer I expected. The next cracker hit the floor. And I admit, I felt relief. I was his mother and knew him better than anyone else did. If anyone could help him, it would be me. But first he had to see what a mess he was making of his life.

"Are you kidding? Mom, you can't do that to me."

"Maybe you should've thought about that before you got yourself in such a mess." I hardened my expression. "I'm at a loss here, Nathan. You don't listen to me anymore. Your grades are falling and your attitude stinks, according to Ms. Graham. Something has to be done. We have to give your father's suggestion some thought."

"No way." His feet hit the floor, and he emphasized the words with a loud fist to the coffee table. "I'm not spending the summer with her and her little brat." The dog sat up and barked in agreement.

"Nathan—don't talk about your sister like that. What happened was none of her doing."

"Okay, so maybe Delilah isn't a brat, yet. But how can she avoid it, living with Misty?"

"You've never given her a fair chance. Admit it."

"Are you kidding? Why should I? As a thank you for breaking up our family?"

"Nathan, it's been several years. You have to get over it and get on with your life—you're too young to wallow in anger. I know it isn't easy, but do it for your own sake or you'll lose your relationship with your father completely."

"Everyone's not like you, Mom. Forgive and forget and all that bunk. I'm never gonna forget, and I'm sure as hell not going to forgive."

"Watch your mouth." I bit my lip. If he only knew what anger and pain I'd gone through before reaching this emotional stage. That's part of the reason I'd cut him so much slack. A mistake I could see now.

"Why do things have to change? I'll look for a job, maybe in Door County. They always need seasonal workers up there."

"Be realistic. You're not quite sixteen so ninety percent of the jobs are out of reach. Besides which, I'd have to drive you up there every morning and pick you up at night. I don't think so. All your salary would go for gas."

"I'm definitely not going to stay with Dad and Misty. That's non-negotiable."

So here we were again at an impasse. I hung my sweater by the door and walked into the kitchen. I needed a glass of wine.

I pulled open the refrigerator door and reached in for the bottle of Chardonnay chilling there. Walking to the china cabinet, I pulled out one of the Waterford wine glasses left to me by my grandmother and poured a glass. The crisp, tart flavor soothed my senses, and I sighed with the pleasure of it. If only I could channel Gram's wisdom to get through this.

The next day was the Friday before spring break. My usual enthusiasm for teaching was definitely lacking as I looked over my group of fourth graders. It was going to be a long day. And as expected, I spent most of it stewing over my predicament instead of being on my game in the classroom. The kids were practically bouncing off the walls anyway, so trying productive work was pointless. We did a few fun math puzzles and word games to pass the afternoon. When they tore out the door at dismissal, I wasn't far behind.

I was barely in the door myself when the school bus stopped at my driveway. Nathan slouched his way from the bus to the front door. My stomach twisted. Wasn't it only yesterday that he'd come rushing in, all excited to describe his day at school in great detail?

"Hi, honey, how was school today?" Had that Pollyanna voice really come out of my mouth?

The daggered look said it all. "I suppose I'm grounded again?"

The look of defeat on his boyish face filled me with an irrational guilt. It was a struggle to remain firm. "You guessed it. And lose the attitude."

How could I help this son I loved so much? I fluctuated between despair and anger. Sam would really put on the pressure if I didn't come up with an answer soon. Could he petition the court for custody in light of Nathan's behavior? I told myself it wasn't possible, but the underlying fear just wouldn't go away. If only I had some relatives or friends we could visit in a big city—like Chicago or New York with all the excitement it held for someone his age. A glimpse into what the world could be for the kid who succeeded in school could make all the difference to someone of his age.

I slumped down on a kitchen chair for a moment, overwhelmed with self-pity. Finally realizing that would get me nowhere, I got up and grabbed a cup of coffee. Time for a new strategy and I needed help.

The Wool Gatherers were scheduled to meet at my house this evening. These were old friends who'd been meeting for years, supposedly because of our love of working with the fiber arts, but in reality, we were our own little support group. They'd helped me through several major crises. Maybe it was time I shared this problem with them, too. I'd seek their counsel this evening. If anyone could help me, it would be these friends. They'd been there for me through my divorce, my bout with breast cancer, and even the pain of watching Sam start a new life with his wife and daughter while mine had seemed to be ending.

Coming Soon from Kate Bowman

ABOUT THE AUTHOR

Born in Wisconsin to an original Brady Bunch, I had the dubious honor of being #14 in the family. As a result, I'll never run out of characters. The early years of my marriage were spent moving around the country with my engineer husband, collecting interesting stories and characters along the way. I picked up my first romance after a particularly stressful shift at a suburban Chicago hospital where I worked as an RN. Hours later, bleary-eyed and exhausted, but able to sleep because the story affirmed that good things can happen to good people, I was hooked. After seventeen years in the Chicago suburbs we returned to Wisconsin and a new life of country living. After a local class in spinning, I decided it would be fun to have my own source of wool. Several years and many animals later, I found a new source of humor for my stories. I've always loved animals and you'll find many of them populate my books. My stories are about real people trying to make it in this crazy, sometimes funny, sometimes sad world— but always with an ending that will renew your faith in love and life.

When I'm not writing, you'll find me with my family or out walking in my fields, spinning wool, knitting or weaving, but always listening to the interesting stories of those characters living in my head.

For more information about me and my books, visit www.Kate-BowmanAuthor.com.

Thanks for reading *It Never Felt So Good.*

~Kate Bowman

"Fill your paper with the breathings of your heart."
—William Wordsworth

Made in the USA
Monee, IL
12 November 2021